"No."

"Why not?"

Lindsey exhaled with annoyance. "I know you're under a lot of stress, Naomi, so I'm making allowances. But do me a favor, would you? Back off."

Naomi's brows rushed together just as her twin brother's did when he was upset. "Someone's got to make you see sense!"

"Your timing's lousy. I have to go out into that blizzard—with a crazy gunman somewhere nearby. Excuse me if my mind's on my job right now."

"Spare me the dedicated ranger act, Lindsey. I know you better than that." Naomi paused. "I thought we were friends."

Lindsey straightened, her eyes narrowed. "We were never friends."

The other woman's flushed cheeks acknowledged the truth of Lindsey's words. "No, but later on, I wanted to be. I know I went about things wrong, but I needed my twin! I swear, Lindsey, I never meant for my relationship with Eric to damage yours. Or to cause bad blood between the two of us."

Lindsey held up a restraining hand. "Naomi, I didn't come back here to assign blame. Eric didn't trust me. Whatever you said to him made no difference in that department."

Dear Reader,

Many of you know that I love to write about my country's national parks. Each park has its own traits—its own character. While some places are definitely "user-friendly," others are not. The setting of this story, Yosemite Park in the dead of winter, can be formidable.

Yosemite is located in the four-hundred-mile-long Sierra Nevada. This is the main freshwater source for San Francisco and the Central Valley. But the huge volume of snow that ultimately provides water for California's coastal population is also the scene of deadly winters. California isn't all beaches and sunshine.

Only two parks in the United States have rangers who live in total isolation due to winter weather conditions. Yosemite is one; Alaska is the other. The heavy loss of life sustained by the Donner Party members is only one of many tragedies to occur in this snow-locked area. During the winter, these mountains are just as inaccessible today as they were in the 1840s, the time of the Donners.

I have taken some liberties by making the existing town of Lee Vining larger than it is and setting a fictional hospital, municipal airport and ranger office there. And in reality, Yosemite has only two rangers on duty in the winter, not four.

Today's rangers must be mentally and physically self-sufficient to survive in a winter climate so harsh that—as in the Antarctic—even snowmobiles and helicopters can't be relied upon. Rangers must also be able to protect and, if needed, rescue any visitors to the parks. Rangers who hold these jobs are very special people.

I hope you enjoy my story about Lindsey Nelson and Eric Kincaide. Welcome to winter in Yosemite! (And please visit my Web site at www.annemarieduq.com.)

Anne Marie

The Replacement
Anne Marie Duquette

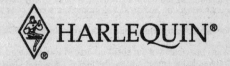

HARLEQUIN®

TORONTO • NEW YORK • LONDON
AMSTERDAM • PARIS • SYDNEY • HAMBURG
STOCKHOLM • ATHENS • TOKYO • MILAN • MADRID
PRAGUE • WARSAW • BUDAPEST • AUCKLAND

ISBN 0-373-71145-X

THE REPLACEMENT

Copyright © 2003 by Anne Marie Duquette.

This edition published by arrangement with Harlequin Books S.A.

® and TM are trademarks of the publisher. Trademarks indicated with ® are registered in the United States Patent and Trademark Office, the Canadian Trade Marks Office and in other countries.

Visit us at www.eHarlequin.com

Printed in U.S.A.

This book is dedicated to my fraternal-twin nephews,
Richard and Patrick Ferraro. And to all cancer survivors,
especially those in my own family.

Although this is a work of fiction,
any resemblance to my old dog Ginger
and my sister's dog Rocky is *purely intentional*!

CHAPTER ONE

Yosemite National Park, California

WINTER SNOW...FEBRUARY SNOW...*killing* snow continued to fall throughout the High Sierra as the rescue party advanced. Aluminum poles in hand, the three rangers probed the white depths in a straight grid pattern, searching for their missing fourth. Seconds ticked mercilessly away, even as the lead ranger, Eric Kincaide, listened to his homing beacon, trying to zero in on the battery-powered locating device all rangers were required to wear.

Neither he nor the other two rangers spoke of the irony of the situation. Tomorrow, following Eric's orders, Keith Arroyo, alias "TNT" Arroyo, planned to set charges in this very area to trigger a controlled avalanche.

Controlled avalanche. Now, that was an oxymoron. Like *walking corpse*...or *buried alive*...

Eric glanced toward his twin, Naomi. The ranger team's emergency medical technician had bitten through her lip. Eric noticed the tiny bloodred bead glittering under the noon sun, contrasting with the bronze of her cheeks. Naomi didn't look up at his scrutiny. Her eyes remained focused on the massive amounts of snow beneath her probing pole.

Keith, however, lifted his head. "Of all the stupid

things to do!'' He spoke in a hissed whisper to avoid triggering any other slides. ''Bad enough we're supposed to find an armed felon and the child he's kidnapped. Eva knew better than to use this shortcut! She's probably got the dog killed, too. How are we supposed to find the missing girl now? Or find Eva without her dog?''

''Shut up!'' Naomi hissed back. ''Just—shut up!''

''That's enough, both of you!'' Eric checked his watch again, unable to help himself. The first ten minutes of searching were the most crucial for any avalanche victim. Sometimes you were given fifteen or maybe twenty, if the victim managed to make an air pocket around his or her face. After that, victims suffocated—if they weren't already crushed to death by the weight of the snow...snow that could pack to the weight and density of thick, wet cement.

It's been thirteen minutes already! Dammit, Eva, why couldn't you follow the rules? This whole area was an avalanche waiting to happen! Keith and I both warned you to go around.

His tracking device pinged more loudly, the pings suddenly rushing closer together until they chimed a single urgent note.

At the same time Keith's pole hit something firm. ''Here! Here!''

Immediately the other two dropped their poles, fell to their knees and started digging. With gloved hands and folding aluminum shovels, all three followed Keith's pole down into the cruel cold.

''It's Ginger!'' Naomi cried. The sandy-colored fur of Ginger, Eva's specially trained search-and-rescue dog, contrasted sharply with the snow's virgin white.

''I've got her collar,'' Eric said after digging around the dog's head. ''I'll pull, you two lift.''

The three braced, lifted and pulled. The golden retriever emerged from the snow, whimpering and coughing.

"She's alive! You pedigreed bitch, you're alive!" Keith brushed snow from the dog's face as Naomi quickly shed her gloves and ran her hand expertly down the animal's legs and across the body.

"Eyes and tongue look good!" Naomi grinned. "She's had plenty of oxygen."

"Come on, girl, let's find your owner," Keith urged.

"Ginger, search," Eric commanded. "Find Eva."

Ginger stood fast, signaled her find with a single whimper, then shook some of the snow from her coat.

"Come on, everyone, dig!" Naomi said, pulling her glove back on and bending over the hole with her folding aluminum shovel.

As Eric followed her example, premonition hit hard. His stomach lurched. Even before the three dug farther down to the motionless blue of Eva's favorite jacket, even before Ginger sat and pointed her nose to the heavens to keen her death howl, Eric *knew.*

Eva Jenkins, the fourth member of their winter ranger team, was dead.

San Diego, California
The next day

LINDSEY NELSON PACED BACK and forth, the hem of her evening dress swishing as she continued to look for her date, peering through her apartment window every few minutes. A revival of *The King and I,* her favorite musical, had finally left Los Angeles to play at San Diego Civic Center. She'd been waiting for this performance for weeks, but Wade—the current man in her life—was late. Very late. Not only that, he had the tickets and she hadn't eaten. Her stomach growled.

If Wade doesn't show up soon, we're not going to have time for dinner.

He'd called twenty minutes ago to say he was leaving work. Lindsey had made reservations at their favorite restaurant, a place with delicious fresh seafood and Napa Valley wines—but Southern California's infamous rush-hour traffic could easily ruin the most carefully laid plans.

Maybe I should order some food. We can have a quick bite here before we leave. It'll have to be pizza or Chinese.... Where is he?

Lindsey impatiently shoved her curtains aside once more, hoping to see Wade's car in the parking lot. *Definitely Chinese. I'm not eating pizza in this dress—and I'll trade the chopsticks for a fork, too!*

She reached for the phone just as it rang. With a quick grab, she answered. "Wade, where are you? It's late!"

"I—" A pause. "Do I have the right number? Is this Ms. Lindsey Nelson? Ranger Nelson?"

"Sorry, I was expecting another call. I'm Lindsey."

"Thank heavens. My name is Jack Hunter. I've been authorized by the Yosemite Ranger Station to contact you. Your office told me I could catch you at this number."

"*Catch* is the right word. I'm on my way out." Lindsey heard the familiar honk of Wade's car outside her window. "In fact, my ride's here," she said, trying to stem her impatience. "How can I help you, Mr. Hunter?"

"Call me Jack. My job is to fill unexpected openings among high-risk ranger positions anywhere in the Historic Monument and National Park system."

"Well...Jack, I'm not interested in moving anywhere," Lindsey said. "Look, could I take your number and call you back?'' she asked as Wade beeped again impatiently. ''I'm really very late.'' Normally Wade wouldn't do anything this rude, but he was obviously trying to save time.

''Forgive me, but this is a matter of some urgency. We need a ranger up in Yosemite. Sadly, the opening's come about because of a ranger down. Dead, I'm sorry to say.''

''Not Eric Kincaide?'' Lindsey asked, her chest tight with fear. ''Or his twin, Naomi?''

''A female—a dog handler named Eva. Did you know her?''

''No.'' Lindsey drew in a deep breath, her chest still tight, but with sorrow, not fear. *A ranger dead? How? Why?* Lindsey listened in horror as Jack explained.

He concluded with, ''As you know, Yosemite rangers are snowbound in the station during winter. We can't fly anyone in due to the danger of avalanche. You're a ranger without a dog, and we've got a dog without a ranger. You also have extensive experience in the snow. I understand you used to work in Yosemite.''

''Yes, but that was more than four years ago. And it's been almost as long since I've worked canine search-and-rescue.'' Since she'd stopped working professionally with dogs and given up cliff-climbing, she'd gone back to her teenage loves—surfing and scuba diving. At present she was a ranger at La Jolla Cove, the only state diving park in California and one of only two in the United States, the other in Florida. ''I've stuck exclusively to diver search-and-rescue.''

''So I've been told,'' Jack said briskly. ''But we desperately need a replacement, Ms. Nelson. I know this is short notice, but it's only until we open the park to the public and the summer ranger staff—maybe three months. Four, tops. I already cleared it with your present park supervisor. She assured me your regular position would be waiting when you return. Call her to confirm if you wish, then please call me back.''

"That's not the point, Mr. Hunter. I've already told you, I'm not interested in transferring anywhere, not even for a few months.''

"I'll be frank, Lindsey. We have a young child and her kidnapper at large in Yosemite. It's her father—he escaped from jail. We won't find them without a dog, and you're the best chance we have of recovering the child.''

Immediately Lindsey's attention focused on the conversation. ''Why didn't you say so earlier?''

''I'm saying so now.''

Lindsey hesitated and regrouped. ''Look, I want to help, but isn't there anyone else? I don't have enough winter gear left for a transfer,'' Lindsey said uneasily, thinking of her present working wardrobe of swimsuit and dive gear. ''I couldn't pack in very much if I have to ski to the station.'' Down below Wade beeped his horn again. Phone in hand, she hurried to the window and waved to him, holding up a finger and pantomiming *Just a minute.*

"You could use the equipment that belonged to the ranger you're replacing. All you'll need are the most basic personal items. She was about your size.''

Lindsey found herself being directed to a place she didn't want to be, and suddenly realized that the man on the other side of the line was very good at directing reluctant rangers. ''I don't know. I'd prefer—''

''Not to use the dog and equipment of a dead woman? Ms. Nelson, excuse my frankness, but we can't pack them out, and you can't pack your own stuff in. I hope you don't have a problem with this. We're talking about a child's life. We need to find her, and we need you to handle the dog. I wouldn't ask if it wasn't important.''

"Oh, I think you would, Mr. Hunter," Lindsey said, deliberately not using his first name. "I also imagine you don't make too many friends in your position—railroading rangers—if you are indeed legit.''

"Call it whatever you want. And I'm legit.''

Lindsey took in a deep breath. "Before we settle on anything, let me explain something. I don't know if you're aware of this, but I left Yosemite because I couldn't work with Eric Kincaide." *The man I loved. The man I was supposed to marry. The man who said he loved me.* "I understand he's still there. Believe me, I'm the last person he'd want to see. And I never got along with his sister, or she with me. In the interests of teamwork and harmony, especially under these circumstances, I'd suggest—''

"Ms. Nelson, we need you," Jack Hunter interrupted. "Up in Yosemite, we've broken the record for the most snow in the Sierra Nevada since the Donner Party tragedy. This is a national park. During the winter it's open to anyone who can trek in and out. We just lost a ranger—one of our own—to the snow, it's so bad. What do you think is going to happen to the kidnapper and his hostage? *Someone* has to find them. He won't turn himself into the police—he faces kidnapping charges, since his wife has sole custody, and he still has time to serve on domestic violence charges. The odds of finding them without a dog drop significantly—and we can't use the dog without a handler. You used to work Yosemite in the winter. You know the area, the routine. And you know dogs. Believe me, I checked you out very carefully. Your father taught you canine search-and-rescue work. Your two sisters work with dogs. Your parents own a kennel, and breed and train law-enforcement canines. I understand you're part of the family business.''

"Yes, but still…'' Lindsey bit her lip and thought. The park maintained strict visitor quotas in the summer, but in the winter the conditions were too primitive for all but a skeleton staff of the most expert winter survivalists-skiers. Even the park horses and mules were trucked out before the snow hit. The bears hibernated, the antlered animals headed for lower country, and the birds flew south toward San Diego and Mexico. Very few species of animal life could survive the High Sierra in winter. Only a few had the skill to live in a land so frigid and snowbound that snowmobiles and helicopters were as useless as frozen water pipes.

"Ms. Nelson, there aren't many rangers with your qualifications. Subtract those who are married or have children and can't leave their families on such short notice, and you're all I have left. And in these circumstances, the fact that your ex-boyfriend's in charge is pretty irrelevant.''

"How did you…?'' Obviously the gloves were off. Lindsey decided to follow suit. "Eric wasn't just an old boyfriend.'' *Eric was more than that. We wanted to start a family. I could've had a son or daughter by now. Maybe both…* "We were engaged to be married. His sister had a hand in our breakup—a very messy breakup. I haven't spoken to either of them in the past four years.''

"I've been on the radio with Mr. Kincaide. He vouches for your competence. Says your arrival won't be a problem for him if it isn't a problem for you. His sister says the same.''

"You talked to Eric *and* Naomi?''

"Mostly Eric. Reading between the lines, I gather he's

willing to overlook any, uh, romantic grudges. He says he'd bet his life on your skills.''

Lindsey's cheeks burned and her heart ached with a pain four years hadn't dispelled. *Too bad he didn't bet on a future with me in it.*

"Ms. Nelson, we need you. There's no one else to ask. As I've said, our head ranger is willing to set aside his personal emotions to try to find the missing child. Rest assured, the two other rangers already stationed there are much too upset over the death of their co-worker to intrude on your past love life or present feelings about it. We have a child taken away from her mother by a madman of a father. He's vowed to kill anyone who comes between him and his daughter.''

"Of course I'm worried about the child!''

"Good. Because right now, I badly need a replacement ranger who can handle a search-and-rescue animal in Yosemite. Are you willing to be that replacement?''

Lindsey closed her eyes. Four years, and she hadn't been able to feel anything for another man even close to what she felt for Eric. Four years, and she still hadn't made peace with the past. Wade was a good man and any woman would be happy to fall in love with him— with all the physical and emotional sensations that entailed—but she couldn't. Wade wanted a wife, a family, a commitment, and he wanted Lindsey permanently in his bed. He'd hinted that he intended to ask her to marry him. Wade expected her to be ready with an answer, but Lindsey felt herself getting older, sadder, lonelier and more confused as the weeks and months went on.

It's time to get over the past. I need to find out what went wrong with me and Eric—and to see if we can fix it. If we can't…then it's time to move on.

"I'm in,'' she agreed. "Just let me touch base with

my boss and family while you make the flight arrangements. Will someone be meeting me at the local airport?''

''It's in Lee Vining, and yes, I will. Your connection will be in Fresno.''

''I can be ready sometime tomorrow afternoon.''

''Tonight would be better. There's a red-eye leaving San Diego at nine forty-five.''

''Sorry, that's impossible. I need tonight.''

She heard Jack slowly exhale. ''Fine. Tomorrow morning, then. No later. I'll call you back with the final arrangements, and you can pick up your prepaid ticket at Lindbergh Field. I'll see you tomorrow. Good evening, Ms. Nelson.''

''Same to—'' The line was already dead. ''You.''

Lindsey replaced the receiver just as a knock sounded on her door. Wade must have given up waiting. Her stomach now churned from nervousness, not hunger, and she hurried to let him in. She quickly explained why she'd been held up on the phone.

''You have to stay home and pack? *For Yosemite?*'' His normally patient voice rose. ''Why you?''

''Because there's no one else. Because it's my job. Because I couldn't refuse when the pushiest supervisor I've ever met forced me into it.''

''Forget it! I don't want you going back to Yosemite and that guy who dumped you at the altar!'' Wade protested.

''We never made it to the— Wait a minute! How do *you* know about Eric?''

''Your parents told me. Your sisters told me. Your friends told me. Said he broke your heart. That you're overly cautious now. That I need to be patient. I have been, Lindsey, but this is too much!''

"What do you want me to do?"

"Say no!"

"I can't, not when there's a child involved. It's like an E.R. doctor refusing to come in for work when there's a major catastrophe. And even if I did say no, I suspect this Hunter could've pulled rank and ordered me out there. I didn't have a choice. I mean, it's not like I'm happy about it!"

Wade peered closely at her. "Maybe not," he said. "But I don't trust this guy." He reached into his suit coat to withdraw a jeweler's box. "I was going to give this to you at dinner tonight." He held it out to her.

Lindsey refused to take it. "Oh, Wade... Tell me this isn't what I think it is."

He opened the box containing the solitaire diamond, since she wouldn't do it herself. "Can I put this on your finger?"

"Please don't. I can't say yes to marriage, yet."

"You aren't saying no, either," he insisted.

"Let's wait. I'll know for sure when I come home. I'll only be gone three or four months."

"Four months—with that bastard," Wade said, his face grim. "Let's hope that's long enough to get him out of your system."

Four years hasn't been long enough. But she couldn't say that to Wade, any more than she could take his ring or be his wife.

Not now. Maybe not ever...

Pushy supervisor or not, deep inside Lindsey knew she couldn't have stayed away, even if a child hadn't been involved. Time to face the past—and decide on the future.

JACK HUNTER DOODLED on the pad of paper before him. Still on hold with the travel agency as they tried to arrange a flight reservation, he found a humorless smile twitching at his lips. Lindsey Nelson had been a harder nut to crack than most of the ranger replacements he contacted. But then, the best of the best were never pushovers, Lindsey included.

He studied the files before him with their official photos and stats. Eric Kincaide: age thirty, never married, with a master's degree in parks and wildlife management from U.C. San Francisco. Six foot two, blue eyes, black curly hair and a lean muscled body that could traverse any winter terrain.... A powerful skier and hiker who had traveled and skied the world, skiing that included obtaining two gold medals for his country's Olympic cross-country skiing and shooting team. Yet he always returned to his native home in Santa Clara county, near Yosemite. He was an excellent lead ranger, and no one blamed him for Eva's death, not even privately. Anyone who died on Eric Kincaide's team had screwed up big time. Period.

Eva Jenkins…young, pretty and dead. She hadn't had the brilliant career of Eric or Lindsey, but was a solid worker and canine handler who'd somehow made a fatal mistake.

Naomi Kincaide accepted Eric as leader, despite their being the same age—and twins. She hadn't started out as a ranger, the way her brother had. Earlier she'd worked in a hospital in San Francisco as an EMT, where she'd eventually met and married her husband, Bruce Palmer; she'd kept her own last name. When he died, she'd joined the ranger service and now worked as Eric's EMT team member.

Enter Lindsey Nelson, tough as nails. Twenty-five, never married. An associate's degree in athletics and sports, and school letters in softball, gymnastics, golf and tennis, she competed harder against herself than anyone else. Despite her long blond hair, green eyes and a trim package of feminine curves and lithe strength, one noticed her looks second, her self-assuredness first. Lindsey Nelson came from a family of women who thrived on challenge. She could climb mountains and sheer cliffs, including El Capitan, at three thousand feet the tallest unbroken cliff in the world. She'd also climbed to the top of Yosemite Falls, its twenty-four hundred feet making it the highest free-falling waterfall in the United States.

She had a talent with animals that other handlers envied. Obviously it ran in the family. Yet she'd given up dogs and climbing and winter sports for an equally flawless career as a rescue ranger at California's underwater state diving park, La Jolla Cove in San Diego county, with fill-in stints as a lifeguard at Carlsbad State Park. Lindsey Nelson was multitalented and successful in all her endeavors—except when it came to her personal relationships with men.

Jack studied the photos of the two rangers. To his discerning eye, the two stubborn chins promised resistance to anyone or anything challenging them. Their faces showed intelligence, determination and more than a hint of steel. Admirable qualities on the job, but from a personality standpoint, Jack figured that as a couple these two were doomed from the start. Their impressive careers and daring rescues proved that neither of them accepted compromise. He doubted either knew the definition of the word.

That might work well for rescues, but not for romance. However, Jack Hunter didn't care about old flames or bruised hearts when it came to a kidnapped child. He only cared that he'd filled the opening Eva had left—

filled it with the best ranger available. Personal relationships weren't Jack's concern. He'd done what he was hired to do. As for anything else—including love and romance—the woman he'd chosen as Eva Jenkins's replacement was on her own.

CHAPTER TWO

THE PLANE TOOK ITS REGULAR flight path north, high above and along the California coast. The green of the ocean contrasted with the beige of the shoreline and the dark greens and tans of the mountain deserts. So far, Lindsey had seen little snow, but she hadn't been airborne long. She turned away from the window, pleased the two seats next to her were empty. She wasn't in the mood for chitchat. Her farewell phone conversations with her parents and two sisters had been full of their warnings—to be careful in the cold of Yosemite, careful around Eric, and to be especially careful not to upset Wade.

It hadn't been easy to say goodbye to Wade. He'd insisted on driving Lindsey to the airport, and had been as gracious, as loving as ever, but she knew he'd been hurt by her refusal to wear his ring. He'd become even more distraught when he learned how isolated she'd be at the ranger winter cabin.

"Can you at least give me your phone number?" he asked.

"I wish I could. There aren't any phones. No cell phone service, either. No e-mail or snail mail. It's strictly ham radio, Wade. The best you can do is phone any emergency news to Mr. Hunter, and he can radio it to me."

Her boarding call was announced. "I guess this is it."

She'd reached for him to kiss him goodbye. When they parted, Wade took her hand and pushed the diamond ring onto her finger.

"If you won't wear it as an engagement ring, consider it protection from the ex. If nothing else, he'll keep his distance."

Before Lindsey could protest, Wade had pulled her close for one more kiss, and whispered in her ear, "I'll be waiting for you when you get back." Then he'd abruptly left. Lindsey stood alone with a ring on her finger, no Wade to return it to, and a loudspeaker blaring out the final boarding call for her flight. She could do nothing, but get on the plane.

Open seating was blessedly plentiful. Lindsey found herself a spot, put a pillow and blanket on the aisle seat to discourage the more sociable, and found herself reviewing recent events. The last-minute frenzy of filling out checks for her rent and utility bills in advance and addressing them for her older sister, Kate, to mail in the next few months had kept her mind off Eric and their history. Her younger sister, Lara, had promised to look after her apartment and water her plants. Her parents promised to look after Wade; a request she hadn't made, but something they'd offered nonetheless.

Then came the check-in line and being searched by airport security, getting a decent meal inside the airport ahead of time in case the airline food was tasteless or skimpy—it later proved to be both—and takeoff. Lindsey politely answered the usual round of questions from the flight attendants in the negative. "Do you want a soft drink? A snack? Care to purchase a headset or cocktail?"

Eyes closed, Lindsey tried to set her thoughts in order. *Eva dead because of carelessness. That poor woman. And now I'm taking her room, her gear, her winter uni-*

*forms, her bed, even her dog. I doubt I'll get much of a
welcome from the dog—or Eric. Not to mention the other
two rangers. I don't blame them, though.*

Eric must be devastated about this ranger's death, she
found herself thinking. As team leader, he'd always em-
phasized safety....

Eric, her ex-lover with the laughing blue eyes, the dark
hair and the capability to surmount any and all obsta-
cles—or so she'd thought. She'd only seen him devastated once before. The day their happiness ended.

Yosemite
Summer, four years earlier

LINDSEY NELSON sat dejectedly in her bedroom at her
summer cabin. The wedding dress she was supposed to
be wearing tomorrow hung unwrapped, untouched, in her
closet. Her suitcases were packed for her honeymoon vacation, boating and hiking at Lake Tahoe, along with
some easy climbing. The dress, the suitcases, the snor-
keling equipment in their travel bag for the honeymoon—
it was all waiting and ready. For nothing, it turned out.

She stared at the floor, unwilling to meet the gaze of
the white-faced man standing before her. Just this time
last week she'd thought her life perfect. Lindsey Nelson,
year-round search-and-rescue ranger for Yosemite, had it
all: a job she loved, a man she adored and her wedding
day tomorrow.

But her last rescue had ruined that; one loss had triggered it all. Lindsey and Missy, her beloved golden retriever, had searched and found a missing five-year-old
boy. Missy might have been getting on in years, but her
nose and her determination to succeed was as strong as
ever. Yesterday, after sunset, when the other searchers

had given up for the day, Missy and Lindsey continued their search alone—and were rewarded for their efforts.

The boy had been found alive, but Missy's great courage was no match for her advancing years. For the first time ever in their partnership, Lindsey knew Missy's rescue days were over.

"It's time to retire, girl," Lindsey had said after rushing her to the vet. "Eric, I don't know about going to Lake Tahoe for the honeymoon. The vet said Missy's still very fragile. Maybe we could go to the coast, instead. She'd get more oxygen at the beach than at the higher altitude of Tahoe."

"It's too late to change our plans now," Eric had replied. His large, capable hand stroked the dog's head. "Maybe we should just board her at the vet's and re-evaluate her health after the wedding."

A warning rang in Lindsey's head. *Reevaluate* from Eric's lips meant *We'll see,* as in *No way.*

"I'm not going anywhere, and Missy isn't going anywhere without me while she's not feeling herself. I'm not leaving her side."

"Even to get married?"

"We'll still get married the day after tomorrow, just as we planned," Lindsey said reasonably. "After that, the vet and I will...*reevaluate* the honeymoon plans." Her choice of his favorite word to stall was deliberate.

Eric drew in a deep breath and changed tack. "Sweetheart, I know you love the mutt. She's—"

"Her name is Missy!"

"She's done great work over the years. You both have. But marriage means we should put *each other* first."

"Then you should respect my wishes. I don't want to leave Missy alone when she's sick."

Eric had been disappointed, but agreed to postpone

their honeymoon for the time being. "I can wait for the honeymoon, as long as the wedding is still on," Eric said. He closed the door to her room with the easy maturity that would soon earn the twenty-six-year-old rescuer his promotion to head ranger.

Twenty-one-year-old Lindsey had sighed with relief and considered herself lucky to have such a great guy in her life. But right now her dog needed her. She fixed Missy a special dinner with the vet's new pills mashed and mixed in. Then they curled up in bed for the night, the woodstove blazing with heat for the invalid. Missy burrowed her nose against Lindsey, while Lindsey encircled the shaggy neck with her arm, her hand resting on Missy's golden head.

Late that night, before the sun rose on her wedding eve, Missy's brave heart quietly, painlessly stopped. Even in death, the nose that had saved so many lives remained snuggled under Lindsey's loving hand.

Lindsey's fellow rangers gave Missy an official funeral in the beauty of Yosemite that dog and handler had served so faithfully, and loved so well. Her family, in town for the wedding, attended. Pet and kennel owners themselves, they understood Lindsey's pain. Eric had seemed understanding himself, until later when they all gathered at a local hotel for what was to have been the prewedding dinner.

"Are we all set for the ceremony tomorrow?" he asked.

Lindsey shook her head, tears starting again. "I can't, Eric."

He grew very still, as did the whole roomful of family and friends, including other rangers. "I think we should postpone the wedding," she whispered.

"You mean...cancel." His voice hadn't sounded like her lover's at all.

"No, reschedule," she insisted. "I just need a day or two and then everything can go on as planned. I'm so sorry, Eric...everyone. I just can't..." Her voice broke. "I hope you understand."

He had, at first. He'd been comforting, loving and compassionate—until that evening when Naomi, who had never approved of Lindsey for her beloved twin, had used her influence with Eric.

That influence was considerable.

Lindsey had overheard the end of one argument. "For God's sake, Eric, Lindsey knows what our work schedules are like! Yours and mine and hers. She's a park ranger! She also knows this park is booked two years in advance. Not to mention plane reservations and rental car reservations and the tight planning it required to get everyone flown in. This is going to throw everything into one big mess. Believe me, twin, Lindsey doesn't want you to *delay* the wedding, she wants to cancel it. She's scared. Her dog's death is a perfect excuse to call it off. She's been dragging her feet all the way to the altar."

Eric had used those same arguments later that evening in private.

"But...you said you were okay about this," a shocked Lindsey had said. "It's only for a day or two."

"I thought it over, and I'm not."

"You mean your *sister* thought it over, and *she's* not," Lindsey had accused him. "You always take her side over mine! Dammit, Eric, I warned you about this. She's never liked me. She'll never like anyone who takes you away from her, and if she has to lie to keep you, she will!"

"You're wrong."

"I'm not! First thing she did after her husband died was come running back to you! Both your parents are alive, yet suddenly she has to be a park ranger herself."

"She's right about one thing. You have been dragging your feet about this wedding," Eric accused.

"Damn right, but not because of you...because of this very thing! Naomi's acting like our marriage is her business, and you two are a package deal. Well, I want to marry *you,* not your sister!"

"So now my family isn't good enough for you?"

"I am *not* trying to call off the wedding. Naomi's the one trying to end our plans. Why can't you see that? Marriage is supposed to be based on trust between two people—not three! Who do you believe more, her or me? Choose!"

Eric's eyes narrowed. "Is this an ultimatum?"

"It's the simple truth," Lindsey stated. "Naomi sees me as competition for you, and she's jealous as hell. She doesn't know me, or care to know me. All I want to do is say goodbye to my dog and not bring that sadness to our wedding. Or to the honeymoon, either. We can still go, now that Missy's..." She swallowed hard. "You should take *my* word, not Naomi's. And if you think she's an expert on me, then you're a fool! I'm rescheduling our wedding for the day after tomorrow."

"Don't bother. The wedding's off," Eric had said. He stood up so abruptly the chair behind him tipped and crashed to the floor. Those were the last words Lindsey ever heard from him, then or in the four years that followed.

Yosemite Valley
Replacement day one, the present

THE SHEER FACE of Half Dome, Yosemite's massive rock of granite, reflected the sun's light downward to the valley. There it bounced against the brightness of the snow and reflected upward again, illuminating everything with brilliant clarity. Lindsey stopped in the snow to adjust her sunglasses and take a breather. She slid her pack off her shoulders absorbing in the beauty of the area.

Already she'd covered more than half the distance toward the rangers' winter lodgings. Her flight yesterday had landed smoothly, she'd been met as promised by Jack Hunter—been outfitted in gear, including a radio, and put up in a local motel in Lee Vining for the night. Early this morning, Jack had delivered her via truck and then snowmobile to Yosemite's rear entrance from the Tuolumne River side. Amid the glittering snow of the high country, Lindsey said goodbye to her superior, and from there skied off toward her old workplace.

I never realized how much I've missed this, she thought to herself. *And missed Eric.* To Lindsey, Eric and Yosemite were forever linked in her heart. It made her travel easier and faster than she would have supposed possible. Once she made it to the top of the pass, she took another minute to rest.

Lindsey reached for a trail bar and her thermos of hot chocolate. Since she'd refused to accept and train a new rescue dog after Missy's death, she'd traded the canine handler spot in Yosemite for the warmer parks in Southern California; it was where she was originally from and where her family still lived. She'd quickly found a new position with the park system, thanks to her surfing and diving skills, and went back to helping her parents around the kennels in her spare time. Being around Eric had been out of the question four years ago. He wouldn't even see her to take back his ring. She hadn't wanted to return it, but felt obligated to do so. She'd left it with the former head ranger; Eric hadn't been awarded that spot until a year after she'd left.

Now she'd come back to Yosemite—Eric's home— again. A sad smile crossed her face. With hindsight, she realized she and Eric had more problems than just the death of a dog or the jealousy of a twin. Eric led with his head, she led with her heart, and neither seemed to find any middle ground except in bed. They were young then. Too young, perhaps. They should've talked things out—*would* have talked things out if Naomi had stayed out of it.

Both of them were close to their siblings. If their situations had been reversed and Kate or Lara had suggested that Eric wasn't good for her, she would've taken their words very seriously, indeed. But she wouldn't have called off the wedding—that much she knew.

Lindsey stuffed her once-short blond hair back under her thick woolen hat. Not having to contend with Yosemite's more primitive plumbing, which made simple hygiene a chore, she'd let it grow long and thick.

Her breath came more heavily than she liked. She was still fit and trim, but four years of living at sea level had hindered her blood's ability to process the high-altitude air. Lindsey reached for a Diamox pill and washed it down with the hot chocolate. The medication was needed twice a day to prevent high altitude pulmonary edema, which could kill. An easy physical pace for the next few weeks would be required until her body produced more blood cells and adjusted to the higher altitude. The rangers' winter quarters were at the highest level of Yosemite—the fabled High Sierra that had taken lives from the earliest Native Americans to the tragic Donner Party, and more recent victims, like Eva.

To live on the edge of survival brought out the best or the worst in people. Sadly, Eva, who had replaced Lindsey, hadn't made it. But for Lindsey, true Nature with a capital *N* brought out the best in her. She thrived in the Sierra, and didn't see death within the snow, but glorious life. She prayed Eric still took joy in his surroundings. Despite their breakup—a breakup he'd said *she'd* wanted—she'd never wished him anything but happiness and health. She still wished that for him.

As Lindsey munched on her snack, she mentally reviewed the three rangers she'd soon share a cabin with.

Eric she already knew. A true wilderness expert, a throwback to the early California mountain men and climbing guides he was descended from, Eric was at home in the High Sierra. Four years ago, he'd been a delightful combination of his intelligent father's outdoor ways, his educated mother's handsome looks, and his own brand of wit, charm and courage. All knew him as a gifted expert on climate with an uncanny sense of snow prediction and ability to navigate in any weather. He usually read people just as well—except for Lindsey.

I wonder if he's still the same man....

The second ranger, Eric's twin sister, Naomi, probably hadn't changed a bit. She and Eric were instantly identified as siblings; their hair and eye color, even their skin tone and facial features, were so similar, their relationship was unmistakable. Naomi was probably as opinionated, bossy and possessive as ever. She rarely stayed away from her twin for long. Her husband, Bruce Palmer, had been killed in a car accident, and she'd returned to her twin for comfort. She'd qualified for a Yosemite ranger position at about the same time Lindsey started working with Eric. From what Jack Hunter had mentioned in a later conversation, Naomi was still working as a ranger and busily finishing up her master's thesis on Sierra Nevada botany. A herbalist and botanist, and the team member with the EMT certification, she was usually found deep in her books and research. Lindsey often felt Naomi would never have left her former hospital job for ranger work if her husband hadn't died.

Naomi had always been more interested in her studies than in the people around her. Although twins, brother and sister were opposites, with Naomi quiet and somewhat pessimistic, Eric openly sociable and cheerful. They hardly ever disagreed on anything—except Lindsey.

Lindsey wasn't looking forward to seeing Naomi again. Eric's sister had always seen Lindsey as competition, since the twins were so close. However, to be fair, Lindsey had to admit that although Naomi had certainly tried to influence Eric, the final decision had been his.

Keith "TNT" Arroyo, the explosives expert, remained the only member of the team Lindsey didn't know. He was a relative newcomer with less seniority than Naomi, and he'd replaced the explosives expert Lindsey had worked with. Supposedly "TNT" lived up to his nickname in both his lifestyle and his skiing. His expertise with explosives had already earned him a place as instructor in setting off man-made avalanches. Like Lindsey and Eric, he had a glowing record and had saved lives more than once. He was the youngest of the party at twenty-three, Hunter had told her during her briefing.

"Despite his youth, Keith's an excellent ranger—but that's not all. The man knows his explosives, and he and Eva made a great two-member team. Keith's a good man to have on any team—and he'll need your friendship. He doesn't have a twin's shoulder to offer comfort."

Lindsey had nodded, finished filling in the final paperwork with Jack Hunter, checked her pack, straps and skis, and set upon her journey. Now, almost finished with her hot chocolate and trail bar, she would soon meet Keith for the first time.

She'd resume her acquaintance with the brother and sister who'd almost become her family.

CHAPTER THREE

Yosemite, Rangers' winter cabin
Same day, late afternoon

"WHERE IS SHE?" Eric asked impatiently, his breath making more fog on the frosted, double-paned window. "It's going to be dark soon."

"She checked in by radio right on time. Stop worrying. She probably hasn't skied in a while," Naomi said calmly. "Better to be cautious and a little late than risk injury like—" Naomi broke off and continued setting the table in the large common room.

Like Eva. She's gone. If Lindsey were gone forever... That thought chilled him to the bone. He couldn't finish it, even to himself. Eric strode away from the window and back to the kitchen area. He picked up the spoon and stirred the stew he'd fixed for their dinner. He suddenly wondered if Lindsey still liked stew. Her mother and sisters were vegetarian, but in primitive conditions such as these, it wasn't practical to cook separate meals for everyone. Cooking duties were shared, as was rummaging in the huge cabin pantry among cases of canned goods, dried meats and a freezer full of frozen vegetables and butcher cuts purchased in advance and stockpiled to last four people six months.

Lindsey usually ate what was on the table. Still...

Maybe she'd become vegetarian, after all. Quickly he tossed some flour and other ingredients into the bread-maker. Lindsey loved hot, freshly made bread—and it would go well with their meal, Eric told himself.

Keith emerged from the small bedroom he shared with Eric. They were built deliberately small, with low roofs to make them easier to heat. "If we're waiting dinner on the replacement, I hope she gets here soon," Keith said with an appreciative sniff. He moved over to the fire, tending it and then stroking the dejected Ginger lying beside it, her tail tucked around her body. "I'm hungry."

"I'll never understand men," Naomi said harshly. "You lost Eva, and now you're waiting for her replace-ment—how can you eat?"

"That's enough," Eric said quietly to his sister. "What would you have us do? Stop eating like Eva's dog?"

"You did when Lindsey left four years ago," Naomi responded.

"If so, I didn't urge others to imitate my example."

Eric saw his sister flush guiltily, and immediately felt guilty himself. Ever since Eva's death, they'd all been on edge. And now the proverbial "blast from the past" in the form of Lindsey Nelson, former lover and fiancée, was about to arrive.

"I'm sorry, Eric. My apologies, Keith. I've been a ner-vous wreck since Eva—and I'm worried about Lindsey," Naomi said contritely. "I just wish she'd get here, that's all."

"We all do," Eric added kindly. "Go ahead and radio her again, if you like."

"I—no, that'll only slow her down more."

"Tell you what. I'll go walk the dog and take a look-see," Keith offered. "I'll check the generator on my way back."

The schedule of cabin chores was strictly adhered to. Wood must be brought in from the woodpile, supplies inventoried, snow cleared from the roof, the generator checked and refueled. As far as meals went, this week Eric was cooking, Naomi setting the table, and Keith cleared the dishes and washed up.

"I'd appreciate that," Naomi said before Eric could reply. "Thanks, Keith."

Keith nodded. "I won't be long…ten minutes. Fifteen at most."

All three checked their wristwatches from long habit. You planned your travel, you traveled your plan, and you always registered an itinerary with your partners. Even Eva had followed that rule. Keith hooked Ginger to the leash and after tugging and coaxing finally forced the reluctant dog to her feet and outside.

The rush of cold air coming in from the double-doored porch sent shivers down Eric's spine as he peered out the closest window from his spot in the kitchen. His sister noticed. She always noticed.

"You're nervous about her coming back," she said without preamble.

Eric continued to stir.

"She'll eat your cooking, you know. She always did."

"That was four years ago. She likes pepper." Eric added a dash of pepper.

"You're still in love with her." Naomi reached for the sturdy dinner dishes and placed them on the table. "Well, I hope you take every opportunity to get Lindsey back."

Eric smiled, but the smile didn't reach his eyes. "This from the woman who never liked my fiancée."

"You're my twin. I'd resent anyone who replaced me

in your life. And yes, I always thought you could do better than some animal lover who put her dog first and her boyfriend second.'' Naomi picked up the silverware. ''But I'm not the one who fell in love with her. And you haven't been yourself ever since you let her walk out of here.''

''She walked away from me.''

''Wrong. You pushed her away by refusing to reschedule the wedding.'' Naomi frowned at a spot on a piece of silverware. She wiped it on her heavy flannel shirt and set it at her usual place. ''If I'd died, would you have wanted to get married the next day?''

Those words got a reaction. ''You're not a damn dog!''

''Lindsey was as close to that dog of hers as you and I are. They were like us—twins.''

''You're dead wrong.''

''I'm not wrong! You know what I'm thinking most of the time. I know what you're thinking. We know each other's actions, movements, likes, dislikes. Each of us knows how the other would react to just about any situation at home or on the job. We're in sync—we work perfectly together. Same with Lindsey and her dog. You and I love each other, we get along better than anyone else could, yet you'd still choose Lindsey over me, wouldn't you?''

''We've had this conversation before, Naomi. Drop—''

Naomi interrupted him. ''Just like she would've chosen you over her dog, if you'd given her a chance. For heaven's sake, Eric, she has a real gift with animals! I wouldn't be surprised to see a grizzly eating out of her hand. She saved more lives with her dog than both of us put together. Because of your hurt pride, you lost a wife. And she lost confidence in her gift.''

Eric abruptly tossed the stirring spoon in the sink. ''What the hell are you talking about?''

Naomi paused, a stack of silverware still waiting to be set out. ''The Park Service practically ordered her back here to work as a canine handler. She didn't want to leave San Diego. She hasn't worked with a dog since she left Yosemite. That's your doing. *Our* doing,'' Naomi corrected herself. ''And she's playing *Baywatch* babe with the surfers and divers. She's not climbing or skiing. She's not the same Lindsey we knew.''

Eric found himself shaken. He and Naomi had talked about Lindsey a few times, but this was news. ''I never heard… No, I don't believe it. She'd never give up her dogs—or her search-and-rescue work with them.''

''That's because you haven't kept in touch with Lindsey's sisters. I have. Lindsey's no better for your breakup than you are—which is why you both need to repair the damage. I'll help in any way I can. Her family wants their old Lindsey back. I want my old brother back. If that doesn't happen, when this winter is over, I leave here for good. I can't stand seeing you like this anymore. Knowing I helped make you so miserable makes it even worse.''

''That was four years ago. Why the sudden guilt complex? Because she's coming back?''

''Because I *am* guilty.'' Eric watched with horror as tears ran down his sister's face. Naomi moved away from him to snatch at the coffee mugs and napkins. ''I saw that you hated the time she spent with animals—you felt it was time she should spend with you. You felt her love for you was somehow compromised by her commitment to her dog. I know how you think, Eric. And I saw what it did to Lindsey. I should've helped you both—but I selfishly stood by. I'd already lost my husband. I didn't want to lose my twin, too. But I lost you, anyway, by letting you walk away from Lindsey."

"You didn't 'let me' do anything, Naomi. I'm a big boy. Right or wrong, I made my own choice."

"It was wrong."

Eric watched the tears slide down her cheeks as she continued setting the table. He asked his sister a question he'd never asked. "Naomi, you only told me the truth, right? Or what you believed to be the truth? You never lied to me, did you? You said she wanted to break off the wedding and her dog's death was the perfect excuse."

Naomi didn't answer. Shaken, he retrieved the spoon from the sink. "Naomi?" He started to press for an answer just as Keith returned with Ginger and announced, "I saw her. Better set an extra plate, Naomi. She should be here in about ten minutes."

Could Lindsey have been right? That all along Naomi had planned to break them up? Never once had Eric suspected that Naomi might have deliberately deceived him. Eric took a deep breath and put the communal pot on the table. He reached for the lid to the breadmaker. He hadn't clicked the switch hard enough to activate the process earlier, he noticed with dismay. There would be no bread with the stew, no bread for the replacement ranger.

Eric couldn't help wishing for a more auspicious beginning. He checked his wristwatch once, twice and a third time, until he caught both his sister and Keith watching him.

"Just seeing if she's still the punctual type," he excused himself—he who never made excuses.

Naomi said nothing, but Keith remarked, "You can see her from the window now, Boss. Take a look."

Eric loped to the front cabin window as fast as he could without seeming to rush. Despite the distance, he immediately took in the gracefully moving figure. The shape, size and movement hit him with a sense of recognition. He could pick Lindsey out in any crowd. The familiar pain he felt at her rejection warred with joy as the figure came closer and then stopped outside the porch door.

Before he could leave the food to hurry outside, she'd removed her skis, stepped inside the unheated enclosed porch, racked her skis and poles, and knocked on the inner connecting door. Eric immediately brushed past the other two rangers to open it personally, eager to see the face whose appearance once gave him such joy.

Lindsey Nelson stepped inside the cabin, bringing the cold air inside. The smile on his face froze as she spoke in a stranger's voice.

"Lindsey Nelson reporting for duty as ordered, sir."

One hour later

ERIC ROSE FROM THE DINNER table to fetch the apple pie he'd warmed for the night's dessert, and wondered if Lindsey would refuse to have any. She'd refused his meat-filled stew earlier. After introductions had been made, Lindsey had declined dinner in favor of sitting on the huge, raised hearth and warming up in front of the fire. She hadn't moved or spoken since, except to answer a few questions from Keith and apologize for her silence.

"I haven't skied for four years, Keith. I promise we'll get better acquainted tomorrow. Right now I just want to catch my breath."

Her answer had shocked Eric to the core. Lindsey loved the mountains and skiing, yet her stiff movements, audible breathing and a repeated dose of Diamox showed she had indeed left the high country behind when she'd left him. Worse, her uncharacteristic detachment matched that of the depressed animal on the hearth. She hadn't made eye contact with anyone, not even the dog.

My God, she has changed—and not for the better. Is Naomi right? Have we really done this to each other?

He brought her the first piece of pie. He remembered she loved apple and preferred it warm with coffee...or at least she used to. "The bread will be ready in an hour. This should hold you until then." He handed her the plate with its fork and the cup of coffee. "Two artificial sugars and cream, right?"

"I'm sorry, sir, but I don't use chemical sweeteners anymore," she said quietly. "I will take the pie. Thank you."

As she reached for the plate, the warm fire caught and reflected a sparkling gleam on her ring finger, a gleam that had been hidden in the dimness of the cabin. He stared at the diamond engagement ring—a ring much larger than the one he'd once bought her and still kept in his dresser drawer. The cup shook in his hand and coffee sloshed over the rim. He watched as she jumped and wiped at her indoor warm-up boots with her diamond-clad hand.

Eric backed away with the coffee. "God, I'm sorry. Did I burn you?"

"I'm okay. You just caught my boots."

"Sorry," he repeated. "I shouldn't have poured it so full," he managed to say.

"No harm done." She turned her attention back to the fire, leaving him to set the cup on the table.

Soon afterward, the table was cleared and wiped. Keith went outside to add more fuel to the generator. Naomi went to the storeroom, as she had cooking detail the next day. Eric, Lindsey and the dog were alone in the cabin's main room.

Lindsey moved from the hearth to the thick hooked rug on the floor. He noticed Ginger had slipped closer to Lindsey and seemed to be watching her as closely as he was.

"What's her name?" Lindsey finally asked.

"Ginger. Although Naomi says her name's gonna be RIP if she doesn't start eating soon."

Lindsey broke off a piece of pie crust, and silently placed it halfway between herself and the animal.

Furry golden head resting on her paws, Ginger studied the crust. Her nose twitched once, but that was all. Lindsey picked up the crust and popped it in her own mouth. The dog's gaze took in the action without any visible response. Lindsey broke off another piece of crust, placed it somewhat closer than before, and waited. When the dog made no move toward the food, Lindsey took back the second crust and put it in her mouth, eating with casual nonchalance despite its having been on the rug.

"Is she drinking, at least?"

Eric nodded, registering true interest in Lindsey's voice and on her face for the first time since her arrival.

"That's good." This time Lindsey broke off a bigger piece of crust with a chunk of apple filling. She placed the food inches away from the dog's alert eyes and again waited a few minutes. Then she casually reached toward the pie chunk again. Ginger lifted her head and gulped the food down, her motions canine-quick. Lindsey reached for the plate of pie, and set the whole thing in front of Ginger. The dog licked the plate, next licked the pie itself, then, still lying down, she began gulping pieces of pie.

"Well. I see you haven't lost your magical touch," Eric said.

Lindsey shrugged. "Nothing magical about it. The dog obviously considers this fireplace area home base. She watched me sit on the hearth, then tensed when I sat on the rug. She hasn't closed her eyes since. She's still territorial. I figured she'd challenge me for that food sooner or later. Besides, she's a golden."

"Huh?"

"She hasn't given up the ghost. Her breed adapts easily to new owners. Some, like German shepherds, don't. That's why retrievers are replacing shepherds as service dogs for the handicapped. They can be trained as puppies and passed on to new owners as adults with much less emotional trauma to the animal. Do you have any of that stew left?"

"Yeah." Eric rose and hurried to the stove to scoop out Lindsey's share of the dinner. Lindsey took the plate and set it on the rug next to the pie plate.

"Go on, Ginger," Lindsey urged. "You had dessert. Time for the main course." Ginger didn't hesitate a minute. She actually rose to her feet to eat. Lindsey took the plate and lifted it onto the raised hearth so the dog would swallow less air. "No gas bloat for you, girl. Eat up. Compassionate leave is canceled. Tomorrow morning— back to work."

Eric watched as Lindsey's hand toyed with the long fur on Ginger's ears. He remembered those fingers, gentle, soothing, skilled, touching him with love during their passion-filled nights.

"Naomi was right. You still have a gift with animals."

"My father has the real gift. I learned from him. Where's the dog food? She's almost done with the stew."

"I'll get it." Eric hurried to the dried food. He dumped

a few cups of it into the empty stew pot and stirred, coating the nuggets with leftover gravy. Lindsey took the pot from him and started hand-feeding Ginger, who allowed the familiarity.

"Naomi told me you hadn't replaced your dog."

"Her name was Missy."

Eric caught the edge to her voice—the first sign of emotion she'd directed his way. "I remember.... Haven't you missed—" *Working with dogs?* Suddenly, what he wanted to ask stilled his tongue. *Haven't you missed working with me? Missed us together?* His eyes studied the diamond on her hand.

Lindsey didn't meet his eyes. "It's always rough to lose a partner, two-legged or four. Sorry to hear about the loss of Eva."

"We all are. Last week there were four of us, and now…"

Lindsey finished for him. "You're stuck with me."

"I wouldn't exactly call it being stuck, Lindsey," Eric said quietly.

"If they could've found anyone else for a replacement… But they couldn't, not on such short notice. I'd never have come otherwise."

His stomach fell at that, but he refused to let it show. He glanced pointedly at her ring. "So I gathered. Who's the lucky guy?"

"No one you know." Lindsey stacked the cleaned dinner dish and pie plate in the empty stew pot and got to her feet. Ginger still watched her closely as Lindsey set the dishes in the kitchen sink. "I'm going outside with the dog. Where did Eva take her to relieve herself?"

"A couple hundred feet behind the summer storage sheds—not the same place you used for Missy. I imagine the dog knows the way."

"I'm not taking any chances. Where's her leash?"

"I—" Eric looked around. "I don't know. Sorry."

"Obviously you never considered this dog part of your team," Lindsey said sharply. "But then, commitment was never your strong point, was it? Excuse me...sir."

Lindsey and the dog headed for the glassed-in porch, leaving Eric feeling as empty inside as the unwashed stew pot.

Women's bedroom
9:00 p.m.

LINDSEY UNPACKED THE FEW belongings she'd brought, the dog alertly watching her from a safe distance.

"I know the feeling, Ginger," Lindsey said softly. "I don't know what to expect from you, either. Or anyone else here, for that matter."

Ginger's ears perked up, but there was no responding tail thump at the sound of her voice, just as there had been no warmth in Eric's eyes at Lindsey's presence. The man she'd once trusted with her body, heart and soul had acted as cautiously around her as the dog had—even more so, truth be told.

"It's not like I bite or anything," Lindsey said. She dug into her meager pack of personal items with a stiff arm and rummaged around for her over-the-counter pain-killers and muscle liniment. "If I feel this sore now, Lord help me tomorrow," she said, easily slipping back into the long-unused habit of talking to dogs. "I hope this bed is soft, girl, because I could sure use some rest before tomorrow."

She stripped down to her long underwear and socks, started to ease her weary body under the thermal sheets, thick blankets and down coverlet, then stopped. "I hate going to bed alone when it's cold, don't you? I'm used to Missy keeping me warm in snow country. I guess you're used to Eva.''

Lindsey knelt down on the floor and took the retriever's face in her hands. Her eyes dampened with tears at the waste of Eva's life, the lost look on the dog's face.

"I know this bed is more yours than mine, Ginger,'' she said softly. ''And I know I'm not who you want in it. But maybe we can share, okay? I promise to take good care of you…no strings attached. Fresh starts for us both, okay? You're still alive and kicking, right?'' Lindsey stood and patted the bottom of the bed. ''Come on, girl. Let's hit the sack.''

Ginger watched her warily. Lindsey climbed under the covers, then patted the bed again. ''The carpet's nothing like a down-filled comforter. Awfully cold on that floor. Eva wouldn't want you to be cold, you know.'' The dog remained on the rug.

"Suit yourself, Ginger. The invitation's open.'' Lindsey turned out the small light by the side of the bed, her disappointment at Eric's coolness compounded by the dog's rejection. ''Good night, girl. Sleep tight. Don't let the snow fleas bite. Yosemite does have snow fleas, you know. When's the last time you had a new flea collar?'' Lindsey yawned. ''I'll check tomorrow. We've got a big day ahead of us.''

Lindsey burrowed under the bed linens, noticing that the sheets smelled faintly of laundry soap and fabric softener. A fresh herb sachet lay underneath the pillow. Only Naomi made those. Eric's sister had been surprisingly kind. Lindsey made a mental note to thank her, then lifted her head from the pillow for one last comment.

"Good night, pooch.''

Silence in the room. Lindsey sighed, tucked one of her

cold feet under the other and waited to warm up enough so she could sleep. She waited in vain. She felt cold inside, cold outside, cold through and through. Maybe she should get up and find Eva's arctic sleeping bag. That meant she'd have to strip to her skin and sleep in the bag atop the bed for maximum warmth. But she didn't know where the bag was—nor did she have the energy to search.

Tomorrow I'll check out this cabin in daylight. Everything feels better in daylight, Lindsey reassured herself, ducking her head under the covers. *Even my nose is cold.* Immediately she popped her head out. It reminded her too much of Eva's death, buried under the deadly weight of killing snow. Her ring caught on a thermal-weave pocket, snagging and making a tearing sound in the blanket.

"Dammit!" Lindsey tried to yank off the ring. It was stuck because of the higher altitude and the puffiness of her fingers. Lindsey licked her ring finger and tried one last time. Nothing. She gave up the attempt, burrowed back down into the covers and forced herself to relax, willing her body to adjust to the cold of the sheets. "Some replacement I am," she said aloud, extremely grateful that her new cabinmates—especially Eric—didn't realize how weak and vulnerable she felt. Worse, loneliness seemed to make her feel colder.

Fine. Feel sorry for yourself—but only for tonight. Tomorrow, chin up. I'm not a coward. At least, I never used to be.

Exhausted and overtired, she tossed and turned until she felt Ginger climb up on the bed to stretch out alongside her, the dog's head resting on her shoulder. She smiled, and only then fell into a deep sleep, so deep that she didn't hear Naomi enter the room an hour later, followed by Eric.

"One short evening—and the mutt's literally eating out of her hand. None of us could get the dog to budge," Eric said in an undertone.

"She has a way with living things." Naomi quietly pulled off her winter boots and socks. "She always has."

Ginger, who had lifted her head at their arrival, laid it back down again. Lindsey moved in her sleep at the motion. Eric watched as Lindsey's right arm came out from the covers to settle around the golden neck. Both dog and new mistress relaxed and were motionless again.

Brother and sister stared at the diamond solitaire on Lindsey's finger. "No wedding band, yet, twin. It's not to late to fight for what you want—if you still want it."

Eric smiled, a predatory smile that didn't reach his eyes. "Oh, I still want it," he said. "I need to know if she does."

Naomi's eyes opened wide in amazement. "You didn't tell me that!"

"I don't tell you everything. Nor do I want you blabbing to Lindsey."

"I won't. Not until her wedding, anyway," Naomi said.

"If there's a wedding, I intend to be the groom. Me— not the bastard who gave her that ring."

"I hope you're right."

"Keep hoping." Eric faced the opposite bed again and shook his head. "Lindsey and those animals. Some things never change."

"Maybe *you* should do the changing," Naomi suggested with a sibling's frankness. "We both should. Start with calling Ginger by name and not 'the mutt' or 'the damn dog.' She's been with us four years. And don't rag

Lindsey about putting the dog first. I won't, either. The last time we did—"

"Don't remind me. Still…I've got three months until the snow melts. I don't intend to make the same mistake twice."

"Three months…" Naomi echoed. "Good luck."

"Thanks." Eric stared one last time at the ring. "But I believe we make our own luck."

And that's why I told Jack Hunter that Lindsey Nelson should be our replacement.

CHAPTER FOUR

Rangers' winter cabin
Day 2, sunrise

THE SMELL OF PANCAKES, maple syrup and fresh biscuits greeted Lindsey's nose, while the golden retriever greeted Lindsey's ears with a particularly high-pitched yip.

"All right, all right!" Lindsey groaned. "I'm awake."

Ginger jumped down from the bed to prance near the closed bedroom door.

"Let me guess. You need to go out."

This was followed by a full-fledged bark. Lindsey sat up and winced as skiing muscles, long unused, protested. The dog barked again, and there was a knock at the door.

"Come in. I'm decent."

Eric poked his head in. "Morning."

"What time is it?" Lindsey asked in a sleep-hoarse voice.

"Eight. We let you two sleep in. Want me to walk the dog for you?"

"Please, and keep her on the leash," Lindsey said, rubbing at a sore shoulder. "Just in case she doesn't come back."

"Will do, but she'll come back," Eric said confidently. *Just like I did.*

"Breakfast is ready." He and Ginger both left, Eric closing the door behind him.

The meal was a quick affair. Ginger bolted her food, and Lindsey finished her pancakes and eggs almost as quickly, but with more delicacy. Soon Lindsey and Eric skied away from the cabin, Ginger at their heels, out into the crisp, pure air of Yosemite.

The crystal-blue clearness of unpolluted high altitudes against the vivid whites and pine greens soothed her soul. The wide-open spaces of Yosemite echoed with the sound of their newly waxed cross-country skis cutting through the crisp snow. Lindsey remembered earlier, happier times, when the silent, brooding man ahead of her had smiled and skied at her side and another dog bounded at her heels. She pushed those dangerous thoughts away. Instead, she took in a deep breath of air tinged with pine, then slowly exhaled. She soaked in the stark beauty of the ancient granite and continued to follow Eric on the packed cross-country ski trail. Ginger trotted between the two of them, easily keeping up with Eric's slow, relaxed pace.

Lindsey smiled, remembering Eric's usual brisk rate of travel. She suspected he was making allowances for her sore muscles, since a dragging pace in anything wasn't his style. In bed he'd made love to her with an easy energy that fully complemented Lindsey's more easygoing approach to life.

Wade was only partially compatible. She never felt the deep satisfaction that went past physical pleasure. Only Eric could satisfy her emotionally and mentally—probably because he was the only one she'd ever trusted emotionally and physically. With Wade, that trust barely extended to the physical level, although both he and her parents believed otherwise. Her sisters, however, weren't deceived. They knew she still had feelings for Eric, no matter how happy she seemed with Wade.

He deserves better, Lindsey thought. *And so do I. I shouldn't settle.... I want Eric to trust me. He used to. I wonder what lies Naomi told him....* Lindsey suddenly realized that her explosive, deeply satisfying sexual relationship with Eric had prevented them from exploring other facets that two people with a future really needed to know. *And why did I let him stop the wedding? Why didn't I go after Eric? Maybe I was too young.*

Those often-asked questions took on a changed relevance as she studied the figure before her with new insight and a weak longing to feel his powerful body once more joined with hers. The image of them together was so strong that she slipped on an icy area, overbalanced and pitched down into the deeper snow on the side of the trail.

Eric immediately turned and Ginger bounded her way to investigate, which only caused more of a tangle of limbs, skis, poles and snow. Despite the serious thoughts of earlier, her mood lightened at the ridiculous sight she knew she presented.

"You okay?" Eric asked, quickly joining her as Ginger licked her face.

"Unless you count feeling stiff, sore and having snow down my neck." Lindsey giggled, pushing the dog off her. "I don't need dog hair in my mouth, either." Ginger bounded at her chest again with puppy playfulness, shoving Lindsey flat on her back in the snow. One ski binding popped open, and a pole complete with leather glove fell across the dog's back.

Lindsey broke into full-fledged laughter. "Some rescue ranger I am. Get off me, you silly dog. Ginger—move!"

The dog came closer, causing a clump of snow to land squarely on Lindsey's face. Lindsey groped blindly about, then felt herself being lifted up and away from the snow. She felt the ground underfoot again. One arm remained around her waist, while strong masculine fingers gently brushed at the snow on her face. Lindsey opened her eyes to see Eric's dear face only inches from hers. Both the intensity in his gaze and the lines around his eyes—lines that weren't there four years ago—made the grin fade from her lips.

"I've missed your smile," he said hoarsely.

"Not enough to postpone our wedding for forty-eight hours so I could bury a friend." The anger in her voice surprised him into releasing her. The words she hadn't been able to say because of shock rushed to her lips.

"I'll never forget that, Eric. I hate what you did to me...to *us*."

"Judging by that ring on your finger, I guess you got over it."

"One has nothing to do with the other! I just..." Her voice trailed off. At his continued silence, she took in a deep breath. "Don't know where that came from," she said shakily, backing away from his grasp to reach for her fallen gear. "Sorry, sir. I didn't intend to start my first day by dragging out the past."

"Skip the *sir* routine. I'm still Eric, same as always."

Lindsey nodded and stepped back into her ski binding. "Not exactly the same."

"It's been four years," he said simply.

"That's not what I mean. You seem—different."

To her surprise, Eric didn't press for details. "What do you want me to say, Lindsey? Right now, all I care about is that you do a professional job. There's no reason to think you wouldn't. You always have. Anything beyond that…'' He shrugged. ''Like you said, it's only your first day. We have time to talk later.''

The stillness of the winter snow, a snow high above the timberline, where neither bird nor insect made a sound, wrapped around them.

''A few months, anyway.'' Lindsey finished retrieving and donning her gloves and poles, then patted her thigh with her hand to call Ginger. She waited for Eric to take off at a smooth glide and followed, her pulse throbbing against her temples with emotion.

Eric didn't speak again for some time, and when he did, he spoke only of business matters in a brisk voice that neither repelled nor welcomed. For her part, she spent the next few hours adjusting to the routine of Yosemite. Old tasks came back easily—checking the snowpack, checking the few trails for signs of human visitors that might still remain visible, and watching the sky for indications of changing weather. When they'd traveled two-thirds of the large circle that would return them to the cabin, Eric called the other team by radio.

''We aren't stopping for lunch?'' she asked curiously. On days with clear weather, Eric preferred to take his meal on the trail. The rangers had more than enough cabin time—and cabin fever—when long storms rolled in. She'd packed enough for two, with a nut-and-carbo trail mix and a second bag of dried fruit, expecting Eric to go with his usual dried beef jerky and coffee, but not positive. As he'd said earlier, much had changed in four years.

''Not on your first day,'' he said. ''I'm assuming you're still on the Diamox. You need a few weeks to adjust to the altitude and cold. We'll go back to the cabin for lunch and you can take it easy for the rest of the day.

Let's take a breather, though. I could go for some coffee. You?''

"I'll pass. But I think I'll step off the trail," Lindsey said, falling back into the expression she used when needing privacy to relieve herself.

"Make it quick," Eric warned. "I don't want you chilled from exposure."

"Don't worry. I'm no rookie," Lindsey replied. She removed the snowshoes attached to her pack, substituted them for her skis, and left pack and gear with Eric. "Be right back. Come on, Ginger," she commanded.

They made their way through the snow—the upper level of loose shallow snow with layers of deep, hard-packed crust beneath. Once she reached some pine trees and scrub that made good cover, Lindsey enviously watched Ginger squat as she herself unzipped thermal-lined ski pants to get to her long underwear.

"Yeah, easy for you, girl," she muttered. Lindsey took care of her immediate need, finished with the biodegradable camping tissue and quickly redressed, her bottom still pimpled with goose bumps. "No more morning coffee for me," she said aloud, thinking of the hot chocolate and healthier orange juice she'd passed up. She never could hold caffeine.

She allowed herself a "Brrrr" before quickly treading forward on her snowshoes, using the brisk pace to warm herself. "Come on, Ginger, let's get back to the trail."

Ginger started, then suddenly stopped. Head held high, nose even higher, the golden retriever sniffed the air. Her tail extended stiffly, a sign of concentration.

"Whatcha got, girl?" Lindsey whispered. "A rabbit?"

Ginger's ears perked higher and her nostrils flared even wider. She whined, her tail rapidly swishing—signaling a "find," a human find.

"There can't be a *person* around here," Lindsey gasped. Maybe she'd read the dog's body language wrong. No matter how well-trained dogs were, when they switched handlers, there were always communication problems, at least initially. Not only that, every dog signaled a find differently. Best to be cautious. She thrust out a hand for the dog's collar, but Ginger evaded Lindsey's grasp and half ran, half bounded through the shadowed snow blanketing the base of the denser pines.

"Ginger, come!" Lindsey ordered, but Ginger remained determinedly on course.

Automatically Lindsey reached for her radio to call for backup, but it remained with the rest of her gear—back on the trail with Eric. She yanked off her glove and whistled through her fingers, the way her father had taught her at the family's kennels—long and loud—then hurried after the dog as fast as she could on snowshoes.

She heard Eric's responding two blasts on his whistle, but didn't slow her pace. Ginger might not have been her partner for long, but she trusted her partner. She always trusted her dogs. Unlike people, they'd never lied to her.

"I'm coming, Ginger! Hold up!" she ordered, but Ginger had already stopped of her own accord and was digging frantically at a large mound of snow. Up close, it looked odd; the snow was cut into crisp, hard-packed blocks and arranged into an igloo-like form. Large boughs of pine across the top both protected the blocks from wind and camouflaged its appearance.

"What is it?" Lindsey asked. She pulled the dog away, searching for the entrance she knew had to be there. "What did you find?"

In the distance she could hear Eric shouting her name. She couldn't answer; shocked surprise at her discovery had momentarily left her speechless. Lindsey reached into the hollow and pulled out a sleeping bag....

With a living, breathing little girl.

Rangers' winter cabin
Afternoon, same day

"GOT IT. OVER AND OUT." Eric switched off the radio at the desk and came out of the ranger office.

"Get a positive identity on the girl, Boss?" Keith asked as he carefully waxed his skis in front of the fire. "She's gotta be the one we're looking for."

"Yeah, she is. The description matched. Pamela Wilson. Daughter of Joyce and David Wilson. He was jailed for assault and battery, then the wife filed for divorce with full custody. The court granted both, and when the paperwork was served, the ex became enraged and broke out soon after."

"If I'd escaped from jail, I'd certainly find better living quarters than the snow." Keith shook his head. "What kind of father leaves a kid alone in the dead of winter?"

"One who's armed and wanted by the police for kidnapping. We're damn lucky he wasn't around at the time." Eric looked toward the women's closed bedroom door where Lindsey and Naomi had taken the child to be examined, tended and warmed. The thought of Lindsey walking into the kidnapper's base chilled his blood. She could just as easily have walked into an ambush with the father! He'd have to have a talk with her—with all of them—about taking extra precautions.

"Is he missing?" Keith asked. "Or dead?"

"Neither," Eric said. "I saw the child's shelter. It was first rate—an Inuit probably couldn't have done any better. Whoever he is, the fool knows his way around the outdoors. He did a good job of keeping his daughter hidden.''

"Speaking of good jobs, it didn't take our replacement long to make the find, did it?'' Keith switched skis. "And with a dog she's only had one day. Talk about luck—and skill. I'm impressed.''

"That's Lindsey for you.''

The bedroom door opened and Lindsey stepped out, much to Ginger's delight. The dog had been shut out of the bedroom and away from the young patient.

"Speak of the devil,'' Keith said, adding, "How is she?'' at the same time that Eric asked, "How's the kid?''

"Naomi says that on the whole, she'll be okay. A small frostbite patch on her nose. Her toes are worse. Naomi couldn't say if she'd lose any. She's a little dehydrated, but not underweight. Ginger, calm down.'' Lindsey searched through the pantry. "Naomi says there's some IV bags with Ringer's lactate solution in here somewhere?''

"On the left,'' Eric said.

"Your sister's more worried about her mental condition. The child's not speaking right now. Do we have confirmation on the name yet?''

Eric nodded. "Pamela Wilson. Goes by Pam. She's six years old, and her mother has full custody. From what I've been told, the father decided to take the daughter and run, after the wife filed for divorce—seems the bastard likes beating his family,'' Eric said with disgust.

"Yosemite is no place to escape—or to hide a child!'' Ginger stopped prancing at the harshness in Lindsey's voice. The dog went back to the hearth to quietly observe the proceedings.

"No, it's not.'' Eric passed Lindsey an IV bag.

"Why did he come to the park in the first place? Why are the police so sure he's in Yosemite?"

"They said he grew up in this county. Used to bring his wife and daughter on camping trips all the time. Considering how well he knows the area, we're lucky you found Pam."

"Ginger did. I got dragged along for the ride. Naomi wants a butterfly needle. Says they're best for little veins."

Eric passed that sterile packet to her. "The father's still out there. He's not going to be happy that we took his daughter."

"Obviously the mother's frantic to see her again. If only we could chopper Pam out," Lindsey said. "And chopper some police in."

"We'll just have to pack her out," Keith said.

"I don't think the weather will hold."

Lindsey and Keith both gazed toward the barometer on the outer porch. "It's falling?" she asked Eric.

"No, but it will. We'll soon have more snow than any of us can handle, let alone a small child."

"Are you sure?" Keith asked.

"He's never wrong about the weather." Lindsey collected the supplies.

"I can hope. Damn," Keith muttered.

"If it grounds us, it'll ground her father," Eric said. "For now, that's a plus."

Lindsey echoed Keith's reply. "We can hope," she said as she headed back to the women's bedroom with Naomi's supplies.

AN HOUR LATER, both women emerged; Lindsey first, Naomi following, leaving the door slightly ajar.

"Poor thing's out like a light. She has a slight fever,

too, but that's probably from the frostbite. I'm hoping after she's rested and hydrated she'll take some broth.'' Naomi headed for the sink to wash her hands. ''And she's on a bedpan until I say otherwise. I don't want this child outside or on her feet for any reason.''

''Is she well enough to be evacuated?'' Eric asked.

''Assuming her father lets us out of here...I think so,'' Naomi grabbed a towel to dry her hands. ''I'm going to go back and sit with her for a while.''

''I'll reassign the chores,'' Eric said. ''With Lindsey here, it won't be a problem.''

''I need to let Ginger out again,'' Lindsey said. She wouldn't bother with the leash this time. Ginger had followed her commands out on the trail. Lindsey didn't feel that Ginger had truly bonded with her, yet, but the dog seemed to have accepted her authority.

Eric reached for his coat. ''I'll come with you.''

Outside in the white stillness of Yosemite snow, Yosemite granite, they watched Ginger sniff and trot and sniff some more.

''Fussy, isn't she?'' Eric said.

Lindsey turned her face to him. ''She doesn't strike me as fussy. I think she just has a great nose. Lucky for us.''

''We're going to need more than luck,'' Eric said. ''I'm sure the father's still alive and kicking, and that means he's a threat. With his skills...''

Lindsey gave him her full attention. ''Yes?''

''He's trouble. Think about it. That shelter was expertly built, and would've served any experienced outdoors person well. You just happened to come across the child when he was out—probably gathering fuel.''

Lindsey blinked. ''I didn't notice any signs of a second person.''

"No, you wouldn't. Because you always watch the dog—and gauge your reactions by the dog's reactions."

She flushed, her cheeks turning red in the evening cold. "That's what a good dog handler is supposed to do."

"Lindsey, you could use your *own* senses as well! It would make you a much better—"

"Person?"

"Ranger. That child didn't start the campfire by herself. I learned a lot studying the campsite and what was left of the fire. Her father's skilled in surviving the wilderness, and he knows we have his daughter. It'll be a lot easier for him to find us than the other way around, and he's a desperate man. An armed man. I'd bet my paycheck he'll be back for her—and us."

The retriever scratched with her back legs, throwing fresh snow over the soiled snow just behind her. Then she trotted over to Lindsey, nuzzled her mitten-clad hand, and waited for the command to head back toward the cabin in the failing light.

"We can't cover our tracks," Eric said. "And we can't get Pam out of here unless we're on foot—not an option right now—even if Pam's condition allowed it. Not with the weather about to sour."

The two stood in silence for a moment. Ginger, tired of waiting, took the lead and ambled slowly toward the cabin.

"Independent, isn't she?" Lindsey said.

"It could've gotten her killed. And you, if Wilson had been at the camp with his daughter. He's packing a gun, possibly a rifle, and he isn't above hitting women or children. He wouldn't have thrown out the welcome mat for you. Lindsey, why didn't you radio me?"

"I—well, I didn't recognize that Ginger was alerting

me to a human, and everything happened so fast.... Plus I left my radio with the pack.''

''You should've had it on you.''

''I know. But I did whistle. It's just that I got out of the habit of relying on you as my partner. I've been working with other people for the past four years.''

Her words hung in the cold air, an almost tangible barrier.

''They're not here. I am,'' he said tersely. ''Finding Pam was a lucky break. But we still have to get her out. That won't be easy. Wilson's got the whole park to hide in. We're easy to find—and sitting targets for him if we make any mistakes. Don't let your independent streak turn you into our weakest link, Lindsey. We can't afford mistakes.''

Lindsey nodded. For the first time since her arrival, Eric's attitude held more than just professional caution. He was worried about her on a more personal level, too, or so it seemed. His next words confirmed it. ''Good. I've got to go talk to the others.'' As he passed her, she felt his hand drop lightly on her shoulder. ''Welcome back, Lindsey.''

CHAPTER FIVE

Rangers' winter cabin
Day 3, sunrise

JUST AS ERIC HAD PREDICTED, the rangers awoke to the howl of the wind, signaling the arrival of a fast-moving cold front. Hard, driving snow obscured vision and drowned out any other sounds as it whistled around the peaks near Half Dome and blew through the open spaces of Tuolumne Meadows. Keith and Eric alternated leaving the cabin on a rope guide to refill the generator; if it stopped, the fuel would freeze inside the engine, and the whole machine would have to be thawed to become useful again.

Lindsey took a few trips on the rope to walk the dog and do bedpan duty for Pam. She mentally contrasted her modern plumbing and deeply tiled whirlpool tub back home with the cold austerity of the outhouse. With a start, she realized she hadn't thought about San Diego once during the past few days, nor had she thought about Wade, except in relation to his ring. It still continued to hold her puffy finger hostage, and catch on glove or mitten every time she pulled one on.

For now, the white wilderness of the High Sierras, and the people inside the cabin were her whole frame of reference. One of them was a former lover, one a former enemy, and the other, a stranger. She stomped the snow from her boots before taking off her mittens and heavy parka inside the cabin's glass-enclosed porch area. Ginger's long coat remained full of snow, but it didn't seem to be bothering the dog. She waited for Lindsey to open the door to the interior cabin.

"Not until you shake," Lindsey said. "Shake, girl!"

Ginger obligingly lifted one front paw.

"No, not your paw," Lindsey said. "*Paw* means give me your foot. *Shake* means clean your coat." She was surprised at Eva, teaching the dog pet commands, instead of working commands.

Ginger's furrowed forehead showed confusion. Lindsey gently caressed the top of the dog's head.

"Obviously no one ever taught you what to do with a wet coat. Time to learn. We don't need melting snow all over the cabin." Lindsey leaned down and lifted a sensitive ear, then softly blew into it. "Shake!"

The irritating puff of air caused the desired result. The dog shook her ears, then her whole body, sending a mini-blizzard of snow flying.

"Good girl!" she praised. "Okay, *paw*," she commanded. "Let me see a paw." One by one, Lindsey lifted the four legs, and gently pulled out any stray pieces of ice or snow that had clumped inside the dog's pads. "Now you're ready to go inside. Come on." Stomping her boots one last time, Lindsey entered the cabin, mentally reminding herself to work on retraining Ginger.

"Took you longer than I thought," Naomi chided from her place at the table. "Breakfast is ready—and look who's joined us."

Bundled up in Naomi's over-large flannels and a blanket sat a little girl in an extra chair. Naomi had boosted her up with a couple of pillows. The child's frostbitten toes were warmly covered with thick loose socks, and straight brown bangs partially hid her eyes, but not her nervousness.

Lindsey sat in the chair closest to Pam, and had Ginger lie down between the chairs.

"You like dogs?"

The bent head lifted a bit, revealing a freckled nose, brown eyes and chapped lips. Keith and Eric joined the breakfast table, bringing to five the number of people sitting there. Lindsey noticed that Keith made a special point of sitting next to Naomi. She realized that Keith always preferred to sit near the other woman and wondered if there was a one-sided romance going on, then turned her attention to the child.

"Would you like to make friends with Ginger?"

The girl's chin lifted a little higher, and her eyes flicked from the dog to Lindsey and back to the dog again.

"She's a very nice girl," Lindsey went on. "She won't bite, so don't be afraid."

"I'm not afraid of dogs." Pam's voice was timid, but the words and emotion behind them were obviously truthful.

"Glad to hear it." Lindsey scooped some scrambled eggs, made from frozen egg liquid, and canned peaches onto Pam's plate. "When you're done eating, you can help me feed Ginger."

Pam nodded. Lindsey shoved the child's fork and spoon closer. "You're a big girl. You use a fork instead of a spoon, right?"

Pam paused, then stabbed at a slice of peach in heavy syrup and popped it into her mouth.

"Pretty good, huh?" Lindsey said, doing the same with her own peaches. "You like eggs?"

Pam shook her head and speared another peach.

"I like to do this." Lindsey reached for the bottle of ketchup and dumped a red blob on the scrambled eggs. "It makes 'em taste just like French fries. They even look like French fries. They're both yellow."

"Not the same yellow," Pam argued. These were her first words since her rescue. Lindsey ignored the suddenly alert adults and continued her conversation in the same soft tone she used with her dogs.

"Well, no, but they still taste like fries. Wanna try?" Lindsey scooped up some eggs and held them up. "Come on…one bite, and you can tell me if I'm right or wrong."

Pam opened her mouth and took the portion of egg, then chewed and swallowed.

"Good?"

"It doesn't taste like fries."

"Well, it does to me. What do you think?"

Pam shrugged. "It's okay."

Lindsey shoved the bottle of ketchup Pam's way. "Help yourself, honey."

"Mommy calls me that." Pam tried to snap the popcap up, and failed. Suddenly her eyes filled with tears. "I wanna go home." She began to cry in earnest, harsh sobs that made Naomi reach for the child, but Lindsey was there first.

Lindsey tucked the little girl under her chin and kissed the top of her head. "Of course you're going home! As soon as we can get you there."

Pam shivered. "Daddy said I couldn't see Mommy again. I have to stay with him forever an' ever."

"Well, he was wrong, wasn't he? You're right here with us, and we've already had the police tell your mother you're safe." Lindsey picked up her napkin and wiped the child's cheeks and nose. "We'll send you home as soon as possible. After you get better—and the weather does, too.''

The child sniffled some more, and Lindsey wiped her face again and rocked her. After a few minutes, Pam settled down. Lindsey speared yet another peach and fed it to her. ''Shall we put ketchup on the peaches?'' she asked.

Pam grimaced. ''Not on mine.''

''Come on, let's try it,'' Lindsey teased. ''I will if you will.''

Pam shook her head, then gasped as Lindsey dunked a peach slice into some ketchup and ate it. ''Umm-umm! Tastes just like French fries!'' Lindsey smacked her lips. ''Your turn!''

Pam wrinkled her nose. ''Yuck!''

''Fine. More for me. Forget the ketchup.'' Lindsey moved Pam's plate closer. ''Let's have a race and see who finishes first. On your mark, get set, go!''

Five minutes later, all the peaches were gone, and a few minutes after that the eggs as well. Pam yawned, drank her milk, then yawned again.

''Back to bed for you, young lady,'' Naomi announced.

Pam reluctantly allowed herself to be taken from Lindsey's lap. She balked as Naomi began to lift her up. ''I was gonna feed the dog!''

''You can feed the dog in the bedroom,'' Naomi said firmly. ''I don't want you getting chilled.''

''Good idea,'' Lindsey agreed. ''You two can make friends with each other there.''

Pam sighed with contentment as Naomi carried her away. Lindsey and Ginger followed, closing the door behind them.

''IMPRESSIVE,'' KEITH SAID, clearing the dishes as Eric studied the storm outside. ''Our replacement always seems to know just the right thing to say or do. Seems to come naturally to her. I'm surprised you ever let her go.''

Eric peered through the small window and pivoted back toward the table. ''No one tells Lindsey how to do her job.''

''I'm not talking about work. I'm talking about personally. Naomi's dropped a few hints here and there about Lindsey.''

''My personal life is none of your business.''

''Look, Eric. We've got enough going on here without adding an ex's angst to the list.''

Eric restrained the sudden flash of anger coursing through him. ''Don't worry about it,'' he said curtly.

The men were silent for a moment, then Keith put down his pile of dirty dishes with a thump. ''You might as well know I've applied for a transfer. Another winter alone with your...moods—and your sister's—isn't anything I'd care to repeat. If I have my way, I'll be leaving when Lindsey does.''

Before Eric could reply, the lights flickered, went out, then went on again, but dimly.

''Hell, now what?'' Keith said. ''I'd better check the generator.''

''I'll go with you,'' Eric said, the hair on the nape of his neck rising with a creepy premonition he'd learned never to ignore.

''Pass.''

''I *said* I'll go with you,'' Eric repeated. He reached for his ranger-issued rifle. ''Naomi—Keith and I are going out to check on the generator!'' he called out. ''Be back in twenty minutes!''

NAOMI LOOKED AT HER WATCH, then continued to bandage Pam's feet. ''My brother has a loud voice, doesn't he?'' she said, hoping Pam would open up with her as she had with Lindsey. Like Naomi, Lindsey sat on the bed. Ginger lay on the floor closest to the portion of bed where Pam sat, sniffing Pam's damaged toes, then sniffing the air, then the child's toes again. Next she shoved her golden head straight at Naomi's chest.

"Ginger, knock it off," Naomi grumbled. "Lindsey, do something."

Lindsey grabbed Ginger's collar and gently tugged, effectively distracting the dog.

"My feet are ugly," Pam moaned. "They're all black."

"Just the toes," Naomi explained. She'd finished bandaging the first foot and was beginning the other. "That black is where the cold damaged your capillaries, and the lifeless tissue is starting to slough off."

"Huh?" Pam pulled her bare foot away from Naomi and started to touch the damaged toes.

Lindsey caught Pam's hands and clapped them together in a patty-cake motion. "Don't touch. The black is like a big scab. Don't make it bleed."

"Oh. Okay."

"And Ginger, get your nose out of here. She wants to lick your feet," Lindsey told her, "because that's how animals help heal themselves, by licking their wounds. The increased circulation helps speed new skin growth."

Ginger shoved her nose underneath Naomi's hands and sniffed at the bandaged foot. Then, before either woman could react, Ginger stood on her hind legs and shoved hard at Naomi's chest again. Naomi overbalanced and slid off the edge of the mattress to bounce down on the floor rug with a thud.

"Ouch!" Naomi cried, rubbing her behind. Pam giggled as the dog jumped off the bed to nuzzle Naomi's chest.

"This dog is always pestering me. Even Eva couldn't stop her. For heaven's sake, Lindsey, do something!"

"CAN'T WE DO SOMETHING?" Eric asked. "We need this generator working!"

"I told you, I'm trying." Keith set down his wrench with a clatter and rubbed his hands together. "If there wasn't a raging blizzard outside, I'd swear someone's been messing around in here. The fuel pump's barely processing, but it was fine yesterday."

Eric froze. "Wilson's been here."

"You sure? The man couldn't have hiked through a storm, waltzed in here, tampered with the generator and strolled back out again. Seems hard to believe."

Eric hurried to the outside of the door that protected the generator. Amidst howling wind and sharp, stinging snow, the faint impression of footsteps into and away from the shed were still visible. Inspecting the keyhole was an afterthought. The bright silver lines stood out starkly among the dull weathering of the surrounding iron plate. For once, Eric hated being right.

"He picked the lock," he told Keith a few minutes later. "The scratches are fresh."

"Could've been a bear. They don't have a true hibernation. One could've left his den and tried here for food." Keith picked up his wrench once more and went back to tinkering with the fuel pump.

"Animals don't leave human footprints. Where's your repair bin with the spare parts?"

"You don't think…" Keith rushed over to the unlocked storage cubby and lifted the wooden lid. He swore viciously at the damage inside.

"Bears don't destroy so neatly." Eric's jaw tightened. "That son of a—"

"So can you fix the generator or not?"

"I do keep a spare set of parts on the cabin porch where we store the skis. It's not as extensive as the missing set, but I ran out of room in here. They're in my yellow tool kit."

"I'll get it. You keep babying the generator. If it stops on us, we'll never get it going again."

Eric reached for his gloves and the length of rope they used to get back and forth to the cabin. "I'll be back in five. Lock the door."

Ginger continued to pester Naomi. Lindsey called off the dog and ordered her out of the room. When Naomi finally finished tending to Pam, Lindsey called Ginger back. "Pam, you stay in bed. Ginger will keep you company. Naomi and I will be back in a minute."

"I don't wanna take a nap," Pam complained.

"No one said you had to nap. I just want you to rest your feet," Naomi said.

"Here." Lindsey opened a dresser drawer and removed one of Eva's old socks. "Take this—" Lindsey tucked it into a ball shape "—and throw it for Ginger. Tell her *fetch*. I'm going to close the door. Come on, Naomi."

In the main room, Naomi looked puzzled. "What's going on? You're acting almost as weird as the dog."

Lindsey checked her watch. "The men will be outside for another ten minutes. We need to use their room."

Naomi sighed. "Look, I have work to do. If this is some kind of game—"

"You know me better than that." *If anyone plays games, it's you,* she refrained from saying. Naomi had been pleasant, even welcoming, and Lindsey had decided to return the favor.

Inside the men's bedroom, Naomi crossed her arms. "Now what?"

"Take off your sweater and shirt." Lindsey locked the door.

Naomi actually grinned. "Yeah, right." She stopped at the serious expression on Lindsey's face.

"This isn't a joke. I want to see what's bugging Ginger. Have you been injured lately?"

"Nope."

"We need to be sure, okay? Take off the sweater and shirt," she repeated.

Clad in her bra, Naomi frowned as her skin broke out in goose bumps from the cold. Lindsey circled her, carefully inspecting the other woman's sides, back and front.

"I see a bruise by your left breast. What's that from?"

"I told you, Eva's dog's been banging me in the chest every chance she gets." Naomi reached for her shirt and sweater.

"No, don't get dressed. Take off your bra."

"What?"

Lindsey ignored the woman's reluctance. "When's the last time you did a self-exam?"

"Huh?"

"When's the last time you checked your breasts?"

"I don't know.... What does this have to do with anything?"

"Last month? More than a few months?"

Naomi shrugged. "I don't know. A while."

"Remove your bra, get on the bed and examine yourself."

"Come on, Lindsey, I have chores to do and a patient to attend! I can do this later."

"Come on, it'll only take a minute. You're already half undressed. I'll watch Pam."

"For the love of… Oh, all right, if it'll make you happy and get Eva's dog to settle down."

"She's not Eva's dog anymore. She's mine."

LINDSEY SAT ON THE BED opposite Pam, watching the girl throw the sock for the dog. Ginger retrieved it over and over, delighted with all the attention. Pam smiled and giggled, but Lindsey found little joy in the pair's antics.

Dogs were used for search-and-rescue and for drug detection, because of their incredible sense of smell. Vets claimed most dogs could detect and remember more than ten thousand smells, while labradors could detect probably hundreds of thousands, even more than bloodhounds. A new smell was like a loose twenty dollar bill on a busy city sidewalk—something to stop and pounce upon.

Dogs could smell the chemicals of those prone to seizures, and if trained, could notify epileptics of an oncoming grand mal attack before the person afflicted even knew. Lindsey was also aware that dogs could smell cancerous cells. A human's porous skin was no barrier to a nose that could sniff out a little girl hundreds of feet away, hidden deep in the snow and pine branches. If Ginger kept shoving her nose at a certain area of Naomi's body, then there had to be a new smell to be investigated and categorized.

Ginger wasn't trained as a clinical dog with any frame of reference for the strange smell Lindsey suspected Naomi carried. Nor did Ginger know what to do after locating it, any more than a drug-sniffing dog would know what to do in an avalanche, or a rescue dog would understand how to react among airport baggage. Human-canine bonds required intimate knowledge of each partner by the other, and specific training to keep the team safe and satisfied while achieving certain desired results. Without it, there was no life-saving team, only a person and his or her pet.

Lindsey's father had been, and still was, a professional dog-handler who owed his life to his military bomb-sniffing dog overseas. Lindsey's retired mother had once been a canine handler for the police force. Both parents bred and trained American Kennel Club registered German shepherds—canine officers that protected the public in numerous ways, including drug detection, bomb detection and criminal apprehension. Lindsey had grown up with her parents' deep respect and even deeper trust in the ability of their dogs. Those same dogs protected the lives of their owners with a fierce loyalty; a German shepherd police dog named Jade had taken three bullets meant for Lindsey's mother and paid the ultimate price, dying in the then-young officer's arms.

Not to trust one's dog was, to Lindsey and her family, unthinkable. Their way of life was too dangerous to do otherwise. Lindsey's oldest sister, Kate, worked her dog with the U.S. Customs Department, searching for contraband at the San Diego Airport and the San Diego Harbor Port Authority. Lara, the youngest, had followed in her mother's footsteps and worked the K-9 division of the San Diego police. Lindsey, not as comfortable around firearms as the rest of her family, had entered the park service and specialized in search-and-rescue with Missy, her first canine ranger partner.

Her family possessed knowledge and experience with dogs that the general pet-owning public didn't. Ginger's actions around Naomi had been a red flag to Lindsey. She desperately prayed that both she and the dog were wrong in their suspicions.

Lindsey heard the men's bedroom door open. She tousled Pam's hair and grabbed a nature book with large pictures. "You can look at this if you want. I'll be right back."

Ginger dropped the sock and followed Lindsey into the main cabin living area. Lindsey closed the bedroom door behind her and faced Naomi. The other woman's face was white, and one hand rested over her breast.

"There's a lump. I found a lump," Naomi whispered in a choked voice.

Despite their past differences, Lindsey opened her arms to envelop and comfort with a hug. Naomi fell upon her as a lifeline. "It'll be all right," Lindsey said.

"How do you know? I haven't done a self-exam since the end of the summer! And I'm the medical ranger, too. I should've known better. Oh, God, what if it's malignant? What if it's spread?" Naomi sank to the couch, then buried her face in her hands.

Eric reentered the cabin to find both of them sitting quietly on the couch, Ginger at her usual spot on the hearth.

"Keith's still working on the generator. I've got news," he said slowly. "It's not good."

Naomi lifted her face, her eyes troubled. "Join the club, twin," she said.

"Sweetie?"

Despite the seriousness of the situation, Lindsey felt the pain of earlier times when Eric spoke. He made the word sound exactly what it was—an endearment between two people bonded since conception—and Naomi did the same in return when she called Eric *twin*. It made her both jealous and sorrowful.

Naomi shook her head and stood. "*You* tell him, Lindsey. I'll be with Pam."

CHAPTER SIX

Rangers' winter cabin
Late afternoon

THE BLIZZARD'S HOWLING WINDS passed by, but the heavy snow continued its fall. Both Pam and Naomi had succumbed to much-needed naps in the women's bedroom after hot bowls of soup for lunch. Keith lounged in his bedroom with a book he'd started, having finally restored the generator to full power and added a chain and padlock to the generator-shack door. Only Eric and Lindsey remained in the cabin's main room, Eric perched on the hearth, his back to the fire, and Lindsey sitting cross-legged on the rug, toying with Ginger's ears.

The dog snored gently on the rug facing the blazing fire as Lindsey waited for an opening to tell Eric about Naomi's health, while Eric summarized the situation with Wilson.

"Pam needs a doctor, and we have a violent felon trying to steal back the child he kidnapped. However, you and Ginger have only worked together a few days, and Ginger could slow us down. We'd have to pack her on the sled to get through the snow—if she'd allow it. Plus we have a blizzard, and although the generator may or may not keep working, thanks to Wilson, Keith has secured the shed and it's working now. I think our safest bet is to stay put. There's four of us, and only one of him.''

Thinking of Naomi, Lindsey asked, ''Isn't there any way to get Pam out of here? Couldn't Naomi and another ranger try?''

Eric lifted his head. ''How? Naomi might've been able to ski out the same way you came in before the storm, but now she'd have to snowshoe out. As for Pam, she can't walk, not with those frostbitten feet. We can't track down her father in this weather, and frankly, I wouldn't risk it. We'd best sit tight.''

''But…after the weather clears, maybe then?'' Lindsey pressed.

''Hard to say. I want you to talk to Pam and find out if her father has a rifle. We need to know how much of a buffer we have. There's a big difference between the reach of a high-powered rifle and a handgun.'' He shook his head. ''I refuse to lose another person.''

Lindsey moved to touch his arm, but Eric bent to pick up a piece of wood to toss on the fire. By the time he'd finished, the opportunity to comfort him was gone.

''Here's the way I see it,'' he said suddenly. ''Once the storm clears, we reevaluate. I'm in no rush to expose our backs. I'm betting the moment we take Pam out into the open, Wilson will show up. There's only one route out of here, and I'm sure he knows it as well as we do. He'll be watching the trail.''

''We won't have an easy time of it, that's for sure.''

''If we have to keep Pam here until the thaw, we will.''

''Until spring?''

''Why not? Then the police can get in to help search

for Wilson, and Pam can easily be transported out. Our job is search-and-rescue, not playing posse for some escaped psycho.'' He shook his head. ''The police have called a temporary halt to the manhunt because of the weather. That new storm front is already causing high winds. So...''

''Spring's a long time off.'' Lindsey chose her next words carefully. ''What if there's a medical emergency?''

''With Pam? I've thought about the worst-case scenario. If that happens, two of us will act as decoy, while the other two take Pam.''

''How?''

''Why go into details? Naomi said Pam's stable for now. The longer she stays here, the better off she'll be, especially with those feet. In the meantime...I was wondering how you and Naomi were getting along.''

His abrupt change of subject took Lindsey by surprise. ''Getting along?'' she echoed.

''Yeah. You two always rubbed each other the wrong way. But believe it or not, I think Naomi's missed you. She was pleased to hear you were coming back, and even fussed with Eva's room.''

Lindsey remembered the herb sachet under her pillow. ''That was kind of her.''

''Naomi promised to do her best to get along during your stay. I know she meant it.''

''That's...good to hear,'' Lindsey said, noncommittal. A few days weren't enough to generalize about a person's behavior. ''Besides, I knew what I was getting into. Jack Hunter was quite clear about the situation when he called me. I could have said no.''

"He told me you almost did."

"Almost."

"Because of the danger, or because of me?"

Lindsey didn't answer immediately. She rose from the carpet and joined him on the hearth so they were both at eye level, the dog between them at their feet.

"Because of you," she said softly. "I didn't know what to expect. Didn't think you'd want me here."

"That was never true. Not then, and not now."

"I wasn't sure you'd feel that way, considering—"

"Considering we couldn't talk out our problems," Eric said, completing the sentence for her. "Missy's death wasn't the issue."

"You realize that now?" she said.

"Yeah. It was just the latest in a long line of events that showed we didn't really know each other well. Didn't understand how the other feels…reacts to things. Not that I'm blaming you," he quickly added.

"We never agreed on anything except in the bedroom." Lindsey sighed. "I didn't postpone the wedding because you thought I chose an animal—a dead animal, no less—over you. How could you think that of me?"

"What else could I think?"

"You could've thought for yourself, instead of letting Naomi do the thinking for both of you. Which proves your point. We weren't ready to get married. Marriage requires more than great sex." A long pause, then Lindsey gathered her courage. "You never told me what Naomi said to you to make you change your mind about delaying the wedding a few days."

"No."

"Will you tell me?"

No answer.

"Why not? I'd really like to know."

"Because I still don't know if Naomi lied to me four years ago. Until I can straighten that out with her, I can't talk about it to you."

"That's me—always the third wheel."

Eric's expression spoke volumes, but he didn't deny it.

The quiet sputtering of the fire behind them was the only sound in the room. Though physically they were only inches apart, the emotional distance between them seemed like miles. She knew this particular topic of conversation had been tabled. Lindsey opened her mouth to broach the subject of Naomi's medical condition, but Eric spoke first.

"So, this new guy in your life. What's his name?"

"Wade."

"He make you happy?"

She shrugged. "Why wouldn't he? He's a nice guy."

"Which doesn't answer my question."

Now Lindsey chose to remain silent.

"So...is he any good in bed?"

"Eric!"

"Does he satisfy you?"

"That's none of your business," Lindsey said, her voice unsteady.

"You brought it up."

"Just to illustrate a point! Besides, sex isn't everything."

"So he doesn't," Eric concluded. "Yet you're wearing his ring."

"I said I—he insisted—" Lindsey broke off at the smug look on Eric's face, angry at having revealed so much. She'd forgotten how Eric's blunt honesty frequently disarmed her. "Damn you, Ric!"

Eric's lips twitched upward. "No one's called me Ric since you left. Or told me to go to hell. I've missed that."

"I haven't missed your lack of tact. Now, would you please drop the subject and listen for five minutes? I need to talk about Naomi."

"What about Naomi?" Eric asked impatiently. "Or is this just a convenient change of subject?"

Lindsey reached for Eric's hand and took a deep breath. "There's no easy way to say this. Naomi found a lump in her breast. Or rather, Ginger did."

"What?"

Lindsey quickly explained, her voice low. "And worst of all, she says she hasn't done a self-exam since last summer."

"My God! How's she taking it?"

"She's shook up. So badly, she asked me to tell you."

"It could just be a cyst. Something harmless."

Lindsey tightened her fingers around Eric's. "I hope you're right. But Eric, Ginger wouldn't act so aggressively toward a cyst. She wouldn't react at all. Cysts are fluid-filled pockets and don't necessarily transmit specific chemical scents like cancer. I didn't tell Naomi what I've read on the subject—frankly, it wasn't the time—but I'm as worried as she is."

Eric's face paled, and he abruptly withdrew his hand from hers to run his fingers through his hair. Her hand felt empty without his touch.

"I know you said it makes sense to sit tight with Pam," she continued. "Wait until her feet heal and the weather clears. Wait here until it's safer. But Eric, if it were my sister…if it were *me*…I wouldn't want to wait that long. Not with this.''

Eric nodded just once. He glanced at his watch and stood. ''Time to check the generator again,'' he said in a clipped voice.

''Need some help?'' Lindsey asked.

''No.'' Eric bent and, to her surprise, kissed her cheek. ''But thanks.'' Then, before she could make any kind of reply at all, he left.

INSIDE THE GENERATOR ROOM, Eric did nothing more than take a perfunctory look at the equipment. He'd used that excuse to be alone for a few minutes, to calm down. He'd barely been able to enjoy Lindsey's presence after four long years before that pleasure had been replaced by the horror of her walking in on Wilson's camp. Then his triumphant discovery of Lindsey's lukewarm feelings for her new fiancé had warred with fierce jealousy that she'd found comfort with someone else. There'd been no one for him since Lindsey. He knew what he wanted, and unlike her, he was unwilling to settle for substitutes. Then after his tactless, but driven, queries about her sex life, she'd changed the subject to Naomi's health.

Two days back in his life, and Lindsey had already turned it upside down—along with everyone else's. Eric knew his twin. Naomi wouldn't want to spend the rest of the winter at Yosemite, nor could he blame her. She'd want to leave immediately, which meant even more danger to the rangers, and no medical personnel left at the cabin. Pamela Wilson needed medical care. If Naomi left the park, should they risk taking Pam on that journey as well?

Two days with Lindsey Nelson had changed so much, yet some things remained the same. Eric still loved her. Her unpredictability was her greatest asset as a ranger, because she saw things differently. She'd climbed Half Dome in the summer just to see the view from the top. Risked her life to scale the rocks above Bridalveil Fall in her quest for beauty. Saw rare dimensions in people and animals that even hard-core environmentalists—like him—could miss.

It was that aspect of her that also troubled him the most. Life was simpler for Eric. Peaceful. Even boring at times. Boring wasn't bad, not to him. No adrenaline junkie, he didn't need armed kidnappers and daring rescues and hair-raising rock climbs to satisfy his soul. He'd never be the type to jump out of a perfectly good plane just to try skydiving. Or bungee-jumping off some bridge to get bounced around for the thrill of it. He wasn't afraid of those adventures; they'd just never appealed to him. He'd always been satisfied with what he had and what he did, and considered himself damn lucky to have such a good life. When things went wrong, he solved the problem as best he could, with as much courage as he could, and continued on. He could enjoy the beauty of Half Dome, and life, from the peaceful comfort of his present world. Most people searched their whole lives for stability; Eric had been one of the lucky ones born with it, and was wise enough to realize that.

Lindsey had never been satisfied with one job, one lifestyle, one home or—he hated to admit it—one man. No matter how high she climbed, there was always the next climb. The next rescue. Or discovering something no one else would even have noticed. Like a missing little girl, or Naomi's lump. With Lindsey, these things weren't blind luck or pure coincidence. They were a normal part of the life she led.

Hence the problem. *Lindsey was right. I don't know her as well as she wants, but I know I love her.* It would take the rest of his life to get to know the real Lindsey, and he'd sometimes worried she'd find him—and life with him—dull. Only when they made love had he felt truly connected with her, confident of her love for him. To have her say "Sex isn't everything" hurt deeply, because without their lovemaking, he and Lindsey were oil and vinegar. They didn't mix well—but he didn't care. She was the only woman for him, and somehow, some way, he'd get her back.

If they all managed to survive the dangers that lay ahead of them.

LATER, THE FOUR ADULTS regrouped once more at the kitchen table and listened to Eric's plan.

"This is a mess," Keith groaned, pouring himself a coffee from the newly brewed pot. "Whether we stay or go, we're sitting ducks."

"I'm not staying here the rest of the winter. I'm leaving as soon as I can," Naomi insisted. "And if I'm going, we might want to consider taking Pam along, too, that's all I'm saying."

"I wouldn't give you five minutes if you did," Keith warned.

"I'm not going three more months without a doctor," Naomi said. "I can't afford to wait."

"No one's asking you to wait, twin," Eric said calmly, resting his hand over his sister's. "I'm just trying to think of the safest way. If you take Pam, you become a target for Wilson.''

"I don't want to leave her behind, either,'' Naomi said, stirring her own coffee. ''Her feet need medical attention, and I'm the medical ranger. She'd be okay for a daytime sled ride, and much better in a hospital.''

Lindsey nodded. The park had small hand-held sleds they used in the winter for transporting injured people, supplies or wood. ''It would take two of us to pull the sled. I'll go,'' Lindsey volunteered. ''I skied in a few days ago. I'm the most familiar with the trail.''

"What's left of it,'' Naomi said. They all turned toward the window and the heavy snow still falling. ''Besides, you're out of shape. You're not up to moving out quickly if Wilson's on our backs. And you never qualified on firearms. I'm medical staff, so I didn't, either. I'd need Keith or Eric with me.''

"If and when the time comes, we'll set out in pairs,'' Eric said. ''We'll split up, and the decoy will be two rangers with an empty sled.''

"That's only gonna work for so long.'' Keith sipped at his coffee. ''There's only one way in and out of the park this time of year. Our sicko will know to follow the couple taking that route.''

"Not once you ditch the empty sled and keep heading out,'' Eric announced.

"Pam will stay here?'' Lindsey asked, immediately catching on.

"For now. I'm guessing Wilson will use a park map and move into one of the cabins or some other building. That's what I'd do. We'll try to flush Wilson out of hiding. If so, we may be able to catch him with no danger to the child or to us.''

''Sounds like a plan,'' Keith said. ''Let's hope the weather cooperates.''

''We're not leaving soon, that's for sure,'' Naomi said gloomily. ''I'm gonna check on Pam.''

''I'll start dinner,'' Eric said.

''I'll do it,'' Lindsey volunteered. ''Eric, go with Naomi and talk to Pam. Time to find out if her father has a rifle.''

CHAPTER SEVEN

Women's room
Same day, late evening

PAM SLEPT FITFULLY IN Naomi's bed while brother and sister sat side by side on what used to be Eva's.

"Her toes are turning blacker. They're worse than I originally thought," Naomi said. "She's going to need surgery, after all, but I don't know how we can pack her out with her father hanging around...."

Eric slung his arm around Naomi's shoulders. "She's doing okay for now. How are you holding up?"

Naomi shook her head. "I can't leave Pam, Pam can't leave the cabin, I'm desperate to get to a hospital, and there's a madman out there gunning for us. I could've caught this earlier, but I didn't bother doing a simple monthly check. How do you *think* I'm doing? Stupid question, Eric!"

Eric pulled her close. "I know."

"Yeah, well, what about you?" Naomi asked, leaning against him. "You've got all this on your hands, plus Lindsey. Talk about lousy timing for romance."

"There's no romance. She didn't waste any time volunteering to escort you out of here," he said.

"She volunteered *because* of you."

Eric lifted his head. "Nice try."

"It's true. You should've seen her give me the third degree about examining myself. She's as pushy as you are when she thinks she's right. And she's talked about everything *but* you—which, from a woman's point of view, is a good sign."

"If you say so."

"I know so."

The two were quiet as they studied the feverish child.

"Things can only get better," Naomi said. "Pam didn't remember her father having a rifle. And if we're lucky, Wilson's frozen solid by now."

Eric shook his head. "I wouldn't bet on it. He knows his way around too well for that. He's probably waiting out the storm in some shelter. They're listed in all the park maps. Maybe the museum—that's the building closest to his original igloo."

"Too bad he didn't use it before his daughter's feet froze. That pathetic excuse for a father deserves a public flogging, bringing a child out here. Or worse."

"Finding him's my job. You worry about Pam—and yourself."

Naomi suddenly smiled. "Remember when we were little? We'd talk about growing up and having our own kids. I was going to have twin girls, and you were going to have—"

"Twin boys. I remember."

"I always felt bad that Bruce and I never had any children after we got married, but he wanted to wait. He waited himself right into the cemetery."

"Getting a bit morbid, aren't we?" Eric said in a soft voice.

''Hell, yes....'' Naomi's voice broke, and she finished on a whisper. ''I don't want to die, twin. Not like this....''

''You won't,'' Eric said fiercely, praying he was right. ''I promise I'll get you out of here.''

KEITH FIDDLED WITH the rangers' ham radio, trying to get through, but having no success. Lindsey watched him from the kitchen area.

''No luck?''

''None. Storm's messing up transmission. Damn! Eric wanted me to check with the police and see if Wilson has a rifle registered in his name. Pam didn't think so, but she didn't know for sure.''

''Eric never did leave anything to chance,'' Lindsey said.

Keith shrugged, then turned down the squeal of the radio, leaving it on, but without the static. ''When's dinner ready?'' he asked with the ravenous appetite of most people in cold-weather areas, where abundant calories were needed to keep the body warm.

''An hour. You want me to fix you a snack? There's fresh coffee, too.''

''No, I can wait.'' Keith glanced at the closed door of the women's bedroom. ''They've been in there a long time,'' he observed. ''I hope she isn't feeling worse.''

''Naomi's keeping her fever down with Tylenol and wet compresses. I hope she doesn't lose any toes. Frostbite's always tricky to assess.''

''I didn't mean Pam. I meant Naomi. How's she doing? Do you think she has cancer?''

Lindsey blinked with surprise at Keith's bluntness, and

at something else she heard in his voice. "You're in love with her," she said, her words a statement, not a question.

Keith's smile was bittersweet. "Yeah, but the opposite isn't true. Still, if Naomi has cancer...I'd trade places with her in a minute if I could."

Lindsey fixed two mugs of coffee, and took Keith's over to the desk where he still sat. She chose her favorite spot on the hearth, Ginger at her feet, and Keith continued.

"Of course, I don't have a chance in hell. When she's not carrying a torch for her dead husband, she's always with Eric. It's like they're joined at the hip. You don't know how many nights I've wished him a million miles away."

Lindsey nodded. "Been there myself."

"How did you stand it?" Keith asked.

It was Lindsey's turn to shrug. "Without going into detail, let me just say that Naomi wasn't our only problem."

"Eva had her dog, Naomi and Eric have each other, and I'm tired of talking to the trees. You might as well know, I've given Eric my notice."

"Sorry to hear that." Lindsey knew some rangers couldn't handle the solitude of a remote station or the lack of contact with other people. Not everyone was cut out for a life of isolation and winter hardship. "So you'll be leaving when this crisis is over?"

"I hope to escort Naomi out of here. She—and Pam, if she goes—will need protection."

"You don't think Eric would want that job?"

"I'm hoping he'd rather chase down Wilson. I'm a good shot, but he's better."

Lindsey was silent for a moment. "He's got a lot of tough decisions to make. I wouldn't want to be in his shoes."

Keith looked at the closed bedroom door again. "Right now, I would."

A few minutes later Eric returned to the main room.

"What's up?" Lindsey immediately asked.

"Pam still has a temperature. Naomi's watching her."

"How's Naomi?" Keith asked.

"Biting the bullet. She'll join us with Pam for dinner."

"If there's anything I can do for either of them, just let me know," Keith said. "FYI, I couldn't reach the police on the radio. There's still too much interference from the storm. I'm off for a quick load of wood before it gets dark—just in case the generator gives us problems and we have to stoke up the woodstove. The fireplace won't be enough to keep the bedrooms warm."

"I'll help," Eric said.

"No. You stay," Keith replied abruptly, hurrying away from them both.

After Keith had dressed and left the cabin, Eric wondered aloud, "What's with him?"

"He's worried."

"We all are," Eric said impatiently.

Lindsey chose her next words carefully, not wanting to betray a confidence. "He's especially worried about Naomi. Said he hopes you'll let him escort her out of here when she's ready to go."

"Why would he assume I wouldn't?"

"I didn't say he assumed. I said he hoped."

"But—"

Lindsey gave up trying to be tactful. Tact was never a

strong point with the Kincaides, anyway. "He's in love with her, Ric."

"*What?*"

She checked on their dinner. "The man wears his heart on his sleeve."

"I haven't noticed. Naomi hasn't, either—she would've told me. Did he come out and say so?"

"Yes," she answered reluctantly. "Ordinarily I'd mind my own business, but in these circumstances, everyone's emotional state is my business—and yours. You're head ranger. Believe me when I say Keith's a nervous wreck about Naomi."

"I...can't believe it. Are you sure?"

"He said he wished he could trade his health, his life, for hers if she has a malignancy. Hardly the words of a disinterested bystander."

The lights flickered again and went dim. Lindsey held her breath until they flickered once more, then went back to full strength.

When they did, Lindsey found Eric's gaze on her. "We can't afford any more problems than we already have, Lindsey. I've got a bad feeling about this weather."

Despite the warm air in the kitchen, Lindsey felt goose bumps rising on the nape of her neck. "How bad?"

"Donner Party bad."

Lindsey's breath caught. The winter of 1846-47 was the worst in Sierra Nevada history, with the heaviest snowfall in one season, more than twenty-two feet, ever recorded. Nine terrible blizzards followed, one after another, causing the deaths of forty-five of the eighty-three hardy pioneers, and the consumption of the dead by the living. Civilization had been replaced by a primitive urge to survive, and cannibalism had been a terrible, snow-forced atrocity.

"The bears' coats and prehibernation fat were extreme this year, Lindsey. The birds migrated early, and the deer moved down country much earlier than usual. The day you skied in and the day after have been the only decent breaks in the weather all winter. And it's only February. Wilson or no Wilson, we may have to pack out of here sooner than I'd like. *All* of us—or, worst case scenario, none of us."

Lindsey shivered. Eric had a sixth sense about weather. He didn't need a meteorologist's reports to predict climate. He'd spent his whole life in the area, and his very survival depended on his ability to judge the elements. When it came to snowstorms, Lindsey had never known him to be wrong. Ever.

"What are we going to do?" Lindsey asked.

"For now…we wait."

Day 4, presunrise

LINDSEY SAT BOLT UPRIGHT in her sleeping bag on the couch. "Who's there?" she asked in the darkness.

"Just me," Eric replied. "It's my turn to start the morning fire. I didn't mean to wake you."

"It's okay," Lindsey said groggily.

"Why are you on the couch?"

"Pam's temp is still up. She had a rough night. Poor thing didn't settle down until a few hours ago. I let Naomi have my bed so she could get some rest, too." She pushed an unruly lock of hair out of her eyes, her bare arm pimpling with the cold. "What time is it?"

"Close to five. You warm enough?"

"My legs are." Ginger's weight covered her legs on the far end of the couch. She tucked her arm back inside the sleeping bag and zipped it up, though she remained sitting. "As for the rest of me, well…this sure isn't San Diego."

"Better get used to it. The generator's been limping along all night." His voice held more worry than Lindsey liked to hear. "Keith had to tinker with it around two. We're going back out for another check and more wood as soon as it's light."

Lindsey nodded. It appeared that Naomi and Pam weren't the only ones who'd been cheated of sleep. "What's it like outside?" she asked, aware that the earlier howling of the wind had subsided.

"We're catching the tail end of the storm, but there's another moving in."

"More snow…" Lindsey murmured.

"Too much snow. If we can't get Naomi out of here today or tomorrow, she won't be going anywhere."

"Hell. Ginger, get down." Ginger opened her eyes and defiantly closed them again. "Hey, girl. Move." Lindsey gently shoved at the dog with her foot, finally sending a reluctant canine off the couch and over to the hearth rug. Lindsey reached for her thermals and wool socks, stuffed at the bottom of her sleeping bag and, starting with fresh cotton panties, began to dress within its warmth. Unlike more stalwart stock, she slept with clean, prewarmed underwear every night to spare herself the shock of dressing in the brutal morning air.

"You don't have to get up," Eric said quietly as first the tinder, then the kindling caught, spreading a faint orange light through the darkened room.

"I'll do Naomi's morning chores. Let her sleep in if she can. With Pam still running a fever, she'll need her rest.'' Lindsey thrust one hand back into the sleeping bag to rummage around for her all-flannel one-piece bra. Like most cold-weather experts, she always wore natural fibers against the skin, reserving nylon and other artificial fibers for outer layers where waterproofing, not heat retention, was more important.

As she reached out and upward to pull the sports-type bra over her head, one arm already through a strap, the sleeping bag shell slipped from her shoulders to puddle in fluffy folds at her waist. She shivered, her breasts re-acting with painful goose bumps to the cold. Lindsey quickly shoved her other arm through the opposite strap and pulled the bra over her bustline, straightening and smoothing the fabric until she was comfortably covered. As she grabbed the sleeping bag to pull it back up to her shoulders, she noticed Eric's gaze. He'd watched her the whole time.

''Umm, sorry about that. I'll be more careful in the future.''

Eric continued to observe, but she couldn't read his expression, backlit as he was by the fire. ''I hope I'm not just an old habit, Lindsey.''

Cheeks burning, she ducked her head, realizing that she was still comfortable undressed around her former lover. As comfortable as she'd ever been… Right then, she knew her relationship with Wade was a sham. Only a woman truly in love could have dressed so casually in front of another man with such lack of embarrassment. She had to face facts. Wade wasn't Eric Kincaide, and Ric was, for better or worse, her ideal for all men. The ring on her finger felt more irksome than ever, and she guiltily yanked at it. She had no success in removing it, nor did Eric say anything else. He'd turned away to feed larger pieces of wood into the fire.

Still embarrassed—not because Eric had watched her, but because she'd so easily fallen back into old patterns with him—she pulled on her wool socks, thermal underwear tops and bottoms, then exited from the sleeping bag to finish dressing in front of the fire. Her other socks and layers of warm clothing, along with her indoor and outdoor boots, were all waiting for her in the neat pile she'd left on the hearth. Ginger quickly took advantage of the situation, hopping back onto the couch and burrowing into the folds of the sleeping bag, tail and legs tucked beneath her.

Eric continued to fuss with the fire. "You've lost weight," he observed.

"That's the Southwest for you. Too hot for an appetite half the time, and working in a swimsuit all day doesn't hide any excess pounds, that's for sure." She tried to speak lightly, matter-of-factly, as though the man next to her hadn't once known her intimately. As though she wasn't hurt that his only reaction to her body had been his comment about lost weight. She gave a nonchalant shrug. "The weight I gained up here disappeared as soon as I readjusted to the heat. I didn't—" She abruptly broke off, aware that she was practically babbling—and more than aware of his closeness, his maleness. She found herself wondering how much *his* body had changed.

"Four years without snow. Four years without a dog," he said, as the fire caught the bigger logs. He replaced the poker in the andiron rack. "Why, Lindsey?"

Lindsey shrugged again, and concentrated on lacing up her outdoor boots for a run to the outhouse. "No particular reason," she said, purposely vague. "I still help the folks at the kennels."

"Seriously, I'd like to know." He went on watching her, standing where she couldn't see his face. For that matter, neither could he see hers as she finished lacing up the first boot.

She reminded herself to be on her guard. She was just "the replacement" to him, nothing more. "Time for a change, I guess."

Eric knelt in front of her and reached for her unlaced boot to rest it on his knee. It was something he'd always done for her in the past, something that made her feel pampered and loved, even though she was perfectly capable of lacing up her own boots.

"Was it because of me?"

Lindsey bit her lip.

"It was, wasn't it?" He held her foot as he waited for her to answer.

"Not directly. Whatever choices I've made, I've made because of *me*. Not you, not anyone else."

"But you'd spent your whole life with animals."

"That's right. I know more about relationships with them than relationships with people. Face it—I know more about dogs than anything else, including search-and-rescue. After what happened to us, I thought maybe I should give myself a chance to concentrate on humans rather than canines."

"Obviously without success."

"What?" she asked angrily, yanking her foot away from Eric.

"You're engaged to a man you don't love."

"I love him!" Lindsey said in a forceful whisper, mindful of those sleeping. "I just love him...differently...than I loved you. There are lots of kinds of love. Like how I love my dogs. Or how I love my family."

Eric picked up her laces again. "You don't believe in true love? You're willing to settle?"

She reached for the laces herself with trembling fingers. "Like you're such an expert," she said disdainfully. "You cut me off—cut me out of your life! Because Naomi snapped her fingers, you changed your mind about postponing the wedding for a few days. A few *days,* Eric! That's all I asked."

"Believe me, I'm sorry about that. I..." Uncharacteristically, he hesitated.

"You want to know what *I* thought? I thought I'd failed with you because I was too caught up in my rescue work. Thought maybe I'd be a better person without dogs, that maybe spending most of my time with them was wrong. Thought I was too selfish when it came to my work."

"God, Lindsey, you were never that!"

"That's not how I saw it," she said. "I figured maybe you had a point. So I decided to see if I you were right. After four years without a canine partner, I've reached the conclusion that I'm no better with men and romance than I was before. All I did was face a few hard truths—and allow myself to come back here to work with an ownerless dog. Maybe I'll never be the expert you presume to be on human relationships, and maybe I'll never find 'true love.' But at least with canines I can make a difference in people's lives. I've already *made* a difference with Pam and your sister. That has to count for something. As for anything else..."

To her horror, her voice shook, and tears came perilously close to the surface.

"Lindsey, please—" He tried to take her hands, but she pushed them aside and stood.

"Excuse me, but I need to use the outhouse." She grabbed at her hooded coat and ran outside, feeling very much the coward, her untied laces almost hidden in the deep, heavy snow.

CHAPTER EIGHT

Day 4, midmorning

THE FOUR ADULTS SAT IN THE common room around the fire, the table cleared, dishes washed and put away. Lindsey and Ginger took their usual places near the hearth, Naomi and Keith shared the couch, while Eric straddled the chair by the desk that held the ham radio. Pam, who had slept through breakfast, lay asleep in the women's bedroom.

Eric studied the faces of his staff. Naomi and Keith looked sleep-deprived, Naomi more so. Lindsey, who'd slept more than all of them, had no shadows under her eyes, but she refused to meet his gaze, her facial features almost inanimate. He suspected he'd been responsible for that. Their conversation earlier had shocked him deeply, but any further discussion had to be tabled. The present meant his personal life had to take a back seat.

"The snow's stopped," he said. "We should have a couple of days before the next storm hits. If there's going to be any backpacking out of here, it has to be done now. Naomi, how's Pam?"

His twin shook her head. "Not good. I can't keep her fever down, and the frostbite's starting to turn the area above her toes black as well. I'm worried. If we don't get her to a doctor, she may end up losing some toes.

Maybe all of them. She needs a circulatory assessment and surgical debridement at a hospital.''

''Can she be safely moved?'' Eric asked.

''As long as she stays off her feet, yes. Lindsey packed in here in one day. If we could do the same with Pam, I'd feel a whole lot better about her chances.''

''I don't know about doing an evac in a day.'' Lindsey spoke up. ''I skied in with a visible ski trail and nothing to slow me down. We've got fresh snowfall. We'll need snowshoes, not skis, and we'll have to hand-pull the sled. Getting through Tioga Pass before dark is a gamble, not a guarantee.''

''She's right,'' Eric said.

Naomi stirred her full mug of coffee, poured from the continually freshened pot. ''Too bad we don't keep sled dogs.''

''Let's not forget about Wilson,'' Keith added.

''Like any of us *could* forget,'' Naomi snapped. She immediately apologized. ''Sorry, Keith. I didn't sleep much last night.''

''I did get through on the radio earlier this morning to check on the weather reports,'' Eric said. ''I also talked to Jack Hunter. He's still waiting to hear back from the police regarding gun registration. Not all the state records are on computer.''

''And what about the rescue party for Pam?'' Keith asked.

''He agrees with me. I don't think it's wise for us all to go. If Wilson decides to stalk the outgoing party, I'd just as soon have backup here at the cabin if there's trouble. But as far as any course of action is concerned, the final decision's up to us, not Hunter.''

Eric noticed Lindsey react slightly to his use of the plural. Four years ago he would have declared that the decision was up to *him*. But those years of solitude hadn't been pleasant. After Lindsey's departure, he'd discovered the meaning of teamwork, realized how much he'd missed it. Obviously he had his faults when it came to interpersonal relationships. He'd been spoiled having a twin—his only true teammate—who knew his every emotion. Eric had never learned the necessary habit of explaining his feelings to others. Because he instinctively knew his sister's thoughts, he'd never learned to pick up on others'. He did okay with work-related issues, but intimacy with others came hard. Life in the isolation of a Sierra Nevada winter didn't do much for his romancing skills, either. *I can admit when I need help, Lindsey. And I can admit when I'm wrong. I was dead wrong to let you go.*

"Let me run this by you all," Eric said. "Naomi and Pam stay here. Keith and Lindsey can start out with a decoy handsled—see if Wilson's watching us, and if he is, we draw him out. I'll cover you. If he doesn't surface, Keith and Lindsey can circle back, and we'll send the real sled out with Pam and Naomi tomorrow."

"You'll need someone who's armed to go with them. I'm volunteering," Keith said forcefully.

Eric, mindful of Lindsey's revelation earlier about Keith's feelings for Naomi, chose his words carefully. "I appreciate it, Keith. Let's reevaluate the generator before we decide. You're the better mechanic." The word *we* came much more easily to his lips than it had four years ago. Once again he noticed Lindsey's reaction.

Keith nodded just once. Naomi stared openly at her brother. "I just assumed you'd go with me, Eric."

"So did I," Lindsey said frankly.

"If I have to be admitted to the hospital, I'd want you there," Naomi insisted.

"I'd want to be there, sweetie," Eric said, reaching for his sister's arm. "But I can't leave a crazed gunman loose to take potshots at your back. If that means I stay behind, then I stay behind. And if we all went, we'd have to tow the dog out as well. That would slow us down even more. Like I said, it all depends on the generator."

Obviously upset, Naomi said nothing.

"Let's do the decoy run this morning with Lindsey and Keith, and see what happens. If Wilson doesn't show, that'll give us the rest of the afternoon to prepare for the real run tomorrow before the bad weather hits. Then we can decide who's going. Naomi, you'll stay here with Pam. Will you be okay with Keith's rifle?"

"I hate guns—but yeah, I'll use it if I have to."

"I'll leave Ginger here, too," Lindsey offered. "The snow's too deep for her, and she'll give you advance warning if anyone comes this way."

Eric nodded his approval. "Any questions? Problems? Comments?" There were none. "All right, Rangers, we have ourselves a plan. Let's get moving."

The men dressed warmly to go out and check the generator and took the dog with them, leaving the women behind.

"I'll pack food and drink for you and Keith," Naomi said.

"I'll do it. I still remember where everything is," Lindsey replied, rising from the table and heading to the kitchen. "If Pam's still sleeping, you should put your feet up while you can. You look beat."

"Later." Naomi followed Lindsey. "What's with Eric?"

"Sorry…you lost me."

"All of a sudden he wants to stay, instead of escorting me out. Why?"

"Maybe you should ask him," Lindsey suggested, reaching for two sealed plastic bins containing the trail bars and beef jerky.

"He's not here. Did you two kiss and make up?" she asked bluntly.

"Are we out of hot-chocolate mix?"

"One cupboard over. So, did you?"

"No."

"Why not?"

Lindsey exhaled with annoyance. "I know you're under a lot of stress, Naomi, so I'm making allowances. But do me a favor, would you? Back off."

"I have a right to know what's going on."

"Professionally, yes. Personally, no. Between your health and Pam's, you've got enough to handle. Don't start playing 'Dear Abby.'" Lindsey yanked open the drawer where the sealed plastic bags were kept and began filling them with the appropriate portions.

Naomi's brows rushed together, just as her brother's did when he was upset. "Someone's got to make you see sense!"

"Your timing stinks. I've got to go out into the elements with a crazy gunman somewhere nearby, a ranger I've never worked with, and no dog. My body's conditioned for swimming, not skiing, I'm freezing my butt off, and I'm still taking Diamox. Excuse me if my mind's on my job right now."

"Spare me the dedicated ranger act, Lindsey. I know you better than that."

"No, you don't. If you did, you wouldn't have spent the past four years spying on me through my sisters."

Naomi gasped. "I wouldn't have had to spy if you'd answered my letters or phone calls. I thought we were friends."

Lindsey straightened, her eyes narrowed. "We were never friends, Naomi."

The other woman's flushed cheeks acknowledged the truth in Lindsey's words. "No, but later on, I wanted to be. I know I went about it wrong, but my husband had died. I needed my twin! I swear, Lindsey, I never meant for my relationship with Eric to damage yours. Or to cause bad blood between the two of us."

Lindsey held up a restraining hand. "Naomi, I didn't come back here to assign blame. Eric didn't trust me. Whatever you did or said to him made no difference in that department."

"I still know you blame me. I blame myself," Naomi said painfully. "I tried to reach you a few months after you left…to try to explain."

"Explain what? You wanted Eric all to yourself, you got him. I can read well enough between the lines to know you lied to him back then. You wanted me gone, and obviously Eric did, too, or he would've listened to me. Not you."

Naomi flushed even more, but doggedly went on. "You're right about me, but you're wrong about Eric. He didn't want out. I stupidly thought I knew what was best for him. After you left, something happened. He shut down inside. I used to be able to tell what he's thinking and feeling. Now he's like some stranger."

"So you decided to undo what you did? Just like that?" Lindsey couldn't keep the sarcasm from her voice.

"Yes! I kept trying to reach you to explain, to apologize, to set things straight. You never gave me the chance. Just like you never gave me the chance to be your friend. For God's sake, my brother wanted to marry you! Why wouldn't I want him to be happy?"

Lindsey stopped packing. "You never wanted to be

my friend until *after* he called off the wedding. By then, I wasn't interested. I'm still not.'' The harshness of her words hung in the air.

They brought tears to Naomi's eyes. "I can accept that. But don't let the past stand in the way of your happiness," she begged. "Or Eric's."

"Naomi, drop it." Lindsey's voice shook. *"Please."*

Naomi's chin stubbornly jutted out, a contrast to the tears in her eyes. "I know Eric still loves you. I think you still love him, or you wouldn't have come back here."

Lindsey's last remnants of control vanished, and the words slipped out before she could control them. "How would *you* know? Keith's wild about you, and you haven't even noticed. If you want to play matchmaker, do it in your own life—and stay the hell out of mine!"

Silence. Naomi's expression registered confusion, then shock. She stared at Lindsey, while Lindsey desperately wished she could take back the words that had betrayed a confidence. Damn the Kincaide twins! No one, absolutely no one, but Eric and his sister, could arouse such powerful emotions in her. Usually she had no problem keeping her mouth shut. "Hell, hell, *hell!*" she ground out.

"That fits this place," Naomi said in a shaky voice. "I'm going to check on Pam."

Lindsey opened her mouth, then closed it as Naomi hurried from the room, leaving her to finish packing up the supplies with only the popping of the fireplace wood for company.

THE MEN RETURNED SHORTLY afterward, announcing that the generator still seemed stable enough. Keith had tinkered with it as much as he could. The air and sky were fairly clear, and within a short time the three rangers were ready for their decoy attempt at snowshoeing out. Lindsey and Keith would lead, while Eric would trail them, keeping out of sight in the hilly, conifer-dotted terrain.

Naomi watched the three depart, holding tight to Ginger's collar. She bolted the porch and cabin doors, turned the portable radio to their walkie-talkie frequency, then carefully placed the loaded rifle—safety on—high on the mantelpiece where Pam couldn't reach it. Naomi had settled the girl in a sleeping bag on the couch. Not only would she not need to overtax the generator to heat the back bedrooms, but she also hoped a change of scenery might perk up the ailing child's spirits.

"When are they coming back?" Pam asked as Ginger lay down by the couch.

"Maybe later this evening—definitely before dark," Naomi said, fussing with Pam's pillow. "There. Comfy?"

"Why can't I go?"

"I told you. They're going to check on the…trail conditions…and see if it's safe for us to get you back to your mother." Naomi brought over a tablet of paper and two pencils and sat on the couch. "Want to play tic-tactoe? Or draw some pictures?"

"I wanna see my mom," Pam said, ignoring the pencil Naomi offered her.

"I know. But we can't take you out in the snow unless it's safe."

"I hate the snow!"

"But snow can be a good thing," Naomi said. "Watch." She began to draw on the top of the paper. "We're right here, at Tuolumne Meadows. It was named after the Indians living in the foothills. Can you say Toool-um-mee?"

Pam dutifully repeated the Native American word.

"We're at the highest part of Yosemite Park. Down here—" Naomi sketched on the bottom left "—is where Half Dome and Yosemite Valley are located. Years ago, glaciers from where we are traveled down to carve out the valley."

Pam didn't seem very interested.

"Keep watching the map, and you'll see the route we're going to use to take you home," Naomi cajoled. She immediately caught Pam's interest. The child scooted closer, and actually leaned into her side as Naomi sketched in the Sierra Nevada Mountain Range with its ten-to thirteen-thousand-foot peaks.

"Okay, here's our cabin. From up here, the Tuolumne River flows down into the Grand Canyon of the Tuolumne, and then into the Hetch Hetchy Reservoir. All our snow melts into water for the people in San Francisco to drink. The grapes in the vineyards drink it, too. The water's so pure, California has some of the best wines in the world. So you see, snow can be a good thing."

"Are we going home that way?" Pam asked.

"No." Naomi sketched in another river. "The Merced flows down from Merced Lake, which is also fed by snow. It provides water for all the valley wildlife, and makes beautiful waterfalls in the summer. There's Vernal Fall, Nevada Fall, the Upper and Lower Yosemite Fall, and one even named Bridalveil Fall."

"Bridalveil?" Pam echoed.

"Yep. The wind blows the water into a white froth so it looks like a bride's lacy veil. You can even hike in to see some of the falls."

"Can we go home that way?" Pam asked.

"Not in winter. The western entrances to the park are closed due to heavy snowfall, and anyway, that's the long way out of here. Plus it's too rugged. We drop from thirteen thousand feet all the way down to two thousand feet above sea level. That's too difficult a terrain for winter travel. It's tough in the summer, too.''

"Then which way goes home?'' Pam demanded impatiently.

"Here's our cabin again. Over here to the right—the east—is Tioga Pass. There's a lot of snow there, too, but the distance to the pass isn't that far from us, and beyond it is the rest of Highway 140. Once we get through the pass, it's open to traffic. That's where one of our rangers—Lindsey—skied in. So we'd put you on a sled and go from the cabin—'' Naomi drew a dotted line ''—to Tioga Pass here and down to the highway. And this—'' Naomi made an *X* and circled it ''—is where your mother will be waiting for you.'' Naomi peeled the sheet of paper from the rest of the tablet and passed it to the child.

Pam took the paper and studied it, her frostbitten nose pointing at the ''*X*-marks-the-spot.''

"When do I get to go?''

"I'm not sure,'' Naomi said, not wanting to raise the child's hopes.

"Daddy will be mad,'' Pam said in a frightened little voice. "He said I'd never live with Mommy again.''

"Wrong. Your father's…a bit confused,'' Naomi said tactfully. "You let us worry about him.'' She handed a pencil to Pam. "I'm going to write down the names of the bigger mammals in our park for you, one on each page. Then I'll get one of my wildlife books and some colored pencils so you can draw them. We'll do some this morning, okay?''

Naomi started writing down bighorn sheep, mule deer, coyote, badger and raccoon in block letters, leaving out any of the nastier predatory mammals, such as mountain lions, bobcats and bears. Even though the big cats were at lower altitudes where food was more plentiful, and most of the black bears were hibernating for the winter—the native grizzlies had been wiped out during the gold rush—the child had been frightened enough. Best not to take chances.

"This will do for starters," Naomi said in a cheerful voice. "Let's read the names out loud, then you pick the one you want to draw first."

FIFTEEN MINUTES OF snowshoeing had Lindsey huffing and puffing like a steam locomotive. Even though Keith towed the hand-sled—which was made up with blankets and clothing to look as though it held Pam—he still had to wait for Lindsey to catch up.

"You okay?" he asked.

"I haven't done heavy snowshoeing in years. I forgot how hard this was," she gasped. "And I thought the ski trip in gave me sore muscles."

"Wanna take a break?"

"No, we just started. But if you'd slow down a tad, that'd help."

Keith nodded and continued breaking a trail atop the fresh, powdery snow while Lindsey gritted her teeth and slogged on.

"Try to step in my footprints," he said. "That'll make it easier."

"'Kay," she managed to get out, but Keith had a larger stride than she did, and that wasn't always possible. Although she had physical stamina, her leg muscles were screaming after thirty minutes. Worse yet, her back felt extremely vulnerable, what with Keith in the lead, and Wilson possibly stalking them. For the first time in her life, she fervently wished for a bulletproof vest.

"Sorry, I've gotta stop," she finally said to Keith, "or I'll fall flat on my face."

Keith immediately slowed, careful that the sled he towed didn't bump into him. "No problem. Why don't you check on our 'patient' and I'll get us something hot to drink?"

"Thanks, Keith." Lindsey kicked out of one snowshoe and gratefully dropped to that knee, taking the weight off her legs. She pretended to fuss with "Pam," adjusting the transport blankets and straightening the tassel of the stuffed ski-cap peeking out.

"Can you see anyone?" she asked, still down in the snow. "I've been watching our backs as best I can."

"We know Eric's behind us somewhere," Keith said confidently.

"Yeah, well, let's hope Wilson isn't. I'm jumpy as hell," she admitted.

"Rescue ranger or not, I'm hoping the last storm put that wife-beater permanently on ice."

"Or at least his feet," Lindsey seconded. She rubbed at a sore calf with a mitten-clad hand.

"Eric said we should take at least an hour heading toward Tioga Pass. We're halfway there. If we don't see anything by then, we'll turn around and head back."

"Another half hour to go?"

"You don't think you can make it?"

"It's not that. Another half hour will put us right out in the open. The farther we head out, the more ground cover we'll lose. Talk about being sitting ducks."

"That's why we have Eric as backup," Keith said matter-of-factly. He poured a cup of coffee from his thermos and offered it to her.

"I'll pass," she decided. She had hot chocolate in her own thermos. Less ground cover made relieving herself a problem, although admittedly that was the *least* of her problems at present. She straightened painfully, wincing at the stitch in her side as she slipped her unshod boot back into the snowshoe, then bent again to fasten the straps.

"Want me to spell you with the sled?" she asked. Fair was fair. Even though they were hauling a decoy, they'd added wood beneath the blankets and clothing to simulate the correct amount of weight on the runners.

"Maybe later. I'm fine," Keith said. "You ready to go?"

"Ready as I'll ever be."

"Here. Give me your hand." Keith bent to the side and downward to help her up. At that movement a rifle shot rang out.

Lindsey saw Keith grab at his shoulder with his glove as he spun and fell face-forward in the snow. Lindsey dove down next to him at the sound of a second rifle shot. She stayed low and on her belly as she unzipped the top half of his jacket. Keith was bleeding from not only the entrance wound, but an exit wound, as well.

She grabbed a smaller blanket from the sled, folding it and hard-packing the wound, applying direct pressure from both sides.

Keith, still conscious, groaned and swore a foul expletive that Lindsey shared, then tried to lift his head.

"Lie still!" Lindsey hissed, pressing hard. "And stay down! That idiot could fire at us again!" Keeping her own head low, she cautiously searched the area for movement, praying desperately that Eric would reach them before Wilson did.

Lindsey's prayers were answered. Within minutes Eric was at her side, his rifle carried at the ready, his face grim.

"You okay?" they asked each other at the same time.

"Yes, but Keith's not," Lindsey answered unnecessarily, continuing to kneel and apply direct pressure.

"Keith—" Eric started to speak, but Keith, still conscious, cut him off.

"Tell me you killed that bastard! Because if you didn't, I will!"

"I never saw him. I heard the first shot and fired blind right after to warn him off."

"Thank God," Lindsey breathed.

"How bad is it?" Eric asked Keith.

Keith's answer didn't bear repeating.

"Straight through the shoulder," Lindsey answered for him. "Ric, if he hadn't bent over to help me up—" She broke off, her voice shaky. At his narrowed eyes, she made a conscious effort to pull herself together. "Sorry."

Eric searched the horizon before flicking on the rifle's safety and slinging it over his shoulder. As Lindsey field-dressed Keith's wound and refastened his jacket, Eric cleared off the sled and rigged it for a real passenger. All the while Eric scanned the open areas for trouble.

With the sled parallel to Keith, Lindsey and Eric prepared to lift him aboard, but Keith crawled onto it himself.

"Stay still!" Eric ordered. "The last thing you need is to go into shock."

"My legs work," Keith said, although a fine sheen of sweat had appeared on his forehead. "I could walk if I had to. I probably should. Lindsey can't tow me, and she can't shoot."

"The hell I can't." Lindsey began to fasten Keith, blankets and all, aboard the sled. "My mother's a retired cop. I don't like guns, but I grew up with them. I have no problem shooting a man in self-defense. Especially Wilson.''

Keith's expression registered surprise. Lindsey noticed Eric's shocked look, too. Four years ago, she wouldn't have been able to make such a statement. She'd refused to become firearms-certified. But those four years had changed her, made her a mature realist instead of a starry-eyed fool in love. She finished securing Keith in the sled and stood up with the towing straps. She held them out to Eric with one gloved hand, holding out the other for his rifle. Without a word, she made the exchange. She carried the rifle in her arms instead of slung over her back.

''Whenever you're ready.''

THE HIKE BACK TOOK MUCH longer than the half hour it had taken earlier. Lindsey, in the point position, retraced their previous trail, while Eric pulled Keith over the mostly level terrain. At some of the more rugged areas, it took the two of them to tow the sled. In one particularly uneven place, Keith actually unstrapped himself so the others could walk him over the obstacle. Lindsey and Eric could have taken another, longer and much more exposed way around, but Keith, who remained conscious, insisted they all stay within cover of the few trees at the subalpine heights. No one argued with his reasoning.

Finally, two hours later, and more than three hours since they'd first left, the trio came within sight of the ranger cabin. Once they reached the front porch, they heard Ginger barking from inside. Keith started to undo his safety straps.

''Would you quit playing macho man and let me help you?'' Lindsey demanded. Keith might be hurt, but he certainly didn't lack physical courage.

"We'll walk you in," Eric ordered. Lindsey flicked on the rifle's safety and put it around her back via the strap for the first time since she'd taken it from Eric. She grabbed Keith's waist, while Eric grabbed his good arm to sling around his shoulders. And quickly, but carefully, they got the wounded man to his feet.

Keith groaned with pain as the three tackled the steps to the porch door. Naomi and Ginger both burst through the inner door to let them through.

"What happened?"

"Wilson," Eric said tersely. "Keith's been shot in the shoulder. Where do you want him?"

"My bedroom. My medical stuff's in there. It's okay, Pam," Naomi said as they passed the child. "Stay on the couch."

Pam stayed, but, after seeing the bleeding man, began to cry.

"Want me to stay with Pam?" Lindsey asked, helping Keith onto the bed.

"Go," Naomi said.

"I'll help get him undressed," Eric said.

"I can undress myself," Keith protested as Lindsey left and closed the door behind her. She hurried to the fire to remove her gear before trying to comfort the child. In addition to having snow and ice on her clothing, her gloves were covered with blood, as were parts of her jacket. Ginger, who had retired to her usual spot on the hearth to watch the proceedings, sniffed at the discarded gloves and whined softly. Lindsey knew exactly how the shaken animal felt.

"What happened?" Pam asked.

"Keith got hurt. We had to come back."

Lindsey removed first the rifle and then her jacket; some of the blood spots were now frozen pink pellets.

Lindsey brushed them into the fire before they thawed, making it hiss and spark. She rubbed her hands together to warm her fingers, then pulled off her woolen hat.

"Is he going to die?" Pam asked.

"No. He's hurt, but it's not serious," Lindsey said confidently.

Pam bit her lip. "Did Daddy shoot him?"

For a panicked moment, Lindsey contemplated lying, but realized that Pam and Naomi would both have heard the gunshot across the open snow with the granite range to amplify it. Lindsey also realized that Pam knew more about her father's violent tendencies than any of them.

"Yes, Pam." She hurried to the couch to wrap an arm around the child's trembling shoulders. The tears that had started upon their arrival continued to flow down the girl's cheeks.

"I wish he wouldn't hurt people," she sobbed.

"I wish he wouldn't, either." Lindsey touched the girl's cheeks with the cuff of her sweater. "Shall we say a prayer for him?"

"It won't help," Pam said in the heart-rending voice of the victimized. "Mom and I already tried that."

"We'll catch him. And after we do, they have doctors back at his jail who can help," Lindsey said bluntly. "He won't be able to hurt anyone, and when he gets out, maybe he'll be a better person."

Pam remained silent and unconvinced. Lindsey reached over to the coffee table and the sheets of paper. "I see you've been drawing."

Pam nodded.

"These are pretty good. Did you do one of Ginger?"

The girl shook her head.

"Maybe you could do one for me later. I don't have any pictures of her. Speaking of Ginger, has she been out lately?'' Lindsey asked casually. She didn't like the way the bloodied clothing had affected Pam.

''Naomi didn't want to unlock the doors.''

''Guess I'd better take her, then. Will you be okay until I get back?''

Pam shrugged.

Lindsey grabbed for her jacket and hat. She picked up the gloves, not to put on again, but to discard on the porch, out of Pam's sight. There were others of Eva's she could wear. Lindsey hesitated, then, under the child's watchful gaze, grabbed the rifle as well and called for the dog.

''I won't be long. Stay off those feet,'' she said.

CHAPTER NINE

ERIC WATCHED AS NAOMI examined her newest patient. Keith lay on the bed, an IV with saline and antibiotics hooked up to his arm, his shoulder deftly wrapped in a pressure bandage. She'd also given him something for the pain, which had finally quieted him enough to first relax, then sleep.

"He looks like hell. Will he be okay?" Eric asked.

"I think so. He's lost blood, but not enough to be life-threatening."

"You can thank Lindsey for that. She had him field-dressed before I made it to the sled, and believe me I was moving fast. Plus, she carried the rifle back while I towed Keith."

"Thank God we have her. And thank God Wilson didn't cause any more harm," Naomi said, her passionate words a contrast to her professional demeanor. She studied Keith's IV line with a practiced eye.

"When you get time, check out Lindsey," Eric said. "Her muscles were sore enough from skiing. From what I saw, she was hurting quite a bit while snowshoeing."

"She'll be lucky if she can make it to the outhouse tomorrow," Naomi said with sympathy, "let alone do any long-distance hiking."

"She won't be leaving the cabin tomorrow. None of us will. I'm sorry, Naomi," he told her. "I know how you feel about this, but it just isn't safe."

"I already figured that out, twin. And I'm okay with it." Naomi glanced at her watch. "The generator needs more fuel. Since Keith's going to be off work detail for a while, you and Lindsey will have to cover for him."

"I'll look after it," Eric said, once more pulling on his discarded jacket, hat and gloves. "Take good care of him. If you need me, yell."

Naomi nodded. "Be careful."

Eric left Naomi's room, closing the door behind him. In the common room, he saw Lindsey with Pam. The woman and child were drawing pictures, Ginger at their feet. Lindsey looked up at his entrance. She'd obviously been worried sick over her co-worker.

"How's Keith?"

"Naomi says he'll be okay."

He saw Lindsey stroke the girl's hair with a gentle touch. "See? I told you." To Eric, she said, "Pam's hungry. I'm warming up some vegetable soup and I've sliced some bread. We all need to eat."

"After I gas up the generator."

"Take your rifle," Lindsey immediately said.

"Planned on it."

"And take the dog, okay? She'll hear anything before you will. If you aren't back in fifteen minutes, I'm taking Keith's rifle and coming after you."

"Stay put. That's an order."

"I mean it. Fifteen minutes," Lindsey repeated, nodding at the cabin clock. "No more."

Eric called Ginger and left, systematically perusing the horizon as Ginger sniffed and sampled the air. Eric didn't notice anything, nor did the dog. After one last look around, he hurried to the generator shack. The padlock and chain hadn't been tampered with, and all seemed in order as he entered, Ginger at his heels. The diesel holding-tank gauge showed it was running in the "low to empty" redline area, and he hurried to the warming plates where the fuel was kept heated. Regular gasoline froze solid in the frigid winters, and even diesel could turn viscous and unusable. Once the generator stopped, not only would the engine freeze, but the warming plates for keeping the fuel liquid would shut down as well.

To Eric's disgust, his fingers shook as he removed the clamp-on warming element from the diesel tank. They'd also shaken when he'd removed his gloves to unlock the padlock, and it wasn't from the cold, either. He was afraid of what further damage Wilson could do to them. His stomach had been knotted since the first crack of Wilson's rife. His joy at seeing Lindsey unharmed had quickly turned to horror at the bloodred evidence of Keith's injury. First he'd lost Eva to the snow, then he'd almost lost Keith to a bullet, and the rest of them were still at risk from a deranged gunman. At least he, Eric, had his health.

The condition of the others—Naomi with a possible tumor, Keith with an injured shoulder and Pam with frostbitten feet—didn't help their odds. Lindsey hadn't had time to adjust to the altitude or cold yet; she was still on Diamox and using "poppers," chemical heaters, in her boots and gloves. But she hadn't complained once on the trek back. She'd even offered to change places and relieve him from towing the sled if he needed it, but she couldn't hide the gasping breaths she needed to function.

He poured in the last of the fuel, clamped the warming plate onto a fresh tank of diesel, locked the shack up again and pulled his gloves back on. *I've done all I can here.* His fingers had stopped shaking while he was doing the chores, but neither chores nor the trek back to the cabin could dispel his gut-sick feeling of worry.

LINDSEY PUT AWAY the washed dishes. Everyone, but Keith, groggy and medicated, had finished big bowls of soup. Even the despondent Pam had eaten. The fire blazed hot, adding its light to that of the dim, generator-powered bulbs. Fretful now, Pam was back in her bed. Naomi had dosed her with more tablets and orange juice for her fever, and settled her down. She was reading to the child from another nature book while keeping a watchful eye on Keith. Only Lindsey, Eric and the dog occupied the common room. Eric had just finished up-dating his superior on the situation, checked on the weather report, then turned down the static on the radio. Lindsey, sitting at the hearth, listened in. Hearing the stark situation described by Eric's grim voice created an almost perceptible gloom that even the fire or electricity couldn't dispel.

"Should we move another bed into Naomi's room?" Lindsey asked Eric. "Might be easier now that she's taking care of two patients. Or should we move Pam out? She could sleep with me."

"I thought about moving you and Pam into my room and sleeping out here on the couch. I could keep an eye on the door."

That made sense. To preserve heat, the bedrooms had no windows; just the common room did. The connecting door to the porch and the outside was the only way Wilson would be able to invade the cabin. The windows weren't big enough to admit an adult.

"I should let Naomi know," Eric said, but he made no move to leave his chair. After a moment, he added, "Thanks for your help this morning."

"Some help. I didn't spot Wilson."

"Neither did I. But we were lucky."

"Only because my muscles gave out and Keith was bending over to help me up," Lindsey said with self-disgust.

"If that's true—and we don't know it is—I don't think Keith's complaining. I know I'm not."

Eric's kind words didn't soothe her at all.

"I didn't even see it coming. So much for women's intuition. I'm just thankful the damage wasn't worse." Lindsey twisted the tight diamond ring on her finger around and around. "Some replacement ranger I am."

Eric rose from the chair to join her, his back to the fire. "You're the best kind of replacement ranger. You're our wild card, and right now we need that. If none of us can guess your next move, Wilson sure as hell won't be able to."

He reached for her shoulders and began to knead them, and the tight muscles around her neck. Lindsey froze, resisting his touch for only a second, then she relaxed.

"Don't move," he said, quickly leaving and returning with a tube. He squirted a dab onto each of his fingertips, thèn slipped them inside her layers of thermal, flannel and sweater. The strong smell of liniment filled the air.

"I hate this stuff," Lindsey said in a more normal voice. "It's just a skin irritant that increases blood circulation to the chemically poisoned area."

"I don't think the drug companies label it 'poison.' Anyway, no one ever died from massaging with liniment." A trace of humor colored his voice as he continued to rub.

"It stinks, too," Lindsey muttered.

"Sorry, but our Jacuzzi and spa facilities aren't open today."

She felt rather than saw his smile.

"You rarely complain about the big things, Lindsey. Just the little ones. It's one of the reasons I fell for you."

His hands stopped their movement on her shoulders. For a moment she thought he'd withdraw them altogether, but after a few seconds his gentle massage resumed. "Where else do you hurt?"

"Mostly my legs. But I'm not complaining," she said, glancing toward the women's bedroom. "I took some over-the-counter tablets."

Eric removed his hands to pass her the liniment tube. "Use some of this on your legs when you go to bed," he said. "I don't want you hurting."

"Maybe I'll try a little." She took the tube and slipped it into her flannel shirt pocket under his watchful gaze.

"Why don't you sit on the furniture?" he suggested. "You'd be more comfortable."

"It's too far away from the fire."

"You're always in front of the fire."

"That's because I hate the cold. Hate the snow. Hate the winter."

Eric couldn't believe what he was hearing. "Since when?"

Lindsey didn't answer his question directly. "I'm a native San Diegan. I grew up in the land of sunshine, citrus groves and Frisbees at the beach. I only came to Yosemite in the summer to rock climb, and to practice search-and-rescue in the High Sierra. It was just supposed to be a summer ranger job."

"But…you stayed for a year when the permanent opening came up," Eric said.

"Because I met you," Lindsey admitted. "But I missed my sisters. Missed my parents. Missed the relaxing life of the Sunbelt. I don't like it here, Eric. These mountains have always been full of death."

Lindsey knew that the valuable resources of the High Sierra had caused the white man to wipe out 250,000 of the 300,000 Native Americans who'd occupied the land four thousand years before them. Then those same newcomers had started cutting down the giant redwoods and sequoias and cedars. They killed off the wildlife, too, including all the grizzlies. Only the smaller black bears remained. Pioneers who'd crossed the mountains for free land in Oregon and then gold in California also died in the mountains.

"I know the history, Lindsey," Eric said impatiently. "But I can't change the past—or allow it to affect the present. The land and wildlife are protected now, as are Native Americans. Things have changed for the better."

"Have they? Weather conditions haven't changed. People like Eva still die in the snow. Yosemite is as remote and inaccessible as ever, despite modern technology and advancements—and the police. Why do you think criminals like Wilson find it so appealing? Criminals and hermits. It's a place for people who want isolation—or want to hide."

"I'm not one of those."

"Your sister is. She came here because of her husband's death."

"I...never knew you felt that way," Eric said. Lindsey heard the surprise in his voice.

"No, you didn't. People like the Donners and Reeds and Breens of the Donner Party may be courageous settlers to you, pioneers who conquered what were almost insurmountable odds. But look at the price they paid! Cannibalism. Even individuals like John Muir paid dearly. Other people didn't see him as a wilderness explorer, conservationist or scientist. He was a university-educated man, yet they mocked him for saying glaciers created Yosemite Valley. They laughed when he said the land and its resources needed to be protected. Instead, they employed him to herd sheep, slop pigs and build henhouses so he could feed himself and finance his wild-life expeditions.''

"That was Muir's choice," Eric reminded her, rising to his feet to poke at the fire. "If it weren't for Muir, there'd be no National Forest Service or Sierra Club. No Yosemite National Park. *Some* people have to dedicate themselves to the land, Lindsey."

"True, but at what cost? Near his death, John Muir's closest companion was his mule, Brownie, not a wife and children. He did most of his work and spent most of his life alone, despite his legacy of conservation and parks. Maybe *he* was willing to pay that price. Maybe you are, too, Eric, but I'm not. I thought I could when I met you, but—" She stopped abruptly. "I wouldn't trade a single child's life for all the wilderness in the world."

Eric replaced the poker. "For God's sake, Lindsey, no one's asked you to," he said quietly. "Certainly not the Park Service."

"*You* expected it, Ric. The assumption was always there. Always!" She rose to her feet. "You assumed I'd spend the rest of my life here—with you. Tell me I'm wrong," she challenged.

A telling pause proved Lindsey's point.

"I can't spend my life protecting a land that kills. Protecting those *on* the land—even sacrificing my life for them—yes. But dying for the land itself? I won't. There are other parks and other places that need me—places where snow doesn't kill rangers...where madmen with rifles don't shoot rangers in the back! There are hundreds of winter jobs elsewhere—and only four here in Yosemite. I'm no John Muir, and this isn't the past. The mountains won't crumble if I leave. The gold diggers won't bring in the saws and dynamite. I'm not indispensable to this park, Eric.''

"I see. And when it comes to your personal life, *I'm* indispensable.'' The words knifed through the air, painful in their truth.

"You haven't listened to a word I've said.'' Lindsey's voice was defeated.

"But I have. Perhaps we should've had this conversation before you agreed to marry me. I'm not a mind-reader, Lindsey.'' She heard the hurt and bitterness, especially the bitterness, in Eric's voice. "I could have saved myself a trip to the jewelry store.''

"I left the ring at the office for you,'' Lindsey said. "Did you get it back?''

"Is that all you care about?''

"You should've been able to get a refund....''

"True enough,'' he spat out. "You never wore it.''

Lindsey found herself on the defensive. "Fine jewelry and rock-climbing aren't a good match. I was afraid of damaging it.''

"Unlike the ring you wear now.''

His cutting tone stung, and her defensiveness changed to a bitterness of her own. "I gave up a *lot* of things when I left here. Rock-climbing, too. Figured I'd flirted with enough danger for a while.'' She rose and deliberately reached for Ginger's leash, which hung from a nail on the mantel.

"You didn't give up using the same excuses, though,'' he countered. "The damn dog doesn't need to go out.''

"So we're not going to be polite and civilized?''

"Think, Ranger!'' Eric said, his demeanor changing from bitter ex-lover to that of a concerned superior. "There's a man out there with a rifle who doesn't mind using it! Better the dog urinates on the floor than takes a bullet. Or you! No more storming-out dramatics. These are wartime rules for everyone.''

Lindsey flushed from shame. ''I...I didn't think...''

''No one leaves this cabin without my permission and without a rifle. We're on the buddy system. We go outside only for emergencies, and only if I say it's an emergency. That includes the dog. Understand?''

She nodded miserably, unable to meet his gaze as she twisted the leash in her hands. Seconds later, the lights flickered, then went out. Lindsey's gaze flew to Eric's. They both spoke simultaneously.

''The generator!''

As Lindsey reached for her coat and Eric his rifle, she didn't bother asking if he considered this an emergency. They hurried outside. As if to add to her fears, it had started snowing again.

CHAPTER TEN

Day 5, predawn, still snowing

LINDSEY YAWNED ONCE, twice, then shook her head. Neither she nor Eric had been to bed, yet. The generator had rattled and breathed its last, despite Eric's efforts and Lindsey's silent prayers. The two rangers had spent the later part of the night bringing in as much chopped wood as the common room could hold. Eric started up the woodstove. After that, he woke his sister. He, Lindsey and Naomi moved the couch far back against the common room wall and shoved the men's two beds out of the bedroom to save space, pushing them together and as close to the fire as safety permitted. After making them with fresh sheets, extra blankets and down sleeping bags, Naomi carried Pam to the couch, wrapping her in a third sleeping bag.

Luckily, the child slept through the whole process. Moving Keith wasn't as easy. It took all three of them to shift Keith, using the blanket beneath him as a stretcher. He tried to help, but the blood loss had made him weak. He groaned with pain as they settled him down. Naomi unzipped Keith's bag, and tucked it around him as best she could, then added more blankets.

"I can't get it under him and zipped without jostling

his shoulder. I don't want to start it bleeding again. Think he'll be warm enough?''

"The cabin's still warmish from the generator, and the coals are hot. Plus the woodstove's running," Lindsey reassured the other woman.

"Yes, but...Eric, can't you get the generator going again?" Naomi asked, desperation in her voice. The two oil lamps now burning revealed deep furrows in her brow. At the moment, she looked far older than her twin did.

"I tried, sweetie, but no luck," Eric replied. "Keith warned us the machinery could fail. But we've got plenty of wood to last out this snowfall."

"And we still have the propane heater for water and cooking. We can use it to heat inside, if need be," Lindsey said, trying to stifle another yawn, and failing.

Naomi fussed over Keith, then turned to Lindsey. "You and Eric need some sleep. Take my bed."

Lindsey blinked. "But..." The thought of her and Eric sharing a bed again jolted her sore, tired body wide awake.

"I'll share the couch and my sleeping bag with Pam. Until the stove really catches, blankets won't be warm enough. There's no room in here for a third bed unless we move more furniture, and it's too late to be doing that."

"Too early," Eric corrected, checking his wristwatch. "And we won't need to share a bed, Lindsey. I'll do first watch." He gestured toward the oil lamps, one on the mantel, the other on the oak kitchen table. "Naomi, you need these?"

"Not anymore. I've done all I can for Keith and Pam tonight."

Silently Naomi started undressing as Eric blew out the kitchen lamp.

"I'm worried that Keith might start bleeding again. Wake me in a few hours so I can check him, okay? Then I'll stand the next watch."

"Will do."

Lindsey stayed in her thermals as well, in case Naomi or Eric needed her. The thought of having to waste time dressing during a medical emergency didn't appeal to her, nor did fighting a madman in the nude. As long as the fire still burned and the woodstove caught, she didn't need to strip to stay warm. However, before she climbed into her sleeping bag, she retrieved Keith's rifle and placed it at her side, safety on, the first slot of the clip empty. She'd lost the love of her life to circumstance, but she'd be damned if she'd lose him—or anyone else, for that matter—to death. Although aware of her motions, neither twin commented as she settled the gun and her sleeping bag. Ginger hopped onto the foot of the bed. Within seconds, far more quickly than she could have imagined, she fell asleep, victim of mental, physical and emotional exhaustion.

"You should lie down, Naomi," Eric suggested from the kitchen chair he'd moved closer to the woodstove. His sister had quietly joined the sleeping Pam on the couch, but sat up with a blanket wrapped around her, watching the hot coals inside the fireplace.

"If I thought I could sleep, I would." Naomi sighed. "Look at Lindsey. She just drops off with a rifle at her side like nothing's going on. I envy her."

"She's not as calm as she looks."

"No kidding. I heard you two arguing earlier. Why is everything so difficult with her?"

"Damned if I know." Eric pulled his flannel jacket more tightly around his body, his gaze on Lindsey. "We never seem to agree on anything. Doesn't matter what it is—from using liniment to wedding dates." He shook his head. "Her legs are gonna hurt in the morning."

"I never heard you two argue in the bedroom," she said with a twin's frankness. "Maybe that's where you should settle your problems."

Eric remained silent, knowing his sister would take the hint. She did and changed the subject.

"Lindsey told me Keith has a...thing for me."

"She told me, too."

"Think it's true?"

"Don't go by me. I can't figure out my own love life. Or lack of it."

Naomi turned from the coals toward her brother; the inside of the room was cast in darkness, save for the dull red in the fireplace and the yellow within the grate of the woodstove. Outside, snow continued to fall, insulating the cabin and accentuating Yosemite's isolation.

"Maybe you should tell Lindsey you love her—while you still can."

"Wilson or no Wilson, I don't plan on kicking the bucket anytime soon," Eric stated. "Besides, now is hardly the time to tell her something like that."

"When *is* the right time? It could've been Lindsey who took a bullet, instead of Keith. It could've been both of them!"

Eric exhaled heavily. "Remind me not to appoint you morale officer."

"You know I'm right."

"Go to bed, Naomi. You volunteered for next watch."

"I know." Naomi carefully unzipped the bag and joined the sleeping child inside. Pam moaned, curled up in Naomi's arms, then relaxed again. "Poor thing." Naomi drew the child close.

"Good night," Eric said.

"Night," Naomi replied.

Time passed. Eric added more wood to the stove—safer to use at night with sleeping people than the fireplace. He thought Naomi was asleep until he heard her quiet voice break the stillness.

"Eric..."

"Hmm?"

"How could I not have known?" she asked.

Eric immediately understood what she meant. "About Keith?"

"Yeah. Am I really so stupid?"

"I thought you gave *me* that award."

"Wrong. I married a man I loved who practically wrecked my life by dying on me. I'm in the middle of nowhere, holding a child whose father may have cost her both feet, and tending a man who took a bullet for me. And I haven't been able to make you happy since Lindsey left."

"What do you want me to say, Naomi?" Eric asked, feeling as weary as he'd ever felt in his life.

"I want you to get her back! If I die, you won't have any close family."

"You're not going to—"

"For God's sake, Eric, I could have cancer. Cancer kills!" she hissed. "If I died, who'd take care of you? And don't say you'd take care of yourself."

"I would. Besides, Lindsey can't replace you. She can't be my sister—my twin."

"No. But she can be part of your life again if you don't blow it. Eric, I was wrong about her—wrong about you both four years ago. I went crazy after my husband died. I wasn't myself. I would have—and did—say anything I could to keep you two apart. I'm so sorry. I hope you can forgive me.''

Eric swallowed, unable to speak. What he had thought of as Lindsey's treachery had been Naomi's all along—and his. Lindsey had remained true to him, but he hadn't remained true to her.

"I can't bear the thought of you alone," she continued. "Twin, you've got to get out of here—out of Yosemite! This place may not kill you as quickly as it did Eva, but it's killing any chance you might have at happiness."

Eric felt the cold inch down his spine, and shivered. Lindsey had said something along those same lines about herself earlier.

"If I have cancer, Mom and Dad will take care of me. Promise me you'll leave here when Lindsey does," Naomi begged. "Promise me you'll stay together."

Eric's throat tightened, his words hoarse with emotion when he finally spoke. "I'll think about it," he said. "That's all I can offer."

"That's enough for now. Good night, big brother," she said, using his old childhood nickname. "Love you."

Even as toddlers, Eric had been the taller twin, in addition to being born six minutes before his sister. "Love you, too."

"See how easy it is to say those words? Say them to Lindsey next."

"Shut up, Naomi," Eric said without rancor.

"I will if you kiss me good-night. Despite my husband's death, I've still taken too many things in my life for granted."

"Just my patience," Eric said, affection in his voice. He bent over and kissed his sister on the cheek, as he had done ever since he could remember. "Good night, sweetie."

He zipped up the bag the rest of the way and tucked an extra down blanket around his sister and her young charge. Then, not caring if Naomi saw or not, he stepped over to Lindsey's bed and gently kissed her forehead. As he dared to push a strand of hair off her cheek, he wondered if he and Lindsey could ever be together again.

Day 5, noon

THE ADULTS, EXCEPT FOR Keith, had risen later than usual. Lindsey herself felt more or less rested as she dressed, though stiff and sore from neck to calf. She and Eric, along with Ginger, were headed outside. It had taken both of them a half hour to clear away three feet of snow from the porch door and the higher drifts beyond. Thigh-high snow covered the short path to the outhouse, where once again they had to shovel a path. The woodpile was no different. Drifting snow had to be cleared there, as well, even though the wood was stacked on the leeward side of the cabin with an extended roof slanted and supported to protect it.

Lindsey turned her attention toward the roof. "I don't think we'll need to shovel the roof, yet," she said. Snow was good insulation against the windchill factor, but too much weight could collapse the cabin roof. The roof was built with a high center and sharply dropping sides, which not only aided gravity in keeping too much snow from building up, it also prevented the more agile mammals from descending the chimney to raid their food supplies in the summer.

"I don't want anyone up there," Eric said sharply. With his gun, binoculars and brisk attitude, he was all business. "Down here we have some cover. Up on the roof Wilson could pick us off easily."

The cabin had been deliberately built in a small copse of trees, rare at these high altitudes. The trees provided a windbreak for the corrals during the summer. The cabin had been set in a small depression in the center of a group of low hills, somewhat protecting it from the harsh, icy winds and subzero temperatures.

"If he's got any brains, he'll stay holed up," Lindsey murmured.

"If the weather doesn't get him, I will," Eric said.

Lindsey couldn't decide which was the bigger danger to Wilson. Despite the lack of wind, it was bitterly cold. The snow continued to fall thick and heavy. Already the drifts against the generator shack were more than halfway up the small building. To Lindsey, the stacks of wood suddenly looked inadequate. Eric must have noticed her gaze.

"We'll have to start in on the dead trees soon," he said. The park kept a pile of dead trees, hauling them down near the corrals to season and dry, then be chopped and recycled into fencing and firewood.

Lindsey mentally groaned. Her snowshoeing aches and pains had replaced those she'd incurred while cross-country skiing. She remembered from the past how using an ax and chainsaw could start new aches and pains, even in muscles used to such hard tasks. "I'm getting too damn old for this," she muttered.

When Eric gave her a quizzical look, she added, "That's how this place makes me feel."

Most of the Sierra Nevada, and even much of the Yosemite area, was unsuitable for cultivation and homesteads. It took the farsighted John Muir to realize its greatest value as the natural watershed for the whole Central Valley of California. Sometimes, despite its beauty, Lindsey wondered if that was all the area was good for. Or perhaps her past unhappiness with Eric, like past tragedies on this land, would forever associate Yosemite with gloom.

Thoughts of the bad times in Yosemite haunted her—such as when centuries-old prehistoric species of trees were cut down by miners, the stumps used for dancing platforms for thirty to sixty couples. Or when pioneers deliberately stole the Native Americans' winter crop of acorns, dooming the tribes to death, and themselves as well. The Indians they'd starved knew to leach the poison out of the bitter nuts. The pioneers didn't. Even recently, the murder of several visitors in Yosemite had continued the sad legacy of a land better left to the few who could survive in it, or those who could appreciate its beauty in the summertime from the safety of their air-conditioned cars.

She suddenly became aware that Eric was still staring. "I'm cold. Are we done out here?" she asked.

"Yeah. Let's get back inside." After one more cautious glance around, they headed inside to the welcome warmth of the cabin.

Lindsey led the way, carrying one last armload of wood to stack inside the outer porch. As Eric followed her and locked the door behind them, Lindsey hurried Ginger along. The trio then stepped into the common room.

"Keith, you're up!" Lindsey said with delight.

"Hardly that," Keith said from his position on the couch, where both he and Pam sat, wrapped in blankets and bandages. "But I am watching an expert artist. Isn't Pam good?"

Pam actually grinned, and continued coloring the

Yosemite animals she'd sketched from Naomi's wild-life book.

"How's the shoulder?" Eric asked, placing the rifle in the gun rack above the mantelpiece before taking off his protective gear.

"If there wasn't a child present, I'd tell you exactly how it felt," Keith grumbled. "Since there is, I'll leave it to your imagination."

"They're both doing well," Naomi volunteered cheerfully. "Pam's fever is down a little, and Keith doesn't have one to speak of—very low-grade. No infection as far as I can tell," she said, looking at the pole that had held Pam's IV bag earlier and now held the saline and antibiotics running into Keith's veins. "Fingers crossed it'll stay that way."

Pam raised one small hand and superstitiously crossed her fingers. Keith did the same, keeping his upper body carefully motionless against the cushions.

"How's the weather?" Keith asked.

"Still snowing. I doubt it'll stop anytime soon," Eric replied. "I'll check in with the main office once I get the batteries in the radio."

"The generator's broke," Pam said knowledgeably as she concentrated on her coloring.

"We know," Eric said. He gently ruffled her hair. It made Lindsey wonder if he'd do the same to his own children someday—if he ever had them.

"I bet my daddy did it," Pam said without hesitation. "He breaks things at home, too."

"Well, he won't be breaking anything else here," Eric said briskly.

"Come on, let's draw a picture of Ginger," Keith suggested. "You said Lindsey wanted one."

"I can't draw dogs. Daddy never let me have one."

"Time to learn, then," Keith said. "Find a brown pencil."

"She's yellow, not brown. I wanna use yellow."

"You can use any color you want, but orange would be closer to her real color than yellow," Eric pointed out. Pam nodded.

"Orange it is, then," Keith said. Pam had assigned him the simple task of selecting and replacing colored pencils from the box.

"Soup's on," Naomi called out. "Roast-beef sandwiches, too." She joined Eric and Lindsey at the table. "Pam and Keith already ate," she said. "I waited for you."

Mindful of her sore muscles, Lindsey lowered herself into the chair, appreciating the attractively set table and the cheerful dried herb-and-flower arrangement in the center.

Naomi poured hot chocolate into three clean mugs and passed them out. "Hors d'oeuvres," Naomi said, pushing the bottle of aspirin and Diamox in Lindsey's direction.

"Bless you." Lindsey sighed.

"How are you holding up?" Naomi asked.

"Okay," Lindsey fibbed. "No complaints."

"Good," Naomi reached over to grasp Lindsey's hand.

Lindsey's eyes opened wide. The world really had turned upside down. Or at least Naomi had changed. But even the other woman's concern didn't change their dire circumstances.

Eric waited for them to start eating, then tucked into his own food. The soup was hot, the sandwiches tasty. But despite the trappings of a civilized gathering, Lindsey couldn't help staring out the window at the heavy snow that continued to fall, and wonder when she'd see the green grass of summer again.

WILSON SHIVERED AS HE brought a small load of scrap wood into the museum. The exhibit narrative, which he'd had plenty of time to read in his boredom, said the cabin once belonged to early settlers, and had been refurbished according to the old ways, complete with stone fireplace, wooden floors and authentic reproductions of wooden furniture.

Leave it to bleeding-heart interior decorators to provide him with a ready source of fuel. He'd already burned two of the chairs to keep warm. Unlike the rangers' more modern cabin, which stood in a wooded copse, this one had been built near a spring. Sadly for him, that spring no longer supported any trees for shelter against the wind. All the old growth had been cut away by pioneers ages ago. In the museum cabin itself, the snack area beneath the old-fashioned metal-tab cash register had been cleaned out as protection against foraging wildlife. Still, he had shelter and fuel, and his own supply of dried food.

He'd moved in shortly after Pam had been taken away from him, before the new snow had fallen. If only he'd been able to hike to this cabin before those damn rangers had stolen his daughter. But he hadn't wanted to risk staying in one of the official structures after breaking out of prison. The escape had been easy. Guards and newer prisoners feared him, while the old-timers had either helped him or left him alone. After getting free and kidnapping his daughter, he'd thought leaving the country would be simple. He'd change his name, find a new wife and mother for his child, and start over again someplace new. Had he been wrong in *that* department!

His wife had already filed for divorce. That angered

him, but not as much as her wanting full custody of Pam
with no visitation rights for him, the kid's own father.

That he could not and would not abide. Wilson had a
mission. His daughter would always be his daughter, and
no one, not his wife or the police or a bunch of park
rangers would take her away from him. His eyes narrowed. His mistake had been in underestimating the rangers. They'd snatched Pam during one of the few times
he'd left her by herself. Then they'd pretended to haul
her away on a sled, when in reality the whole performance had been a ruse to draw him out into the open.
He'd missed a kill shot when one ranger had bent over
to help another. His blood had run cold when he'd heard
another rifle fire at him.

But he'd escaped detection. Now he waited for the
snow to stop, for the weather to clear. His museum cabin
was a little less than a one-hour hike in good weather
from where Pam was being held. He'd crippled one
ranger and damaged the generator. He'd get his daughter
back if he had to kill them all. And if that proved impossible...

If he couldn't have Pam, no one would.

CHAPTER ELEVEN

Lee Vining Ranger Station, main office
Day 5, afternoon

JACK HUNTER TAPPED HIS pen on the top of Lindsey's folder. The action wasn't one of nervousness. Jack had never been the nervous type. The tapping spoke of frustration and justified worry. As the personnel ranger who'd transferred Lindsey Nelson into this Yosemite mess, he took more than a personal interest in her welfare. He took responsibility for her safety.

Safety meant everything to Jack. He'd once been head ranger of the winter team in Yosemite himself, until he was awarded his present slot at Personnel.

Jack continued tapping his pen, light reflecting off it. He didn't open the folder. He knew what was it in, along with the notes that had led him to first entertain, then finalize Eric Kincaide's request for Lindsey Nelson as the replacement.

Despite her lack of physical conditioning for winter activities or canine rescues during the past four years, Jack knew Lindsey Nelson's job performance was sterling. She was definitely a winner. He also knew that she and Eric had worked exceptionally well together until the engagement was called off. Shattered romance aside, Jack was positive Lindsey and Eric were a professional team that deserved another chance. So far, going by the radio reports from Yosemite, he'd been right. Lindsey had performed brilliantly.

What was more, Eric Kincaide was winner material, too. Maybe his personal life had some turmoil—whose didn't?—but like Lindsey, his professional skills had never been in doubt. Despite Lindsey's many talents, Eric was the stronger, more stable of the two when it came to judgment. He knew how to utilize his ranger team's talents, talents he might not have, without feeling insecure about it. Eric was definitely an excellent stand-alone ranger, but he excelled even more as a head.

Lindsey Nelson was just the opposite. Jack recognized her as a woman whose extraordinary, but specific, skills increased exponentially with the right partner or the right team. Stick Lindsey with the wrong partner, and that spelled disaster.

There would be no disaster if he had his way about it. Jack shoved his pen back inside his uniform shirt pocket, a frown on his face. So far, the working team of four rangers had been cut down to two by a bullet and by health issues. He doubted Naomi Kincaide was working at full potential due to mental anxiety about her own health.

Cancer… No matter how well he tried to anticipate the skills needed by any replacement, Jack hadn't counted on Eric's sister having a health scare. That was one variable not yet in play when he'd phoned Lindsey in San Diego.

Still, Lindsey *had* been able to work with the dog and find the missing child, and in record time. Now it remained for Eric Kincaide to keep them all safe. Sooner or later, they'd have to evacuate the park, and with a dangerous gunman aiming for their backs. Jack knew it.

Eric knew it. They'd spoken about it in private, when the rest of the team had been out of the common room. The only question was...*when?*

Jack didn't envy Eric the task he had ahead of him. But if anyone could do it, Eric could, with Lindsey on his team.

Jack opened his lower right-hand desk drawer, placed the file back inside and closed it. He debated contacting the remote ranger station again, anxious to hear the latest status report, but refrained from doing so. The radio was running on batteries now, and if Eric had anything out of the ordinary to report, he would have done so. Jack would just have to wait for the regular call-in.

His lips thinned. At times like these, he almost wished he was back in the field again.

Rangers' winter cabin, afternoon

LINDSEY CLOSED THE BOOK she'd retrieved from the cabin's small library as the snow began to fall again on the granite peaks of the Sierra Nevada. Or had it ever stopped? She couldn't help recalling the worst winter ever recorded—the winter that killed almost half the Donner Party. Twenty-two feet of snow had fallen in 1846. Everything from sedate snowfalls to nine howling blizzards that lasted days, even weeks, without letup.

Lindsey's gaze swept over the sleeping patients. She hoped it wouldn't take Naomi and Eric much time to clear snow from the woodpile on this fuel run. The thermometer read fifteen degrees below zero. Even without the wind, that temperature was dangerous. So dangerous that Naomi had allowed a stiff, sore Lindsey to watch her patients while joining her twin for the outside chores.

Lindsey's brow wrinkled in a frown. Sore muscles

were the least of her problems. Ever alert, she'd noticed
Ginger's renewed interest in Pam's feet. The dog sniffed
and downright worried over the bandages. As the child
slept, Ginger stood at the base of the bed, sniffing and
snuffling, her ears perked forward with concentration.

Gangrene? Despite the antibiotics, it was a distinct
possibility, Lindsey thought ruefully. The whole replacement expedition so far had been a big reinforcement of
Murphy's Law: "Whatever can go wrong *will* go
wrong."

*We're going to have to pack Pam out of here. If she
doesn't get to a hospital, she could lose more than her
feet. She could die....*

Lindsey quietly motioned Ginger to her side, not wanting the dog to wake the sleeping child. Keith moved
once, moaned, then settled back to sleep again. Lindsey
knew with certainty that sooner or later Keith would need
to be evacuated, too, despite the snow and a deranged
gunman at large. She rose to her feet, muffling a groan
as her back and legs protested. Time for more Tylenol
and that stinking liniment, then she'd begin packing for
the journey she knew she'd soon face.

LINDSEY'D ALMOST FINISHED when Eric entered the female rangers' chilly bedroom.

"There you are," he said. "I wondered where—" He
broke off, seeing her backpack with attached snowshoes
and sleeping bag resting on one of the beds. "Been listening in on the radio conversations?"

"Nope," Lindsey replied honestly. "But Ginger's
been sniffing around Pam's feet far too much for my
liking. I hope she doesn't have gangrene."

Eric's expression was grim. "So does Naomi. She just

told me she's worried about it, but didn't want Pam or Keith to know.''

''So that's why she wanted me to stay here.'' Lindsey tightened the last strap of her backpack with a yank that spoke less of need and more of emotion. ''Well, I figured it'd be you and me packing Pam out,'' she guessed. ''And Keith and Naomi will have to wait for a second trip until his shoulder stops bleeding.''

''Right again,'' Eric said. ''Though I wish I could take Naomi to the hospital, as well.''

''Does she have a problem with staying?''

''No, she volunteered. Said Keith wasn't ready to be moved, nor were you as well equipped to take care of him as she is.''

''Poor Naomi— I wish she could be with us for Pam.''

''I hate to think of that kid going under the knife. Naomi says she's going to lose some toes. She needs a good doctor.''

''She needs her mother, too. Oh, I packed your gear.'' She noticed the startled lift of his head. ''You always hated packing. Socks on top of underwear, just the way you liked it. I used to do it all the time, remember?''

''I remember. Thanks.''

There was an awkward silence, then she took a deep breath and went on. ''We still need medical gear, but I didn't want to mess with Naomi's things. And of course we'll have to get Pam fitted out on the evac sled. I figured Naomi and I could do that.'' Lindsey stopped fiddling with her backpack strap. ''God, what a mess. I hate feeling so helpless.''

''I know.'' Eric gathered her in his arms, holding her blissfully close. Even the rough wool of his shirt against her wind-chapped cheek felt good. She found that her arms automatically remembered the way she liked to hold him, her senses taking in his strength and closeness.

Lindsey let her eyes drift shut for a moment. "When are we leaving?" she asked. "Tomorrow morning?"

"Late tonight."

She didn't bother asking for an explanation. She knew why. The windless weather was in their favor. They could both navigate the familiar pass with the aid of artificial light. The element of surprise was also a plus; Wilson probably wouldn't predict a night evacuation.

"I want you to get in a nap," Eric ordered. "And maybe get Naomi to rub down your muscles." He slowly released her and took a step back.

"She's too busy now, but I'm game for the nap when I'm done here." Lindsey wished she had the nerve to ask Eric to join her. "This has been one hell of a reunion," she observed.

"Typically Lindsey-esque," he said with a smile. "Complete with your usual fireworks."

"Yeah, well, this kind of show I didn't plan on."

To her surprise, Eric actually chuckled. "You never do, love. You never do."

Lindsey let the sound of the old endearment warm her chilled heart, then reluctantly turned back to business. "I'll go ask Naomi about those medical supplies."

"Wait," Eric said. "I have a question. Have you examined *your* breasts lately?"

"Isn't that kind of personal?" she asked, startled by the abrupt change of subject.

"Under the circumstances, no." He grasped her arms, not painfully, but tightly enough to keep her close. "I'm serious, Lindsey."

"So am I. And I haven't missed any monthly self-exams."

Eric sighed. "I could've said something to Naomi—but I never thought she had anything to worry about."

"No one ever does," Lindsey said softly, placing her hand on Eric's arm in a gesture of comfort. "But, Eric, it's Naomi's body…Naomi's responsibility. You can't blame yourself."

"I can wish things were different. Since that's a waste of time," Eric said, his curtness breaking the mood, "let's get started on those medical supplies."

PACKING THE SUPPLIES didn't take long, but convincing Keith to stay put did. The moment he woke up and realized the situation, he demanded that he and Naomi be allowed to join in the exodus.

"Don't be ridiculous," Naomi said. "You're not ready for such an arduous trip. You'd bleed to death."

"I wouldn't. I'd be better off in a hospital than in this cabin," Keith insisted. "That goes for you, too, Naomi!"

"We've weighed the odds," Eric said. "You and Naomi stay here."

"What kind of brother are you?" Keith spat out. "You'd deny your own sister medical care?"

"Keith, please," Naomi begged. "I'm the paramedic. I volunteered to stay. You need me."

"I'm not dying," Keith said. "I—"

"You're not up to the journey, either," Eric interrupted. "The decision's been made. Drop it."

"The hell I will! I'll go pack my own stuff if you won't do it for me."

Keith sat up in bed. When Naomi tried to restrain him, Keith argued, and Pam suddenly began to cry. Lindsey gathered the sobbing little girl into her lap.

"Dammit, Keith, you've started bleeding again!" Naomi snapped.

"Done showboating?" Eric asked as he went to Naomi's assistance and helped lay the man flat again. "Or do you intend to make matters worse than they already are?"

Keith's answer was a swearword that echoed the feelings of every adult present. Sweat broke out on his pale forehead as Naomi lifted his bandage.

"Naomi, please go with them!" Keith pleaded. "You don't have to stay with me. Get to the hospital, for God's sake!"

Tears started in Naomi's eyes. Lindsey watched as Eric grabbed the medical bag and passed it to his sister, her heart going out to both of them. Rotten timing for Keith, for Naomi, for Pam, for everyone... Suddenly she couldn't bear all the pain in the room, the missed chances at life, the close encounters with death. Before she could start crying herself, Eric spoke in the firm, kind, confident voice she'd always loved.

"Keith, buddy, lie back and let Naomi do her work. Pam, don't cry." He spoke gently to the child as Lindsey rocked her. "I know things seem scary, but don't worry. By this time tomorrow, you'll be back with your mom. I promise."

Pam hiccuped and buried her face in Lindsey's shoulder. Eric stroked the child's head as he said to Lindsey, "We'll leave right before sunset. The three of us."

Rangers' winter cabin, sunset

"IT'S GETTING DARK FAST," Naomi called out from her position at the window. "Pam's ready, and so is Lindsey. You'd better get started."

Eric nodded, and took one last look around the cabin's common room. Pam had been bundled in warm clothes, a sleeping bag and blankets, then strapped securely to the flat-bottomed sled. His skis and Lindsey's were also strapped to the sled, their radios, survival packs and snowshoes just inside the porch. He and Lindsey would put everything on once they'd carried Pam and the sled outside. They'd have to snowshoe up to the incline leading to the pass, but if at all possible planned to ski downhill to prearranged coordinates, where a medi-chopper would be waiting outside the avalanche zone.

"Be careful. Don't forget to load your gun," Naomi said in an undertone that Pam wouldn't hear, but Keith did.

"He wouldn't. You loaded mine, Boss, like I asked?"

"And it's under the bed like you asked," Eric replied. "Within easy reach."

Keith nodded. "I'll take good care of your sister."

Eric caught Naomi's tremulous smile as he said, "You'll both take care of each other. I've brought in plenty of wood. We'll be back as soon as we can. Hopefully within a few days."

"Don't play hero," Keith warned. "If the weather's bad, hole up someplace safe in town. Make sure you radio and let us know."

"Hey, who's the head ranger here?" Eric asked. He briefly squeezed the other man's good shoulder in farewell, then Naomi flung herself at Eric for a desperate hug, despite the bulk of his full outdoor gear.

"Be careful, twin," she whispered hoarsely.

"You, too." He kissed her on the cheek. "I'll check in later by radio."

"You'd better call on time," Naomi warned. "Come on, I'll help you carry Pam out."

"Just a sec," Lindsey said.

Eric nodded as Lindsey locked the dog inside one of

the empty bedrooms. There was no question that Ginger would have to remain behind. She couldn't maneuver in the deep snow and, like Pam, would've had to be drawn by sled. Lindsey stroked the whining dog's head before closing the door.

Under Keith's worried gaze, the three other adults lifted the sled and bore it outside into the snow. A few minutes later, with Pam's face covered, packs and rifle on their backs and snowshoes on their feet, the party of Eric, Lindsey and Pam started out.

Rays of the setting sun still gave off faint illumination to the east with its lower elevation. The snow picked up some of the light and reflected it back just enough so that they could make their way through familiar territory. With herringbone steps, they snowshoed away from the small copse of trees and the protected shelter of hills surrounding the cabin. By the time they'd reached the open meadows, the sun had dipped below the horizon. Eric continued towing Pam on his own, wanting Lindsey to conserve her strength for later. They weren't making fast time to begin with, since travel was uphill. He made frequent stops so Lindsey could catch her breath and check on Pam; once full darkness set in, they'd be forced to go even slower.

It wasn't until they'd been out for a few hours that Eric dared to hope they had indeed evaded Wilson. Although he didn't relax his vigilance for a second, he did feel confident enough to stop for a longer break and to get out the hot chocolate. He even loosened Pam's traveling straps.

Pam's face popped out from her cocoon. "Are we there yet?" she asked excitedly. Her straps hadn't been loosened during previous stops.

"Sorry, not yet," Eric said, pouring liquid into the

thermos cup. "Here, have a sip. Be careful in case it's still hot."

Pam took a sip, then a bigger swallow. "Not that hot. How much longer?"

"You'll probably see your mother close to morning. We'll be traveling most of the night."

"It's dark. I hate the dark. What if we get lost?" Pam shivered.

Eric couldn't tell if her shiver was from the cold, the dark, her fever or a combination of all three. "We won't get lost," he said. "Lindsey and I have been through this pass on skis, horses and on our feet." He remembered those sunny summer rides when they were off duty, and the many times they'd enjoyed the beauty of the land and the beauty of their love—the two mingling, increasing, until it seemed as if nothing could intrude on their personal paradise.

"Plus, out here, there's no such thing as light pollution," Lindsey added. "We can see the stars, and we can use the moon's light to find our way."

"In the snow?"

"It's stopped snowing, silly," Lindsey said. "Look up."

The snow had decreased earlier, then stopped. Once again, Eric's acute sense of weather had proved accurate, although Pam hadn't noticed from the safety of her cocoon.

"Is Daddy around?" she asked nervously.

"We haven't seen him," Eric replied.

"We purposely left at night so he couldn't see us," Lindsey said.

Pam nodded, and Eric hoped she was reassured. "Are you warm enough?"

"My face is cold."

"Then finish up your drink and get back under the covers."

"Do you have to go potty?" Lindsey quietly asked as she checked the chemical heaters inside the sleeping bag and decided the poppers were still working.

"No," Pam said, yawning. "I'm tired, but the sled keeps bouncing."

"Sorry, I can't do anything about that. You want to stay awake to see your mother, don't you?" Lindsey asked before Eric could explain that sleeping in the bitter cold wasn't a great idea, especially for someone not physically active enough to generate much body heat, despite her fever.

Pam's yawn changed to a vigorous nod.

"Then get your head back inside the covers, and we'll get going again. If you need anything, just yell, okay?" Lindsey tucked the child in, then tightened the stability straps around the small body.

"Eric, let me pull now," Lindsey suggested. "I've got my second wind."

"I'm good for a while, yet."

"I'll take a turn, anyway," Lindsey insisted. "See if I can give Pam a smoother ride than you," she kidded. "Unless," she said very quietly, "you don't think I'd be fast enough. No trace of you-know-who?"

"I told Pam the truth. There's no sign of him. If he knew we were here, we would've heard from him a lot sooner." He was rewarded with Lindsey's sigh of relief. "As long as the weather holds, we should be okay. We need to keep warm and keep moving. You ready to go?"

"Just make sure you let me take my turn." She motioned at the sled straps. One thing about Lindsey—she'd never let him down on the job.

"I'll keep the sled and the rifle," he said. "But you could carry the torch for me if you're up to it."

"I'm up to it."

He thought of all she'd been through since he'd asked for her as Eva's replacement. "I don't doubt it for a minute," he said.

CHAPTER TWELVE

Rangers' winter cabin
Day 6, past midnight

"I WISH THEY'D RADIO IN," Keith said, fretting from his bed. "Isn't it two o'clock yet?" he asked, the prearranged time Eric had agreed to check in. If Wilson *was* monitoring their radio with one of his own, Eric hadn't wanted to tip him off about their escape plan, until it was far too late for the threesome to be caught.

"We've got an hour, yet," Naomi replied. She sat crossed-legged on the other bed in the common room, with only one oil lamp lit. Earlier she'd pushed both beds away from the dying fire and closer to the woodstove, which she'd fueled for the long night, and closed the fireplace damper against the cold. She'd told Keith to rest, while she stayed awake to turn on the radio at the appointed time. They couldn't afford to waste batteries with the generator down. "I thought I told you to sleep. Why aren't you?"

"Easier said than done. You know, for an intelligent woman, you ask foolish questions."

"I'm just trying to be helpful," Naomi protested.

"Three good people are out there facing God knows what. Until I hear from your brother, I won't be able to rest." Keith drew his uninjured arm out of his sleeping bag and gingerly propped himself up in a sitting position. "Anyone with brains could figure that out."

"Thank you so much," she replied, stung. "So I'm brainless?"

"You should've checked your breasts every month," Keith continued. "If you didn't learn that in sex ed at school, I know you learned it in your paramedic classes."

"So I screwed up," Naomi said, angry with Keith for bringing up the subject, even angrier at her own stupidity.

"Your husband's dead, so you don't care anymore? You just go to hell in a handbasket and leave the rest of us in the lurch?"

"That's not true!"

"Then what's the reason?" Keith demanded. "Your family obviously loves you, your co-workers admire you, you have a highly skilled job with responsibility—but you can't be bothered to act like an adult when it comes to your own health?"

Naomi rose to place her hand on Keith's forehead. "Is your temp spiking? Is that where this is coming fr—?"

Naomi suddenly broke off, realizing that Keith's emotional outburst wasn't from anger at all, but fear—fear for *her*. Lindsey's conversation flashed in her memory, then the meaning of that conversation sank deep into her bones. It was one thing to hear Lindsey say Keith was in love with her. It was another to hear it from Keith himself. Keith, who'd never been married. Keith, who had seemed the loner in the group. Keith, who was a good five years younger than she. A man who couldn't sleep, despite a hole in his shoulder, worrying over her health, her safety, her life.

The realization created an awkward moment that seemed to stretch on and on.

"I'm an idiot about a lot of things." Naomi's hand

shook as she withdrew it from Keith's forehead. "Sorry."

He reached for her hand so quickly that he winced with pain, yet he still held it within his own. "No, I'm sorry. Ordinarily I can keep my big mouth shut."

Naomi joined him on the bed, careful not to jar him. "Are you really quitting and not coming back next season?"

"Yes."

"Because of...me?"

"No, because of me. I'm tired of playing with explosives."

"But you save lives!"

"I start avalanches. I was thinking of going into anti-terrorist work—getting hired with the bomb squad."

"But that's so dangerous. And depressing."

"Yeah, like this job is so safe." He shook his head. "This place is getting to me. At least if I worked with the police, I wouldn't be so isolated. I'm tired of being the odd man out."

"Oh." She didn't know what else to think...to say...and was afraid of thinking and saying too much. But she did let Keith continue to hold her hand.

"Your fingers are like ice," Keith observed. "What's the temperature outside?"

"I didn't want to look," she admitted. "It's so cold out there, and Pam already has frostbite."

"They'll radio after they reach the top of the pass. Then we'll know."

Naomi noticed her fingers didn't feel so cold anymore. Nor did she seem as fearful. She realized that this time Keith was taking care of her, instead of the other way around, and she didn't mind that, either.

"Then we'll know...." she echoed.

HOUR AFTER FRIGID HOUR passed as the trio made it to the top of the pass. Even with the aid of chemical warm-ers, state-of-the-art winter gear and high-tech torches, it was a bone-numbing business made slower by the dark terrain. Lindsey kept Pam awake for her own safety, though privately she doubted anyone could sleep while being jerked along on a sled—except perhaps herself. Every muscle ached, and those that didn't had progressed to outright pain. She'd taken her turn towing Pam when even Eric's strong muscles needed a breather.

"We're almost at the top," Eric said, his confident voice giving her both encouragement and warmth. "Then we'll radio the cabin, get onto our skis, and it's downhill all the way. A few hours from now we'll be eating breakfast in civilization again."

Lindsey smiled. "I'll settle for a cup of hot tea and sack time in a soft hotel bed—with the room heat set on high."

"I get to see my mom first," Pam said, raising her face from her cocoon of blankets.

"Only if you cover your head. If your poor nose gets any redder, we'll have to rename you Rudolph," Lindsey teased. Pam immediately ducked back into the blankets. "Don't come out again until we call you. Talk through the blankets." Lindsey smiled at the muffled agreement and at Pam's childlike faith in the ability of adults to solve any problems.

A short time later, they stood on the summit of Tioga Pass. Lindsey felt no joy in having come so far. She was glad the child couldn't see what she did.

Sloping downward lay a huge expanse of snow. Even in the limited darkness, they could see that the sheer volume of snow had completely covered every rock, tree and even the very contours of the landscape. It glowed with a strange luminescence, reflecting the light from above in eerie waves. Lindsey began to sweat in spite of the freezing cold as fear sucked at her lungs. This place was a deathtrap. Beneath that deceptive calm lay tons of snow and ice that could and would kill. Any noise, any movement, could trigger a slide. The skiing necessary to maneuver through such potential danger would be tricky. And towing a sled down the incline exponentially changed tricky to deadly.

"Oh…my…God." Panic raced through her veins. "We can't go down there," she whispered, keeping her voice low. "We'll have to go back." She felt Eric's arm around her shoulder. It did nothing to dispel her terror.

"We wouldn't make it back before the next storm hit," Eric said. "And there'd be even more snow to navigate if we dug in now. I think we can manage it. Trust me."

Lindsey's heart sank. The two of them stared at the scene before them, which resembled a giant bowl.

"It's now or never, love." His endearment brought tears to her eyes, but didn't take away the feeling of dread in her heart. "I'm sorry I dragged you into this."

"You didn't drag me into anything. I volunteered."

"I'm glad you did. I missed you. Wanted you back."

Disbelief, shock, joy and anger tumbled inside her. "So you had to wait four…whole…years…to tell me this?"

He didn't answer.

"If Eva hadn't died, would I *ever* have heard from you?"

Again, no answer.

"You've got a hell of a lot of nerve! And you—"

"Got you to stop shaking in your boots, didn't I?"

"I—" She was aware that anger had shaken her out

of terror's grip—aware of a deep sense of loss, as well. Had he told her the truth or not? "So...you didn't miss me after all?"

"Get your mind back on the job, Ranger," Eric said brusquely. "Now's not the time for hearts and flowers."

Lindsey bit back the retort on her lips. Now *wasn't* the time. But there never seemed to be any right time when it came to the two of them. "Our plan of action—sir?"

"Let's not go overboard, Lindsey. We'll ski down the north side of the bowl," he said. The Dana Fork cut its way through Tioga Pass on the south side, leaving sheer edges and unnavigable terrain. "Less chance of triggering a slide. I'll go first and pick out a short path. Then you follow with Pam. I'll negotiate some, you follow some. That should get us down safely, as long as we avoid the center of the bowl. We'll keep to the edges as much as possible."

"Sounds good except that I need to blaze the trail. Not you."

His head snapped sharply up at that. "As head ranger, that's my responsibility."

"Maybe, but I'm in no shape to ski towing a sled. I don't have your strength, and my skiing muscles are out of condition. I don't trust myself with Pam on this incline. But without the weight of the sled, I can easily stay on my feet and blaze a trail."

"You lead, I follow? I don't like it."

"Neither do I, but at least this way if I make a mistake, Pam won't suffer because of it."

"Lindsey—"

"We don't have time to argue! I'm getting cold just standing here."

Eric swore. Lindsey ignored his temper as she took off her snowshoes and switched them for skis. He helped her remove the backpack. Then he lashed it to the sled, along with his pack and the rifle. The removal of the excess weight felt heavenly to her overtaxed muscles. She quickly substituted new poppers for the cooler ones inside her gear and in Pam's sleeping bag.

"Thanks," she sighed. She watched Eric fiddle with his radio unit as he attempted to reach the cabin. "What's wrong?"

"Nothing, but static," he said with disgust. "If we can't get through to them at this height, we never will."

"Try again after you put on your poles and skis," she suggested.

The result of the second radio attempt was the same. "We can't stand here any longer. Let's go."

After a final check on Pam to adjust her blankets and straps and offer a reassuring word, Lindsey straightened. "I guess I'm ready."

Eric maneuvered close to her. "Turn on your locator beacon. I've turned on mine. Just to be safe."

She complied. "I know we won't need them," she said firmly.

Taking her face in his gloved hands, he kissed her full on the mouth. "For luck," he said.

Lindsey didn't return the sentiment. "Did you request me as a replacement or not?" She had a driving need to know.

"I never said I did."

"I'm asking, anyway."

"Tell you when we reach the bottom. Let's get going."

"I'm gone." She deftly poled her way toward the incline. The top of the pass had hard-packed snow from the harshness of the winds—the same winds that consistently prevented helicopter flight—but the bowl beneath them was covered with the newly fallen powder, which lay over its harder snow. Different temperatures produced a layered effect—hence the avalanche danger. Heavier snow, such as a layer that had melted a little in the sun, then frozen at night, would mix with fresh snow. The various layers built up and up until gravity disturbed the delicate balance. The loose powder provided a moving, sliding plane for the more solidified layers. When one layer sheered away from another, it tended to have a chain effect on the others—like sheets of snow falling from a roof, but over and over and over again until the whole roof—or mountainside—reached stability again.

Lindsey was an excellent powder skier, but skiing prowess meant nothing in these shifting slabs of snow. She cautiously tested her balance and began with slow, easy movements. This was no time for overconfidence, let alone hotdogging. Without her added burden of pack and torch, she made fair progress, only a bit clumsy in the darkness. If she took her time and was very careful, they would all reach the bottom, none the worse for the wear. Eric shone the light ahead for her, then followed.

He'd attached the sled to himself with a body harness and long leads, since—unlike earlier, when he wore snowshoes—he needed ski poles to negotiate. His S-shaped descent was even slower than Lindsey's. He couldn't allow the sled to run into his skis or upset on its own at the end of each turn. He ended each traverse down by skiing off the powder at the end of the bowl, and waited inside the relative safety of the trees and rocks at the edge while Lindsey descended some more.

Time passed with agonizing intensity. The three picked their way down the shallower edge of the bowl, where the snow wasn't as heavy as it was in the center.

Only now the shallower edge of the bowl turned into

rocky ledges and outcroppings for a good two hundred feet. They'd have to enter the deeper curve of the decline—and hence the deeper area of the bowl—to clear the rocks.

Lindsey stopped her progress, and allowed Eric to catch up to her. "We've got problems," she said, staring at the snow and wishing it was warm San Diego sand. "Look at these rocks!"

"My turn to lead," Eric said immediately.

"No. I told you before, I can't handle skiing and towing the sled. Pam's safer with you."

"I—"

"Don't argue. You know I'm right."

"I hate it when you're right. Keep as close to the edge of the bowl as the rocks allow. If you hear anything suspicious, head for the downside of the bigger rocks and hunker down. Let the snow shoot over you."

Lindsey studied the rocks. The granite blocks and rounded stones from the last glacier age didn't look like much protection to her. If they moved, she could easily be crushed. She started to state the obvious, then realized she'd only be stalling.

"Is your beeper working okay?" he asked.

Lindsey checked the test light on her jacket's locator beacon. "Yep. Yours?"

"Yes." He paused. "Be careful...take your time."

She nodded, adjusted her ski poles and slowly glided past the rocky edges of the bowl and into the deeper snow. Ever so gingerly, Lindsey carved out a path with an extremely shallow rate of descent. Eric watched from the edge, then followed, the sound of the flat-bottomed sled scraping against the top layer of snow and echoing strangely in the bowl. They made it safely past the first set of rocks, rested on the side above the second, and started again.

Lindsey slipped, but managed to right herself before she fell. She forced herself to relax muscles she'd tightened in concentration, and negotiated the second set of rocks without further incident. Eric followed and again joined her. Together they studied the third and last obstacle—this set of rocks was even taller and nastier than the other two. The only consolation was that once they were past these rocks, they'd be almost at the bottom of the pass. Which meant helicopter rescue for Pam.

"You know what they say. Third time's the charm," Eric said. She noticed the hoarseness of his voice and knew it wasn't just from the cold or fatigue.

She leaned forward and kissed him, repeating his earlier words. "For luck." Then she was off.

The snow felt dicey below her skis as soon as she left Eric and Pam and the safety of the bowl's edge. Her skis sank through powdery layers and sliced into harder, icier layers below, her ski edges cutting into ice with a harsh grating sound. Worse, more boulders loomed, their rounded tops high above the snowpack, and she was forced to move deeper into the bowl to avoid them.

The sudden crack of what sounded like a rifle shot caught her by surprise. She was facing directly away from the boulders. From above came the groaning of thousands of pounds of snow beginning to move, at first slowly, then picking up speed at an ever-increasing pace.

Lindsey's horrified mind recoiled from the truth and refused to trust in her hearing, but that was only for an instant. Then instinct took over, instinct for survival. Lindsey pushed off for greater speed than ever before, and headed straight down the incline. Her muscles, now responding perfectly in an adrenaline-heightened state, followed her commands as she raced down through the snow. Her life hung in the balance, and Lindsey realized with the calm, detached logic that appears in times of great stress, that decisions had to be made—and quickly, because seconds were all she had. The slide was gaining on her; the roaring in her ears had increased with terrifying intensity to that of a runaway freight train, except that trains never reached hundreds of miles per hour, like this snow. There was no way she could get to the bottom of the slope before the snow got to her.

She had to aim for a clear section below the boulders and ski back up the side of the bowl. She wanted to live! But was it possible? Already her overtaxed muscles were trembling from the extra demands being made upon them. She skied too fast for comfort, for balance, and a fall now would mean certain death. The wind whipped past her face as she crouched as low as possible, offering the least wind resistance for the highest amount of speed. She silently prayed ''Please, Lord,'' the only prayer she had time for as the end of the boulders approached.

All her concentration was focused on her muscles, willing them control, willing them not to collapse and fail. She watched for the end of the boulders, and as the final granite edge confirmed it, Lindsey prepared herself. At the last possible moment, she leaned in to negotiate the deep powder turn to safety. Lindsey could have cheered aloud as she successfully managed the turn; she was shooting up the bowl's inclined side, higher and higher. Her joy vanished as she felt the huge gust of wind on the backs of her legs from the approaching mass of snow. She dared not turn around and look, but she knew the snow was almost upon her.

Faster! she prayed as her uphill progress to the safety at the base of the rocks began to ebb due to loss of momentum and gravity. Just a little faster, a little farther! And then she was at granite. Lindsey dug her ski edges into the snow, the metal rasping, biting into the crusty surface of the wind-swept bluff. Before she could stop, a wall of force hit her in the back and knocked her flat, covering her with icy darkness.

Her safety bindings released and her poles straps snapped around her wrist during her forward momentum. Lindsey was flipped onto her back, her hat and one glove ripped from her body. She immediately thrust her hands before her face, cupping them and making an air pocket while she still had the chance. She waited to be tumbled, rolled and broken into bits. Instead, with a sudden jerking motion, her body ground to a halt. Lindsey lay still, winded and drained, as she listened to the roar of the slide. It filled her head and shook the ground with tremors of power. And then there was only silence.

CHAPTER THIRTEEN

Rangers' winter cabin, 4:00 a.m.

"NAOMI, STOP TRYING the radio," Keith said, resting on the couch, but upright and dressed. "You're only wasting the batteries."

"Since Eric and Lindsey haven't answered me, I'm not wasting batteries," Naomi said, worried. "I hope nothing's gone wrong."

"With those two?" Keith asked incredulously. "Your brother's a tank, and Lindsey seems to have more than her share of luck. If they don't have Pam in a hospital by now, they're damn close to it."

"From your mouth to God's ear," she said fervently. "But why haven't they called? Why can't we reach them?"

"Maybe the problem's at this end."

"You already checked the radio. And you tested the batteries. What else could it be?" Naomi wondered.

"We didn't check the antenna."

"When it's light, I'll go look," Naomi said, playing with the radio again, then stopping. "You don't think the antenna's blown down, do you?"

"Wouldn't be the first time. If it has, I can't get up there to fix it."

"Maybe I could…"

Keith shook his head. "You'd be a clear target for a man with a rifle."

"But what if it *is* the antenna?" Naomi asked. "What are we going to do?"

"We keep warm—and wait."

LINDSEY OPENED HER MOUTH to take in a gulp of air, and succeeded. She felt snow in her hair, and hoped her fingers wouldn't get frostbitten. She hoped the snow hadn't torn the diamond from the setting of Wade's ring. Once she got home she intended to give it back to him, preferably intact. Maybe then she and Eric could find some kind of middle ground. The ridiculousness of her concerns—definitely minor concerns in her present situation—almost made her laugh out loud. But the blackness of her prison didn't allow for laughing. Panic attacked her, but she fought it off. Instead, she did the things all potential avalanche victims were taught to do.

She moved her hands from her face, pressing the snow away from her mouth to allow herself more air. That action alone heartened her. If she'd been buried deeply, she wouldn't have been able to shift the snow; the sheer weight would have immobilized her.

Next she tried to move her legs. They shifted just a bit, but she couldn't lift them. The same applied when she tried to sit up. However, she could move her arms, another encouraging sign. Although she was buried, it appeared that her race for the side of the bowl had placed her in the shallower part of the slide. She still breathed easily; the snow wasn't packed into the consistency of ice or wet beach sand, which meant oxygen might be able to permeate to her layers.

The next step would determine her further actions. First she worked up a ball of saliva in her mouth. Then she turned her head sideways. Slowly, cautiously, so as not to inhale snow, she opened her mouth and let the saliva drool down the side of her face. She noted the downward track gravity imposed on the liquid, and mentally established up, down and her horizontal plane. She needed to dig toward the surface with the truest perpendicular she could. All rangers had read of victims trapped in shallower depths who'd lost their sense of direction in the blackness. They had panicked, and dug sideways or even downward, instead of toward the surface. It was just as easy as losing your bearing in water; there you blew air bubbles to navigate. Trapped in snow, you spit out saliva. The warmth of the liquid against the cold of your face would tell the story, if you kept your head. But nothing could save her from the weighty, pressing darkness.

Don't panic. Stay calm. You aren't in deep, or you couldn't move. You have a locator beacon, and Eric saw your last location.

With her one gloved hand still keeping a protective air pocket and shelter over her mouth, she slowly maneuvered her bare hand to the correct perpendicular position in the heavy snow. With scratching, clawing motions, she began to dig toward what she hoped would be the surface.

AT THE SOUND OF THE rifle-shot crack of snow and ice sheering away, Eric had screamed Lindsey's name at the top of his voice. Then, despite skis and poles, he'd thrown himself over Pam's sled, his body protecting the child. They were out of the snowslide's main path, but the overspill's sudden wind and snow spray could buffet them at the edges of the bowl; the furious pocket of air created by the massive displacement could reach hundreds of miles an hour. Eric couldn't ski himself and Pam to safety. Unlike Lindsey, they were in the safest position they could be at the time, as long as they stayed prone.

After what seemed like an eternity, but wasn't even a full minute, the sound of the freight train stopped. He lifted himself to his hands and knees, kicked out of his bindings, then knelt next to the sled to discard his poles. A light dusting of snow fell off him as he parted the blankets to get to the crying Pam.

"It's okay," he said, glad she hadn't seen the whole terrible spectacle—Lindsey being swallowed alive—as he had. "Just a little delay, that's all."

"Where's Lindsey?" Pam asked, continuing to sob, her face almost as pale as the snow.

"She's below us. I need to go help her out of the snow. Can you be a brave girl for me and stay here alone for a few minutes?"

Fifteen minutes max. Then suffocation sets in.

"Don't leave me," Pam begged. "Please."

"I have to, but I'll be right back. Here, take this." He took off his watch and gave it to her. "Here's the flashlight. It still works. Get back under the covers, and shine the light on the watch. When the last two numbers say fifteen, I'll be back here."

"With Lindsey?"

"That's the plan." He covered her up, removed first his pack, then the body harness and sled traces. He took the radio locator from his pack, hooked it to his jacket and jammed the pack securely against the sled. With the addition of two iron spikes, pegs from the sled itself, the sled became immobile. "Fifteen minutes, Pam," he said, hating the way his voice shook. *Dear God, I can't lose Lindsey again.* He reached for his poles and stepped back into his bindings. "Stay warm, you hear me? I'll be as quick as I can."

THE COLD SEEPED PAINFULLY into her body, causing tingles in her extremities. Her nose and cheeks were already numb, and her ungloved hand burned with the cold. She'd been able to raise it, but even fully extended, it didn't reach the surface. The only thing worse than the dark cold was the weight.

Eric, where are you? How long have I been in here? She slowly retracted her raised arm to check her wrist-watch, but she couldn't reach the button to light it up. Carefully, she took off the remaining glove and put it on her frozen hand. Then, after pushing more snow away from her face and fighting against the weight of snow, slipped her hands under her armpits.

Her frantic thoughts became morbid. She remembered one summer as a child at the beach, when she'd lain on her back and innocently asked her sisters to bury her in the sand. Only her head had been left uncovered. When they'd finished, she'd tried to sit up—to discover that she couldn't move. Lindsey had starting crying, then scream-ing, until her sisters had scooped away enough sand to allow her to free herself. Even then, she hadn't stopped crying until her mother had taken her to rock in her arms.

Lindsey remembered another summer, when the whole family had vacationed in Colorado, and the three girls had begged to be taken to Denver's wax museum, a spooky collection of Americana horror.

There were sinking ships and doomed souls in frigid waters, and desperate treasure hunters in dangerous mines. The Donner Party was depicted there as well, but Lindsey decided the worst scene wasn't the grisly feast. The curator could have done a more terrifying scene us-ing the scariest part of all...the snow that had melted down beneath a Donner Party campfire while they slept and trapped them in a pit more than fifteen feet deep.

Stop it! Lindsey told herself. *Save your oxygen!* Her own labored breathing filled her ears, reminding her of another wax museum exhibit. During the Salem witch-craft trials, one accused woman had been put to death "by press." She'd been staked out, and a wooden door placed on top of her. One by one the townspeople had filed by with the largest rocks they could carry. They placed them atop the door, slowly and surely pressing with more and more weight against the woman's chest. The loud, harsh breathing that had been piped through the museum speakers to re-create the victim's suffocation filled her memory now.

I don't care how hard they beg, I am never, ever taking my children to any spooky wax museum, she promised herself. *If I ever have any children... If I ever get married... If I ever get out of here... Don't panic. Stay calm. Conserve your oxygen.*

Eric, you didn't get covered, too, did you? You and Pam should've been free and clear. Where are you?

ERIC DESCENDED THE ICY cover of what remained on the surface. The unstable snow was far below, but the hard ice that remained was just as dangerous. His skis cut hard into the pack, his poles not always penetrating the crust as he made his way downhill. He had a strong signal from the beeper, and the large boulders had apparently remained in place. If it weren't for them, he wouldn't even have recognized Lindsey's last location. The land-scape had totally changed, except for the massive glacial granite. He angled toward the rocks, praying Lindsey hadn't been smashed against them, praying she wasn't too deep, praying he could find her in time.

A beeper was no substitute for the pinpoint accuracy of a trained rescue dog. And one tired head ranger in just the barest glow of sunrise wasn't a strong search party. He resisted the urge to scream out in sheer frustration, resisted the urge to scream out her name. He didn't resist gravity, however, and skied as fast as he dared to Lindsey's last location, listening to the homing locator beeper sounding at his jacket.

He reached the boulders and kicked off his skis. Then he pulled the basket off one of his poles so he could use the rest as a snow probe. Homing beacons were more two-dimensional than three-dimensional. They could only locate a specific area above the snow. They couldn't tell him how far down to dig. He checked his receiver and started stabbing the snow with his pole.

Lindsey hadn't taken the full brunt of the snow, he thought. She made it to the side of the bowl. She shouldn't be too deep.

The minutes ticked by as he advanced, probed and withdrew, advanced, probed and withdrew, over and over again. Once his pole hit something firm, but his frantic digging only unearthed a broken tree limb. He rose again, keeping to a grid pattern as best he could.

How many minutes has it been? he wondered. *I wish I had my watch.* He'd hated leaving it with Pam, hated leaving the terrified child, too, but had no choice.

The quicker I find her, the quicker I get back to Pam.

He stabbed again, withdrew, stabbed, withdrew, as he mentally ticked off the minutes.

I should never have let her lead. If anything's happened to her...

He couldn't finish the thought. Didn't dare dwell on it or he'd go insane. Right now he had a job to do. Bent low he probed, withdrew, probed and withdrew. The beacon receiver pinged rapidly at its highest frequency, indicating close proximity to Lindsey, yet despite his search, his pole continued to sink until he arrived at the boulders, the end of his grid. Could she have sunk deeper than his pole could reach? Frantically Eric dropped to his hands and knees and retraced his grid, shoving the pole down to the snow until his hand rested on top of the snowy surface.

You've gotta be around here somewhere. The damn receiver hasn't slowed or shut up. Lindsey, where are you?

He felt the pole hit something, but something that yielded. He tried again, and felt the same thing. Immediately he clawed at the snow, digging like some wild beast in a frenzy. The snow came away in clumps and sprays until, more than a yard deep, he uncovered the top of Lindsey's ski boot.

A strangled cry burst from his throat and stilled his hands for just a second. He changed position and began digging even faster where Lindsey's head should be, willing her foot to move or her ankle to bend, anything that would give him a sign that she was still conscious...still alive!

Snow fell into the hole he was digging. Eric swore, taking time to clear more snow between the head area and exposed boot, hating the extra seconds that ticked away, yet knowing that he could work only so fast. Thoughts of Eva filled his memory at that motionless boot, driving him to dig with more fury than before. A few more minutes...an eternity later...he had her face uncovered.

''Lindsey?'' he said as he cleared more snow from her chest. He couldn't administer CPR with it there. ''Speak to me, sweetheart. It's Eric.''

Nothing. He peered closer, hoping he'd see her eyes

flutter, her lips move, her chest rise and fall with respiration.

"Please, Lindsey, open your eyes," he begged, taking off his gloves and brushing the snow from her eye sockets and nostrils. He lowered one bare finger to rest beneath her nose, and felt the faint pulsation of warm, exhaled air. That was all the inspiration he needed to finish clearing off the rest of her body. As he started examining her arms and legs for breaks, she opened her eyes.

"Lindsey?" He spoke her name like one demented, barely able to form the syllables.

"No, it's Frosty the Snowman, you idiot," she said faintly before she coughed and gasped in fresh air. Then, in a slightly stronger voice, she added, "What took you so long?"

First-aid techniques and the head ranger's calm, collected demeanor flew out the proverbial window. Eric grabbed Lindsey and pulled her into his lap, his arms crushing her to his chest. "Thank God," he whispered, overjoyed that she had the strength to raise her arms and place them around his neck. "Thank God."

They clung to each other. Eric drew strength from her, and felt his professional manner return as he slowly went through the required questions. "Do you hurt anywhere?"

"Um..." She considered that, still slightly dazed.

"Can you move your arms and legs? Are you bleeding? Did you hit your head anywhere?" he asked.

"My head aches," she answered.

He noticed that her hat was gone. His gentle fingers found a large knot on her head, but no bleeding. Her pupils were both reactive and equal. "That's gotta hurt," he said, "but I guess we can skip the ice pack."

She watched him take off his hat and put it on her

head. He removed the scarf from his neck and wrapped it around her bare hand. "That'll keep your hand warm. I can't find your glove. Ready to sit up?"

"Sure." He noticed that her hands were shaking. She looked light-headed, and obviously felt it. Eric laid her back in his arms again as her eyes closed.

"Breathe," he murmured. "It wouldn't do to have you fainting now, Lindsey."

"Pam okay?" she managed to gasp out. "You, too?"

"She's okay, but I left her up above us. We can't stay here for long, Lindsey. We've got to get moving."

Her eyes opened. He saw that the first trace of sunrise shone in the east. That sunrise showed a totally different contour in the bowl, a massive shift in snow now exposed to the light of dawn. Eric shook as he realized just how close she'd come to death. He gave silent thanks for her deliverance, and then in a sudden release of pent-up tension, bent over and kissed her lips with rough joy and deep gratitude.

"Thanks for coming after me," she breathed.

"Thanks for taking point," Eric said, silently vowing to take the lead from now on. He gave her one last kiss, then said, "I'm going up to get Pam. Will you be all right?" he asked.

"I—my skis are gone!" she said. "And my poles. What are we going to do?" She raised her scarf-wrapped hand to feel his hat. "This is your hat," she said inanely. "I can't take your hat."

"You packed me a spare, remember? Stay here," he ordered. "I'll get us all down."

"How?"

"Calm down, love. I'll tow you with Pam. It's downhill all the way. We're almost there, Lindsey. Almost to the checkpoint. Okay?"

She nodded as he lifted her out of his lap and made her as comfortable as possible. He put the skis and poles back on. "Soon as we get to town, I'll get us some coffee. Stay calm, stay put and I'll be back in ten minutes," he assured her.

She glanced at her watch. "My watch is broken," she said, surprised. "Look, Eric." She held up her gloved wrist. "It's broken." Eric ignored the watch. He kissed her wrist above the raw skin where the snow had ripped away the strap of her ski pole.

"I'll buy you a new one.

"Then how will I know when it's ten minutes?" Her voice sounded like that of a fearful child, more like Pam's than Lindsey's.

"You'll know when I zip right back to your side. Lindsey, love, I have to go, but I'll be back. I promise." He touched her cheek with a gloved hand, then started the tedious uphill track on skis.

LINDSEY TRIED TO sit quietly during his journey, but couldn't. The panic she'd managed to suppress earlier had left her shaking with reaction, and with cold. Her wrist and head started to throb, her cheeks and forehead were freezing, and her scarf-wrapped hand, which she now held beneath the bottom of jacket, ached with pins and needles as the numbness of her fingers began to fade. Suddenly she was crying, silent sobs that shook her shoulders and made her eyes water. Reaction mingled with adrenaline letdown and the chilling cold, causing her to shiver so violently her head throbbed even more.

The only good thing about all of this was that she'd been the one leading. She hadn't had to see Eric and Pam get buried alive. She cried and shook until she tired of both, and managed to calm down when Eric returned, although she still shivered slightly from the cold. Eric pulled off her ski boots and bundled her into the sleeping bag with Pam, put on the replacement hat and strapped both of them securely onto the sled.

"We're almost there, ladies," Eric said as he placed the blanket over their faces. "Half a hill more, a half hour or so, and we'll all be home."

But where's home for me? Lindsey wondered. *Back with my family or here with Eric in this deathtrap?* She continued to wonder until she heard the sound of a helicopter. She pushed away the blankets, raising her face to the light of the sun. And she watched the chopper land as tears of relief and happiness streamed down Pam's cheeks.

CHAPTER FOURTEEN

Rangers' winter cabin
Day 6, midmorning

NAOMI AND GINGER RETURNED from a quick trip outside, the dog vigorously shaking her coat, Naomi stamping her boots before rejoining Keith, who sat in front of the cabin fire.

"It's down," she said bluntly to Keith's silent query. "The whole damn radio antenna is down."

"Hell. Was the wiring intact, or could you tell?"

"I dug some of it out of the snow. It's in pieces, Keith. It'll need more than a simple splice. The cable must've been shredded when the wind blew the tower over."

"The tower went, too?"

"Oh, yeah." Naomi tossed her hat and gloves onto the table. "Even though the mounting bracket screws are still on the base."

"The storm pulled the whole thing out of the ground?" Keith asked incredulously. The radio tower had been bolted and cemented into solid drilled granite.

"Yeah. Tower and antenna went down together and traveled a good distance."

"We're damn lucky it didn't come through the ceiling," Keith said.

"Lucky. That's us. Guess we'll have to get the portable antenna up on the roof."

"You're not going up there. You'd be a sitting duck for Wilson!"

"Like I'm letting you break open that wound again," Naomi said. "Someone's got to do it."

"You couldn't manage the portable antenna by yourself, anyway. Last time the tower was down for repairs, it took both me and Eric to get it on the roof, and that was in the summer, no less."

"Still...we could try." Naomi bit her lip. "We need that radio, Keith. We could wait until dark, I could climb onto the roof, and if you could manage to hand me the portable antenna, I think we'd be in business."

"Or out of business, if Wilson has an infrared scope on his rifle. I'm the senior ranger, and I say it's not worth the risk."

"You're on the sick list, so I'm in charge," Naomi countered.

"Either way, I'm not handing you the antenna," Keith said. "Without my help, you have no choice but to stay off the roof and safely inside."

"My brother's out there! I need to know if he's all right."

Keith's expression hardened. "There's more to this job than your personal wants, Naomi. If Eric was here, he'd be the first to agree. If all went well, Eric, Lindsey and Pam are on the other side of the pass by now. No portable antenna could reach them."

"What if everything *didn't* go well? What if they're hurt? Still on this side of the pass?"

"Either way, there's nothing we can do for them. Getting yourself killed trying to prove me wrong won't help. It's not worth the gamble."

"I think it is!"

"You've got to have confidence in your brother, Naomi. And in Lindsey. And in me. If you can't trust any of us, you're no better then Eva, and you'll end up the same way she did."

Naomi felt tears start in her eyes. "How can you be so cruel?" she whispered.

"Not half as cruel as you are to yourself. You act like we're all incompetents—even Eric—and only you can save the day. At least I know the definition of teamwork. Grow up, Naomi. This is real life!"

Her tears overflowed and ran down her cheeks. Without another word, Naomi stood up and walked into her chilly bedroom and firmly shut the door behind her.

Keith sighed. He adjusted the sling keeping his shoulder immobile, and reached for the keys to the generator room, where the portable radio antenna was stored. He wouldn't be able to get it onto the roof, but he could probably mount it on the woodpile and string the cable through the cabin's radio hole. It wouldn't transmit or receive outside the park, but at least it would function inside Yosemite for some distance. With any luck, it would pick up Eric and Lindsey after they'd cleared the pass on their return journey. As Eric struggled to get his good arm into his coat, he thought, *Naomi's gonna be the death of me, yet.*

BINOCULARS TO HIS FACE, Wilson continued to watch the cabin from the outcropping he'd hiked to earlier. He'd seen one female ranger and the dog outside earlier checking on the downed radio tower that held the antenna. That destruction was a piece of luck for him, since without the right tools he couldn't have done it himself, not like the storm did. But his jubilant mood turned decidedly sour when he'd noticed the wounded male ranger outside near the woodpile struggling with what looked like a miniature antenna.

Where was the healthy male? Where was the other female? There could be only one reason for a wounded ranger to tackle such an important chore alone. He was protecting the remaining woman—which meant the other two had left…probably with Pam.

Fury pumped through Wilson's veins. They must've left during the night, because he'd kept vigil on the cabin the rest of the time. On snowshoes, the hike from his present shelter to his lookout point didn't take him too long. Weather permitting, he'd checked regularly on the rangers who held his daughter. Only it appeared they'd outsmarted him. Pam was long gone. By now they'd probably taken her far enough to make recapture difficult, if not impossible.

He'd have to try something else, like holding the female ranger hostage and exchanging her for his daughter. As for the male ranger— Wilson had missed eliminating him the first time. He'd make damn sure he succeeded the second time around, but he didn't have a good shot right now. That damn cabin was too sheltered, too low among the surrounding hilly terrain. He'd have to let the one-armed ranger finish getting the antenna rigged. It would save Wilson some work later on. Might as well leave the man alone—for now. Tomorrow would be a different story.

Lee Vining City Hospital
Same Day, late afternoon

UNDER ERIC'S GAZE, Lindsey sat on the emergency room table, her raw, sprained wrist dressed and wrapped. The aching lump on her head—a glancing blow from a flying ski, she seemed to recall—had been X-rayed at the same time as her wrist and pronounced not serious. No frostbite, no exposure, no serious damage, thanks to good fortune and the helicopter that had carried the three of them to safety. She felt passable physically now that she'd warmed up. Emotionally, though, she'd been better. She glanced at the door to the cubicle, wondering how Pam had fared.

"I'm glad Pam's mother made it here," Lindsey said. "It doesn't seem fair, what those two have gone through. I hope things turn out better for them."

Mrs. Wilson had arrived with tears of joy at the reunion, then tears of pain at her daughter's condition. She'd briefly, but fervently, thanked Eric and Lindsey, then gone to consult with the pediatrician, who planned emergency surgery that night. He hadn't been optimistic about saving all the toes on the child's feet. No further treatment was needed for Pam's frostbitten nose, and her fingers were fine.

"You'll see her again," Eric said.

"I won't." *I won't be here. We have to go back to Yosemite.*

Lindsey's attending physician walked in. "You're all set to go, Ms. Nelson," he said. "Sign these papers and you'll be on your way." He went on with the usual safeguards, warnings, come-back-ifs, and concluded by passing her a prescription for mild painkillers and a recommendation to take a week off from work. He'd also asked one last time if she'd consider spending the night under observation, but Lindsey refused.

"You sure she's okay?" Eric asked, signing the workers' comp statement that attested Lindsey was injured on the job. "Maybe she *should* stay."

Lindsey answered for herself. "I'm fine. Let's go!" she insisted. She collected her gear, thanked the doctor and took her copy of the paperwork. With Eric at her side, she left the hospital.

"Where's the nearest hotel with room service?" she asked, glad a rental vehicle had been left for them in the hospital parking lot by staff from the rangers' main office. Their sled, Eric's ski gear, Lindsey's ski boots and their packs were already stowed in the trunk and back seat.

Eric turned the heat on high when they'd climbed in. "They made a reservation at a motel for us. We're headed there now." Eric placed a hand around her waist and pulled out the seat belt for her, sparing her sore wrist. "No one's going anywhere tonight. There's another storm coming in."

"How's Keith holding up? And Naomi? Have you heard from them?"

Eric's brow furrowed with worry. "I never got through. God knows I've been trying."

"Hell. Did the main office get through with their radio?"

"I asked them while you were down in X ray, but they had no luck, either."

"You don't think Wilson—"

"*No,*" was Eric's immediate response. "The antenna could've been damaged by the weather. It wouldn't be the first time."

"How will we know if they're doing okay?" Lindsey asked worriedly.

"We won't until I get back up there."

"You mean until *we* get back up there."

"You're not going back," Eric announced.

"Yes, I am."

"The doctor said to take time off."

"I can't. I'm fit for work as long as I don't lift anything heavy. A good night's sleep and a full meal, then we both go to Yosemite."

"You'll stay here."

"I'm going back to help you with Naomi and Keith."

Eric stopped at a red light, the truck's tires crunching on the ice. "No, you're not," he said.

"Come on, Ric." Lindsey sighed. "Both of them have health issues. Two sick rangers require two able-bodied ones to relieve them."

"Technically, you're not fit for duty, and Naomi's still able-bodied."

"Maybe, but she's not fit for duty. Ever since she found that lump, her mind hasn't been focused on her job, whether you want to believe it or not."

The subject remained unresolved as they drove up to the motel.

"Sorry about the room arrangements," Eric said, "but since the doctor suggested you stay overnight at the hospital, the main office only paid for one room. I tried to get you another, but they're already filled for the night."

"The main office should've listened to me and not that doctor," Lindsey grumbled. "So should you. I'm not going back to the hospital."

Eric parked in front of their door. They entered their single room, which had two beds and was clean and surprisingly cheerful.

"I suggested to the main office that you stay here at the motel until they arrange for you to fly home," Eric explained, taking the bed nearest the door and window. He threw his pack on it, and placed Lindsey's on the bed closest to the bathroom.

"I suggest," she said, using his same words, "you get on the phone and correct yourself while I take a bath. I'm going back to Yosemite with you." Lindsey sat down on the bed. She pulled out some clean panties, socks and thermals from her pack, then started taking off her hiking boots and socks.

"I'm not calling them." Eric bent to unlace his boots.

"Then I will. I'm going back. I don't trust Naomi's judgment any more than I trust Keith's shoulder to heal overnight. The last place a widow needs to be is in the middle of nowhere with a looming health crisis and an injured man. His judgment's probably just as off kilter."

"I didn't say I was going back alone," Eric argued. "I'll get a replacement."

"*I'm* your replacement. Besides, you've forgotten something. Ginger's there."

"Your life is more important to me than the dog's."

"She's my partner! I can't just abandon her!"

"Why not? I used to be your partner, and that didn't stop you from walking away. You're wearing another man's ring, yet you left him to come back here. Seems to me you change your definition of *partner* as you see fit," Eric said.

Lindsey gasped at his words. She noticed that he watched her carefully as he waited for her to speak. If he thought he could push her into tears or hysterics to prove his point about her return to San Diego, he had another think coming. She took a deep calming breath.

"Ginger is a rescue dog, so that makes her safety my responsibility."

"That's not necessarily true, since there are already rangers on the scene."

"They aren't experienced canine handlers, or the dog wouldn't have been starving herself to death before I showed up."

"She's eating now."

"We hope. I am not trusting Ginger's welfare to a wounded ranger—or a paramedic who doesn't have the good sense to take care of her own health!" Her statement was accompanied by the loud thud of his boot hitting the floor. "My God, Eric, cancer is no joke!"

"I'm well aware of that. However, I'm not worried about Naomi right now. I'm worried about you."

"You're just as scared about Naomi's situation as she is. And Eva's death and Keith's injury have shaken you up more than you realize—or you'd see that you need my help. I know the terrain, I know dogs, and I know how you all work. That's an edge some other replacement wouldn't have. You wouldn't have got Pam to the hospital without me, and you won't get Keith and Naomi there without me."

Now in her bare feet, she grabbed the clean thermal long johns. "I'll be in the tub." She closed the bathroom door determinedly behind her.

ERIC HEARD THE SOUND of running water, yet couldn't let the argument drop. "It's not as if you're thinking logically yourself," he said through the door. "First, you leave your San Diego boyfriend behind—"

"Fiancé!" he heard her yell back.

"Then you nearly get shot—and then you get caught in an avalanche. Like you're any calmer than I am!"

"I'd be perfectly calm if you'd let me take a bath in peace. In fact…"

He couldn't hear the rest of her response over the running water. "What did you say?"

The water abruptly stopped, and she yanked open the door. "I said…"

He didn't hear the rest of her words. He stared, but not at the sensible winter flannel pullover bra and cotton panties she wore. Her body was covered with bruises, her arms and legs showing large dark areas. The area above her bandaged wrist was already turning blue, and the fingers on that same hand were puffy.

"My God, Lindsey…" He stared at her from head to toe and then looked back up to her face. He had to swallow to clear his tight throat before he could finish. "How hard did you hit the rocks?"

He saw confusion replace anger, then her gaze tracked down to her body.

"It wasn't the rocks. It was snow. And one of my skis."

He didn't think, he acted straight from the heart as he pulled her into his arms and held her as close as he could without hurting her. "You could've been killed," he whispered, his stomach in knots at the bashing her body had taken.

"I doubt it," she said. "My professional life's always charmed. It's my personal life that usually takes the hits."

Eric couldn't speak, he could only hold her, rest his cheek against her head and close his eyes, absorbing her nearness and letting his fear melt away. He felt her arms on his shoulders and for a moment time stood still. Nothing existed but him and her, together. Then he became aware of the goose bumps on her arms, the almost-overflowing tub, and he reluctantly returned to reality.

"You'd better get in the tub before you freeze all over again," he said, moving away from her. "If you need any help, just yell. I can wash your hair if you're too sore. Or I can do your back."

He caught the slight smile on her face, and knew she was remembering the old days when her playful question "Would you wash my back?" was always followed by "Need me to wash your front?"

"I'm just interested in soaking my muscles," she said. "But thanks, anyway."

"Can you get your bra off?"

She hesitated.

"Let me help. Turn around if you want," he said.

"Thanks." She didn't turn, but continued to face him, and painfully lifted her arms. He grasped the bottom of the bra and carefully pulled it up and over her head. One of his hands brushed gently against the side of a breast. As his eyes took in her torso, he breathed a sigh of relief that her hips and not the more sensitive areas had taken most of the bruising. He stared as he held out her bra. "You sure you're all right?"

"It was just a bit of snow, Eric. Not the whole mountain."

It was a hell of a lot more than that. If anything had happened to you... He stood there until Lindsey, clad only in panties, reached for the doorknob to pull the door closed, a barrier between them both except for an inch or so left ajar.

"Don't fall asleep in the tub," he warned her. "And don't lock the door, either."

"I won't," she assured him. "Order us some food and a pot of hot coffee, okay? I'll be out soon."

Eric nodded. "Don't be long."

Slowly the door closed all the way. Eric couldn't make it to his own bed. He barely made it to hers before his knees buckled. He half sat, half fell onto the mattress, buried his face in shaking hands, taking deep breaths and trying desperately not to get sick on the motel carpet. The scene of that avalanche, with its characteristic freight-train noise, replayed itself in his head. She'd been flung forward and out of his sight in seconds, while his chest pounded with fear, frustration and, most of all, a horrific sense of loss that hadn't disappeared until he'd dug her free and seen her eyes open again.

And I asked for her as the replacement. If she ever knew... If anything had happened to her, I'd never forgive myself. Never.

He forced himself to calm down, order food from room service and unpack a clean set of thermals. When Lindsey exited the bathroom, he quickly showered, emerging in time for the food's arrival from room service. He was almost himself again, at least on the outside.

"I feel like I'm at a slumber party," Lindsey said, digging into pizza, onion rings and an antipasto. They each sat cross-legged on her bed, both dressed in their thermals.

"I doubt you had men in underwear at those parties."

"With my mother a policewoman? Hardly," Lindsey said. He watched her take a final bite of salad, then drop her plastic fork into the two-thirds-empty container. "God, I'm tired."

"That makes two of us."

"I don't even have the energy to clean up," she said, glancing at her bed-turned-picnic area with a sigh that turned into a big yawn.

"Leave it," Eric said. "Take my bed." He stood and

extended a hand to her, helping her up. He pulled down the bedspread and blanket, waited until she'd climbed in and covered her up.

"I think I've died and gone to heaven...." she murmured blissfully.

Eric felt a chill run down his spine at her words. "You're too lucky to die anytime soon. Or too damn stubborn. I haven't decided which."

"I guess I was pretty lucky today," she said. "Thanks for digging me out."

"All part of the service, ma'am."

"I mean it. Thanks." She closed her eyes as he tossed away trash, picked up the remainder of the food, sealed the containers and placed what was left in the minifridge.

"You never answered my question," she said suddenly.

"What question?"

"Whether or not you were the one who asked for me as your replacement."

He shrugged. She didn't see the action and opened her eyes.

"Well, did you?"

He threw away the crumpled napkins and turned off the overhead and bathroom lights, leaving just the bedside light on. "No matter which way I answer, you'll get upset."

"Huh?"

"If I said yes, you'll be mad that I nearly got you killed. If I say no, you'll be mad that I wrote you off. Either way...it's a no-win answer that you don't need to hear when you should be resting. The doctor said take it easy."

"He probably says that to everyone. Come on, tell me. So...?" Lindsey prompted.

"So, I'm not saying." He deliberately didn't meet her gaze as he crossed the room to bolt and chain the motel door, and adjust the thermostat. His body felt heavy from overuse and not enough sleep. He could only imagine how much worse hers felt. "You bring that liniment with you?"

"Somewhere in my pack. Are you sore?"

"I thought you might need some. I'm fine." *You're alive and well, here with me, instead of in some hospital.* "I'm just tired. Nothing a good night's sleep won't take care of," he said lightly.

"I'll pass."

He didn't argue, but reached for the night-light, and was startled to see Lindsey sit straight up in the bed and grab for his arm.

"Lindsey?"

"Please don't turn it off. Not just yet...."

He instantly thought of the total darkness, the tomblike weight of snow against her chest. He didn't blame her for being nervous in the dark. It scared him to death whenever he thought of her beneath that white shroud.

"Hey, we can leave it on all night if you want. No problem." He dropped his hand from the light switch. Then, without asking or waiting for an invitation, he crawled into bed with Lindsey. She didn't argue. Instead, she cuddled against him as if four years hadn't passed since the last time they'd shared a bed. He drew her closer, careful of her bruises, and pulled the covers over them both.

"God, I'm such a big baby," she said.

"No, you're not. Go to sleep, Lindsey."

"I can't."

"Why not?"

"Because when you hold me, I'm not thinking about sleep."

Eric knew the day's events must really have taken their toll. Lindsey would never have admitted such a thing otherwise.

"I don't think flannels are romantic," he said, deliberately ignoring the quickening of his pulse and memories of her wearing bits of lace or, better yet, nothing at all.

"Neither do I. But at least I don't stink of liniment."

Eric fought against his body's responses. He thought he was doing a pretty good job until, still in his arms, she turned and faced him, and her soft curves pressed against his. Even thermals couldn't disguise how well the two of them fit together. Nor could another man's ring disguise what he had always hoped—that Lindsey still had feelings for him. Still cared for him. In a sudden moment of insight, he realized she'd let him take off her bra because she wanted to know how he felt about her.

"I didn't want to take advantage of you in the bathroom," he said quietly. "It wouldn't be right."

She lifted her face toward his, the lamplight full upon them both. "I don't know if I should be happy or furious. I do know I'm disappointed."

Eric couldn't resist any longer. His lips moved toward hers, uniting them in relief and comfort, then pressed harder with the heady combination of love and lust. Their arms wrapped around each other, their legs intertwined, and it was as if the past four years hadn't happened at all....

Until Wade's ring caught on a thermal-weave pocket on his sleeve. The stark coldness of the large diamond sobered him as nothing else could. He lifted her right hand away from him, untangling the ring. By the time that was done, he'd gained control of himself once more.

"And you said thermals weren't sexy," he said, settling himself apart from her.

"What the hell do I know?"

"We need rest, Lindsey. Either close your eyes, or I'll take you back to the hospital right now."

"All right," she sighed, but he noticed she scooted a little nearer without actually touching him. "You don't mind the light on?" she asked as she relaxed against the pillow.

"I'm not paying the electric bill. Besides, I'll be asleep in five seconds, if it takes that long."

She nodded, her cleanly washed hair rustling against the pillow. "Night, Ric."

"Good night, Lindsey," Eric replied. He ached to wrap his arms around her again. He didn't. His conscience said he should go and sleep in the other bed. That Lindsey was engaged to someone else. He told his conscience to take a flying leap. Willpower could only go so far. And if she had a problem, she could get up herself and change beds.

Lindsey didn't go anywhere. "Thanks for digging me out today," she added sleepily.

"You already thanked me. Thanks for breaking the trail for me and Pam."

"No problem." A pause. "I'm still going back with you," she murmured. "As soon as I catch up on my sleep."

"I know."

She said something else, something that sounded like "I've missed you, Ric."

Only he wasn't positive and he couldn't ask her, for she'd fallen fast asleep beside him, bruises and all. Only then did he dare hold her close against his heart. Despite his exhaustion, Eric stayed awake for a long, long time.

If she goes back to Yosemite, the shape she's in, I could lose her. But if I don't let her, I could still lose her. I'll never understand women...especially this one. How can I let her go?

Even worse, how can I let her stay?

CHAPTER FIFTEEN

Yosemite
Day 7

NAOMI STARED OUT the cabin window. The snow had started again sometime during the night, along with a wind that signaled the front's intention to settle above the valley and take its time before moving on. She'd already brought in a huge stack of wood.

The woodstove was stoked and hot, with a pot of soup simmering on top. The room was comfortably warm. Ginger snoozed on the floor near the stove, her tail tucked neatly around her body. Yet Naomi took little pleasure in the hominess around her. Keith still slept on his bed after having spent a restless night. She was definitely worried.

If he hadn't been out mounting the portable antenna yesterday, his shoulder wouldn't have hurt so much.

But he'd mounted it while she'd been alone in her chilly bedroom having her ''temper tantrum,'' as Keith had termed it when she discovered his action and took him to task. He'd also refused any pain medication.

''If Wilson comes storming in here, I need to have my wits about me. For all I know, you could be hiding in your room again. A helluva lot of good that would do us.''

Naomi looked away from the window and took in Keith's sleeping form. *He's not a very diplomatic person,* she thought. *Even if he is right....*

She closed her eyes, hating the sight of all that snow, hating this feeling of being trapped. Her hand dropped to her breast, then inside her wool shirt, fingers feeling for the small mass to reassure herself that it was the same size as yesterday. She'd had terrible nightmares the night before about its growing and spreading and taking over her body.

"Does it hurt?"

Her eyes popped open, and she self-consciously pulled her hand away from inside her still-buttoned shirt. Keith was awake, although his head remained on the pillow. The fact that he wasn't sitting up disturbed her. Yesterday's exertion had obviously been too much for him, she thought guiltily.

"Does it?" he asked, his gaze still on her.

"No—I just worry that it's getting bigger."

He continued to recline, his face pale on the pillow. "Is it?"

"Not as far as I can tell."

"That's good." He continued to watch her. "Is it large?"

"What?"

"BB-size, pea-size...what?"

Big enough to scare me to death, she wanted to say, but she fought down the urge. He had his own problems, yet he was worried about her. She was supposed to be his caretaker, ease *his* pain. She worked out her answer carefully, hoping to allay his fears. "A little smaller than a pea..." *Large masses are usually cysts. It's the small ones that can kill.* "But it's near my cleavage, away from my armpit and lymph nodes, and those don't hurt, so I'm confident the mass is contained.'' *What a lie. I don't feel convinced at all. Any mass could be dangerous, no matter the location.* ''If I'm lucky, a lumpectomy and some treatment will put me right.'' *Heavy-duty treatment, like chemo and radiation therapy—and possibly a mastectomy. Which still might not get it all. Oh, dear God.*

His good arm was now resting beneath his head, the other arm and shoulder propped up on a second pillow to keep them immobile. He hadn't worn the sling or been up and about at all, except to get dressed and check the rifle. He seemed quiet—too quiet for her liking. Naomi went to his side and sat down on the bed, her hand automatically reaching for his forehead. It definitely felt warm.

''You don't look good,'' she said, unbuttoning his shirt to see if there was any seepage through the dressing she'd replaced.

''I don't feel good.'' He sighed. ''I ache all over, not just my shoulder.''

His admission unnerved her. Keith never complained. Naomi gently lifted the tape from a corner of the bandage, then another, to take a look. The wound glowed an angry red in the area around the bullet hole, while the seepage wasn't clear or pink fluid anymore, but a disturbing yellow.

''I think you're gonna need some different antibiotics. Maybe put you back on the IV for a while, too.'' Like Pam, he might need a surgeon.

''Whatever…'' he said listlessly. ''I haven't tried the radio lately. You should see if you can get through to anyone.''

''After I've taken care of you.''

''Try the radio first. I know you're worried about your brother.''

"After I've taken care of you," she repeated, trying not to show how upset his wound's appearance had made her. *Can things get any worse?*

WILSON TRAMPED BACK to the museum cabin, his snow-shoes bogging with every snowy step. He cursed the weather that had upset his plans. Unlike the rangers, he didn't have a winter's supply of food and wood. He'd only planned for a short stay in Yosemite before crossing the border into Canada, and from there, even farther north to hide. Alaska, maybe. This falling snow would have rabbits or other edible mammals heading for shelter, and he certainly couldn't stay outside himself for long. The weather could easily change for the worse and leave him stranded, unable to find his bearings. He'd have to head back to the cabin—where he'd burn some more chairs, more wood, and eat the dried jerky, trail mix and other lean pickings he'd brought with him.

Time for new accommodations. First chance he got, he'd kill the male ranger and take over the rangers' main cabin. There was plenty of food and fuel—and the hostage woman to do the chores until he could trade her for his daughter. If not, he'd just kill her. It didn't matter one way or the other to him. What women wanted never did. After all, it was a man's world, and he was—above all things—a man.

Motel
Same morning

LINDSEY AWOKE FIRST, the light from the bedside lamp assaulting one eye, the light through the curtains hitting the other. She blinked, squinted, turned out the bedside lamp, then turned away from the window. Confusion died as she registered where she was.

In Eric's arms.... She smiled and remained motionless, forgoing her usual morning stretch so as not to disturb him. It was no wonder he was still asleep. She'd had the easy job of lying on a sled with Pam, while Eric had spent another couple of hours skiing down safely. Unlike Pam, Lindsey was no lightweight. Worse, the avalanche had totally blocked off the prearranged coordinates at the bottom of the bowl. Too much snow remained for any kind of chopper landing. That meant Eric had to negotiate down and through the snow, then even farther below to the more stable landing area, which the avalanche hadn't reached.

He'd also had to help load them, load the gear, unload them at the hospital, contact headquarters, reload the gear into the ranger vehicle and deal with police, Pam's mother and the doctors.

No wonder the man's out cold. Poor guy, he must be exhausted. She stayed quiet for a long time as memories, past and present, good and bad, washed over her. *Why can't it always be this easy?* she wondered. But she knew the truth. *It was always easy in bed. It's the rest of the time that nailed us. We fought about work, each other, our professional lives.*

She sighed. As tempting as it would be just to linger in bliss, she couldn't, not if she expected to hike back into Yosemite. She pressed a soft kiss on Eric's forehead before reluctantly slipping out from the covers. She started the minipot of coffee, called the motel's main desk to see when they stopped serving the free continental breakfast, then grabbed a fresh flannel shirt and wool pants, and headed for the bathtub. She craved another bath for the therapeutic effect.

I feel like I've been hit by a freight train. She turned on the faucet and rubbed her sore neck with one hand before bundling up her hair in the motel shower cap. If this was a luxury hotel, she mused, there'd be a whirlpool in a big tub. Eric loved the Jacuzzi. They both did.... She remembered the passionate times they'd spent in Yosemite's plusher guest resorts, such as the Ahwahnee Hotel. One of the parks earliest hotels, it was a favorite of many, including photographer Ansel Adams, whose internationally known gallery still remained in the park. Presidents, European royalty and Hollywood celebrities all stayed there for its panoramic beauty. But to Lindsey and Eric, it had much more than a great view. They would rent a luxury room on their days off, and the loving would begin, with Eric's lips and hands on her—and hers on his.

I could sure go for one of his massages right now. I'll have to settle for a couple of Tylenols and moving around to work out the stiffness. But the bath should help.

She took her time, grimacing as she worked the washcloth over some of her sore areas. At least she felt better mentally and emotionally than yesterday. The panic and hysteria of being buried alive—literally—had almost suppressed her professional abilities.

I wasn't seriously injured...just chilled and shaken up. Even without my skis, I should've changed into my boots and hiked down the mountainside...helped Eric with Pam. Hell, Keith had a hole in his shoulder, but he sometimes got off the sled to walk over rough terrain. What did I do? Let myself be bundled onto a sled, then cried for a night-light like a little kid.

She flushed with embarrassment as she stood up and reached for a towel to dry herself. *I'm definitely better at rescuing than being rescued. I'd better get my act to-*

*gether or Eric will never allow me to go back, no matter
how much I argue.*

Lindsey was determined to return. Keith and Ginger
needed her. Naomi needed a hospital and Eric needed his
twin well. Even if Keith and Ginger weren't at the cabin,
Lindsey would never desert Eric's sister. He loved her
too much to do without her.

That thought stabbed painfully, but it didn't change her
mind. If the only way she could show her love for Eric
was by going back to help his sister, so be it. She didn't
care if there were a thousand other rangers willing to take
her place. She wasn't giving up her spot to anyone. Lindsey knew the definition of loyalty. As a ranger, and as a
policewoman's daughter, she also knew that once she'd
taken the assignment, she was duty-bound to follow it
through to the end. Now wasn't the time to fall apart—
yesterday's embarrassing lapse with the night-light not-
withstanding.

She finished dressing and carefully ran the brush
through her hair so as not to touch the bump on her scalp.
Her hair caught in her engagement ring. *This damn thing.*
She yanked at it, and to her frustration, the ring still refused to budge. *Once I'm home, I'm definitely going to
give this back. I wish I could mail it, but Wade deserves
more than a "Dear John" letter. Or does he? I've tried
to tell him no in person, but he won't listen. And who
knows when I'll get out of Yosemite...or if I'll even want
to leave?*

Lindsey pulled at the ring one more time, then her
wrist started to ache again. She gave up and braided her
hair in one loose braid. When she left the bathroom, she
found Eric awake and sitting up in bed.

"You okay?" were his first words.

Her smile was genuine. "Much better than yesterday. I almost feel like my old self."

He ran his hand through his hair and stopped and rubbed his neck. "Did you eat?"

"No, but they have a continental breakfast in the lobby."

"I'll pass. I need more than stale doughnuts and watered-down orange juice."

"We can go out to eat," she offered. She firmly shoved aside her dismay at the idea of leaving the warm room, hiking through the icy parking lot and navigating through a snowy town. She needed Eric to know she was fine again. "I've got coffee made. Shall I pour you a cup?"

"Bless you," Eric breathed. He waited as she fixed two cups, his with two sugars, no cream, the way he liked it.

"How'd you sleep?" she asked.

"Like the proverbial log." He smiled, and he looked years younger, happier, like the Eric she'd fallen in love with. "You?"

"Great."

"Sore?" he asked.

"Some, but not as bad as yesterday," she said honestly. "I took another hot soak and some painkillers. All things considered, I have no complaints." She passed him his coffee, and noticed how his glance zeroed in on her ring.

"Lucky you didn't lose the stone," he said.

"I guess…"

"Maybe you should take it off—for safety reasons," he suggested.

"I can't," she replied.

Some of the light drained from his face. He set the coffee down.

"I can't *get* it off. My finger's swollen. Not enough so that a doctor has to cut the ring off, but enough to keep it stuck." Lindsey sat down on the other bed to face him as he lay on his. *No, ours. Our bed—even if it was just for one night.* Lindsey stared at her coffee with a bittersweet smile. "All that snow on top on me yesterday, and you know what I remember thinking? How much money Wade paid for it—and hoping he could get it back if I died."

"Is that all you thought about, Lindsey? The damned ring?"

Lindsey almost spilled her coffee. "Of course not! I worried about you and Pam—prayed you hadn't been buried. Hoped you'd find me."

"Well. At least that bump on your head didn't knock you *totally* senseless."

Lindsey blinked, aware of the change in his mood, yet unable to determine what had triggered it. *Here we go again. I never know where the two of us stand.* She waited a few more seconds for him to speak and, when he didn't, reached for her coat and gear.

"I'll go check us out while you dress and warm up the truck," she suggested. "Then let's get that breakfast."

ERIC NOTICED LINDSEY'S fresh coffee left behind, aware he'd upset her. *Again.* But he'd woken up to find her missing, then before he'd recovered from that shock, he'd brought up the damned ring. The woman was near death, and all she'd worried about was that bastard's diamond? Not if she'd live? Not whether she and Eric would ever be together again?

A sudden thought popped up. Lindsey had always been somewhat jealous of his relationship with Naomi—though certainly not as jealous as Naomi had been of his relationship with Lindsey—and he'd once asked her why.

"Because you talk to your sister—really talk. There's no male-to-female nonsense, no boss-ranger-to-subordinate stuff between you. You can talk about anything and everything honestly, completely. I know that's what's special about siblings, especially twins. But you and I don't talk that way. I wish we could."

Eric remembered her long sigh, and her "I'm lost" look, a look she often wore when the two of them were together on a personal basis. He knew that look, and could identify with it.

He also wished he could talk to Lindsey the way he did to Naomi, but he hadn't shared his life—literally his whole life from conception through college—with her as he had with Naomi. He and Naomi could communicate without thought. Each knew how the other reasoned, acted and reacted in almost all situations. How could he ever have that with anyone except Naomi? She was his twin. No one could replace her. By the same token, Lindsey was his dearest love. No one could replace her in his heart, either.

He and Lindsey had never had it smooth. He wondered if he'd taken too much for granted with her—and with other women, too. He was so used to Naomi's knowing his every thought, he'd taken it for granted, and he'd done the same for her. Once he'd even tried to talk to Naomi about it, asking if she and Bruce had ever been in sync. The conversation hadn't gone well. Naomi had said the only place they'd ever been in sync was in bed. Not only that, Naomi's husband had been jealous of Eric until the day he died. After that, Naomi and Eric had drifted back into their childhood pattern of being together as much as possible. Naomi—admittedly with Eric's blessing—had taken up much of his time, and left Lindsey out in the cold.

Lindsey never complained once, he remembered. She'd envied Naomi's ability to communicate so easily with him, but nothing more. She'd said she would never make him choose between his family and her.

Thoughtfully, he took a sip of the too-hot coffee and set down his cup to reach for his clothes. He hadn't understood how wrong he'd been until he'd nearly lost the one woman he truly loved. His soul mate. When the snow cracked, heralding the avalanche, his scream had torn from his throat like a madman's. If he hadn't had Pam with him, he would have dived into that maelstrom after her. As it was, those fifteen minutes he'd spent searching for Lindsey had changed him, aged him and scared him to death.

Time to find out what Lindsey wants—what she wants from life, from me. I've wasted four years without her. And what do I do? Get upset because she thought about her fiancé and not me.

He should be turning handstands with joy that she'd survived, instead of driving her out of the room. She'd fallen in love with him once. Time to see if he could make her love him again…. Time—they didn't have a lot of that, and he'd let her leave him to go and check out of the motel. What an idiot he was. Maybe they'd have a few hours to themselves, without all the official business, before they had to head back to Yosemite. *Three rangers needed him.* But for as long as the snow continued to fall, he and Lindsey were free.

Cinderella liberty—that was what the sailors called it. A few free days in port. He was tired of being lonely.

Sometimes Yosemite seemed like his own personal prison. He missed Lindsey too much. Loved her too much. There was no one else for him. There would never be anyone else for him. He couldn't lie to himself anymore, not after yesterday.

I've got to do more than just keep her alive. Time to find my way back into her heart before the bastard slips a wedding ring on her finger.

THERE WAS A LONG LINE of people waiting to eat at the restaurant Eric had suggested—a combination motel-truck stop just outside town—but the food was great, and the line moved quickly. It was near the crossroads of Interstate 395 and State Highway 120, with a lot of truck traffic heading to Southern California or Reno or Las Vegas. The waitresses took orders and delivered hot food just as speedily as the cooks prepared it. It wasn't long before Lindsey and Eric sat in front of a large trucker's breakfast of eggs, toast, sausage, pancakes and hash brown potatoes, with the best coffee Lindsey had tasted in years—and their waitress provided refills without being asked.

Lindsey dug into her breakfast with the hearty appetite prompted by a body needing extra calories to stay warm. Other travelers crowded around them in the warmth of the restaurant; they included truckers, winter sportsmen on their way to Lake Tahoe, gamblers on their way to Nevada, and a few local families with children headed to school and work.

"Lord, but it's good to be back in civilization," she sighed, popping another bite of pancake into her mouth, her glance taking in the traffic outside. "Another cup of coffee and a newspaper, and I'll be in seventh heaven."

Eric nodded. He seemed somewhat quiet to her.

"You okay?"

"Just thinking about Pam's surgery," he said, peeling back the top of an individual tub of grape jelly.

"I didn't forget, either, but visiting hours aren't until ten," Lindsey said as she checked her watch. "That gives us a few more hours. I wanted to pick her up a card and a stuffed animal, but hospital gift shop choices are usually so limited. Though I doubt any toy stores will be open. Maybe a twenty-four-hour drugstore... It's been so long since I've been in this neck of the woods."

Eric spread the jelly on his toast. Lindsey searched through her little stash and passed him her grape.

"Still eating strawberry, I see," Eric said.

"Yep. Southern California grows the world's best strawberries. Too bad this place doesn't have strawberry syrup, but the boysenberry's pretty good. We grow those, too, you know."

"I know. You're awfully chatty this morning," Eric observed. "You usually don't come alive until noon."

"Nothing like a near-death experience to make one appreciate every minute." Lindsey raised her coffee cup in the air. "To the simple things in life." She took a large slug. She'd barely set it back down on the table before their waitress refilled it.

"Thank you," she said, then addressed Eric. "See? Life is good."

"So, after you're finished, then what?"

"Find a drug store. I want to call home, too, before we head back to the hospital."

"I meant, after you finish your stint as replacement ranger."

"Oh." Lindsey popped some more pancake bites into her mouth and swallowed before answering. "Well, I'll have Ginger, so I'll quit working the beaches, for starters.

I'll have to go back to search-and-rescue school so Ginger and I can be recertified. Make sure we both know the drill and understand each other. Then see what openings come up, I guess. No more snow country, though," she added. "It's too hard on dogs."

"And on you?"

"Yes," she said honestly, "and not just because of yesterday. Both of my sisters put their lives on the line every time they go to work. My mother lived the same way. I don't want that kind of pressure. That's why I never went into police work or Customs like they did. Search-and-rescue isn't the kind of job where I fight to stay alive—I fight to keep others alive. But this place..." Lindsey almost shivered. "Snow country like Yosemite is too demanding. One mistake and you're dead."

"You did it for a full year," Eric reminded her.

"I had my reasons," she said lightly. "But I didn't get the watch, the guy and the gold ring, the way I'd hoped. I ended up burying a partner—same as you did with Eva. That's not the kind of environment for a woman who wants a husband and kids."

"You want kids?"

Lindsey mopped up the last of her egg yolk with a half piece of toast. "Don't sound so surprised."

"You never talked about it," he said.

"Well, you never seemed interested. But having kids has always been a given for me." She paused. "I've raised dogs all my life. Loved them, taught them, disciplined them and cleaned up after them. I figure raising kids will be pretty much the same. Actually, even easier, because children can talk and let you know how they feel."

"Dogs and children aren't exactly the same."

Lindsey shrugged. "True. Dogs do better in remote

locations than children. Truly remote areas don't have schools and churches and playgrounds and parks and other things kids need. I want my children to know my family—their aunts and grandparents. And cousins some-day, too, I hope." She finished her toast. "And I don't want my kids worrying that their mother might be killed on the job, like I worried about my mother. And still worry about my sisters."

She broke off as she noticed that one of the four pay phones continuously busy with callers had become empty. "Excuse me, but I really do want to call home." She tossed her paper napkin on her chair and hurried, glad for the opportunity in another way, as well. She had no intention of debating Eric on any serious subject over the breakfast table, especially the subject of rangers hav-ing children. Since they weren't engaged, anyway, it was a moot point.

Lindsey lucked out. Not only did she get to the empty phone before anyone else did, she was able to reach her older sister, Kate, in her office. Lara, the youngest, worked the police department's swing shift, and still lived at home to help out with the kennels. Lindsey knew calling home meant talking to her parents. It was always easier to talk to her sisters, especially Kate.

"It's so good to hear your voice!" Lindsey sighed. She asked about her parents and Lara, then filled Kate in on everything except the avalanche.

"My God!" Kate's soft voice came through loud and clear on the telephone. "You've really had yourself a workout. That poor little girl! And you still have to go back for Naomi and Keith and that dead ranger's dog. Ginger, right?"

"Yeah. Beautiful golden retriever—big brain, bigger heart. I'm worried about all of them."

"You haven't said much about Eric. Is he still acting like a heartless bastard?" Kate asked with a sister's frankness.

"That heartless bastard saved my life!" Lindsey blurted out in his defense.

"What?"

Lindsey rubbed her forehead in dismay. There was no avoiding the truth now, and she quickly glossed over her ordeal with the avalanche, concluding with, "You can tell Lara if you want, but you have to promise you won't tell Mom and Dad."

"All right—but you know they'll want details on Eric, especially Dad. He and Eric always hit it off."

"Tell them Eric's too upset over Eva's death and Naomi's health to be losing sleep over lost love. Which reminds me—you've done your monthly self-exam, haven't you?"

"Yes, I have, and you sound just like Mom. Damn, there goes my pager! I'm either off to the harbor or the airport. It's contraband time."

"You and your dog stay safe," Lindsey said.

"You, too," Kate responded. "Will we hear from you again soon?"

"I'll try to reach Mom and Dad later. Lara, too. We'll be heading back as soon as it stops snowing."

"Tell Eric thank-you. We're all in his debt."

"Maybe later."

"Tell him now."

"All right. Love you," Lindsey said, carrying on the family tradition. Lindsey's mother had always said "Love you" instead of "Goodbye" when she went off to work. She knew that not all police officers came home, and refused to miss a chance to say those words to her family one last time. With Lara now working for the police, Kate with the Port Authority's contraband squad, and Lindsey employed as a rescue ranger, the family had continued that tradition. Because of their desire to help others, the Nelson women had always lived on the edge.

"Love you, too," Kate said. "Gotta go."

"Bye." Lindsey reluctantly hung up, vacating the spot for the next caller, and returned to the table.

"Everything all right at home?" Eric asked.

"Seems that way. Kate says thanks, and the family's in your debt."

"I always liked your family."

"Yeah, they're pretty lovable. Are you through?" Lindsey asked. Her remaining pancake had grown cold, and Eric's plate and coffee cup were empty.

"I am if you are."

"Then let's find a drugstore and go back to the hospital," she said. "I want to visit Pam before the snow gets any worse."

CHAPTER SIXTEEN

THE SNOWPLOWS WERE BUSY on the roads by the time Eric pulled into the small hospital's parking lot. He'd found a drugstore earlier, and Lindsey had purchased a gift for Pam and some personal items for herself. She'd also bought a "get well soon" card for Pam, the kind that had slots for quarters to be slid into, to go with the darling stuffed teddy bear in pink ballerina shoes and a frilly tutu. Eric had purchased a stuffed dog that looked amazingly like Ginger, complete with silky yellow fur and a ribbon tied in a bow around its neck. Lindsey contemplated buying the child a huge, multicolored lollipop, then decided against it in case Pam wasn't up to solid food after yesterday's surgery. She'd picked up some gift bags and tissue paper, and once they were back in the ranger truck, she wrapped the gifts as Eric drove.

"It's really coming down," he said, shifting the vehicle into four-wheel drive at their next stoplight.

"At least it's not icy. We don't need chains, yet," Lindsey said, inwardly wincing at the thought of having to tackle that task. She still felt stiff and sore. "Think Pam's mother will still be at the hospital?"

"She spent the night with her daughter. Didn't leave the room. They're both under police protection, too. I talked to her while you were choosing the card," Eric explained as he stopped at the light, snow crunching under their tires.

"But police protection down here?"

"Mrs. Wilson figures if *we* could ski out, then her husband could, too. So do I. Can't say I blame her for being worried. She says he has friends who might give him a hand, too."

"He won't get far in this weather."

"Don't underestimate him." Eric met her gaze. "You okay?" he asked, his eyes filled with concern.

"You bet," she said firmly. "I've got all my fingers and toes, and I'm sitting in a warm truck with good company and a full stomach. What more do I need?"

He nodded, then the light turned green. He shifted his eyes back to the road.

"You're a nice guy, Eric Kincaide. My family aren't the only ones who owe you. I do, too. Big time."

"You don't owe me a thing."

"Is this where you say *just doin' my job, ma'am*?"

"I've always wanted you happy and safe. Especially safe. You don't have to go back to Yosemite, Lindsey. No one would blame you."

"It's my job. No one else's."

"I know you're hurt. I can tell by the way you move."

"Yeah, I'm stiff, but it's nothing serious. Certainly not enough to incapacitate me."

"Enough to slow you down."

"My 'slow' beats anyone else's 'fast' when it comes to dogs. What if Naomi or Keith gets covered in snow? You wanna dig them out, or do you want me there to work the dog? And before you answer, think back to how long it took you to find me via beeper, and what kind of shape I was in when you did. I'll be honest, Eric. I was out of air. You barely found me in time, despite being right on the scene. I can't let that happen to anyone else—and I won't, until they find a replacement for me."

"Dammit, Lindsey, do you have to make my life so hard?"

"Hey, just returning the favor," she said with a grin, some of her old spirit returning. She resettled the two large gift bags on her lap. "Come on, let's go see Pam."

THE POLICE OFFICER outside Pam's door had been told they were coming, and, after checking their IDs, waved Eric and Lindsey inside. Mrs. Wilson rose instantly to her feet as they knocked and entered. She hugged first Lindsey, then Eric, despite Eric's arms being full. She also insisted they call her by her first name, Joyce. Pam was awake and, typical of any child who sights a gift, asked from her bed, "Are those for me?"

"Yep," Eric said. "If it's okay with your mother, you can open them."

Joyce Wilson nodded.

"Give her the card first," Lindsey suggested.

Pam quickly tore it open, squealing happily over the twelve quarters arranged in a circle around a Ferris wheel, each quarter slot cleverly designed to be a seat on the amusement ride.

"I'm rich!" she said in an awestruck voice, opening the card to see a cheerful clown holding balloons that spelled out "Get well soon!"

"Hey, we're just getting started," Eric said, then asked Lindsey, "Which one next?"

"Save yours for last."

Pam instantly pulled away the tissue paper to expose the ballerina bear. She smiled and hugged it tight, then started investigating the dress and shoes. "Do the shoes come off?" she asked.

"Oh, yes. The dress, too," Lindsey replied.

Pam took off one elasticized ballerina shoe, then the

other, and checked out the bear's toes. "She only has three toes on each foot. Just like me. They cut off my littlest ones yesterday."

Lindsey felt a moment's horror. She hadn't known until now how last night's surgery had gone, and Pam's feet, resting on a pillow, were heavily bandaged. At a loss for words, she felt tears sting her eyes, but to her relief, Eric filled in the awkward gap.

"I'm sorry to hear that," Eric said in a matter-of-fact voice. "But you'll learn to compensate and your balance will be back to normal in no time."

"Are you sure?" Pam asked, suspicion replacing joy.

"Positive."

Pam's smile returned, and she held out her arms for the other gift. "Give it!"

"Honey, manners!" Joyce Wilson reminded with a mother's embarrassment.

"*Please* give it," Pam amended.

"It's okay, Joyce. Let's not stand on ceremony," Eric murmured as Pam tore into the second gift bag with as much gusto as she'd shown with the first. This time she didn't squeal with delight, but stared with awe at the stuffed toy.

"Is this Ginger?" Pam asked.

Lindsey had her voice back, and she'd managed to blink away the tears. "It looks like her, doesn't it? Eric picked it out."

"Thank you, Ranger Eric," Pam said politely, remembering her manners this time. "Where's Ginger now?" Pam toyed with the bow of the ribbon, then stroked the soft plush of the dog's fur.

"She's at the cabin with Naomi and Keith."

"Who's taking care of them?" Pam asked.

"They're all taking care of one another," Eric said.

"Are you going back to get them?"

"Yes, we are—*both* of us, just as soon as the weather clears," Eric said, his gaze traveling from the child to Lindsey. She was cheered to hear the confidence in his voice—confidence in *her*.

Joyce gathered up the discarded tissue paper and gift bags as Pam tried the slippers and skirt of the teddy bear on the stuffed dog, studied the results, then transferred the dress and shoes back to the bear. A knock on the door sounded, and as it was Pam's doctor, the two rangers said their goodbyes to the child and left the room. Joyce went with them.

"When will we see you again?" she asked when they were safely out of Pam's hearing.

"There's too much to factor in—between how long it takes us to get in and out...the weather... I just don't know," Eric replied.

Tears filled Joyce's eyes. "I'm so sorry your ranger got shot."

"We'll do our best for him, just like we did for Pam," Lindsey reassured her.

"Be careful around my husband," Joyce warned. "You've seen how he treats his family. He's even more dangerous around strangers. Don't trust him. Don't *ever* trust him."

"I appreciate your concern," Eric said. "But for now, you just focus on your daughter."

Lindsey nodded her agreement, and after more thanks from Joyce, the couple left the hospital for the parking lot. It was still snowing outside.

Back in the truck, Lindsey sat motionless.

"I can't start the car until your seat belt's on," Eric reminded her. All of the newer vehicles had a safety lock on the ignition until the belts were fastened.

"I know." Lindsey reached for the belt-shoulder-harness combination and began to pull it out, only to be thwarted when the tightly coiled spring yanked it out of her hand. The belt retracted. Lindsey didn't reach for it again.

"I'm such an idiot," she said, her voice perilously close to breaking. "If I'd realized there were only three toes on the bear's feet, I would never have bought Pam that stupid thing."

"How could you know? It's only a toy, Lindsey. And Pam did seem to like it."

"I didn't know what to say when she said they cut off her toes. What kind of man could be so cruel to his own wife and child? To subject them to such pain?"

Eric threw his arm around Lindsey's shoulders and pulled her close. "An evil man. Or a very sick one. Does it matter? We got her out, Lindsey, you and me. You were right. I couldn't have done it without you. And we'll do it again for Keith and Naomi and Ginger."

Lindsey sniffed, working very hard not to break down completely. Even being buried in snow hadn't affected her like this. "I really, *really* hate my job some days."

"Yeah, well, you and every other hardworking American." He gave her a squeeze and kissed her forehead. "Buckle up and I promise to buy you lunch later."

"Sounds good. Maybe I'll order a beer." Lindsey sighed. "We can drink to Pam's recovery."

"Let's settle for wine at dinner. Right now, we've got to get over to the Lee Vining Ranger Station and get you a purchase order for some replacement gear."

"About time you realized you weren't getting rid of me. Though I'm not exactly in a shopping mood."

"Me, neither, but unless you plan on flapping your arms, you need skis and poles and gloves to get back.

We could both use a good, long nap, too. The sooner we get this done, the sooner we can get back to the motel. I want you rested before we hike over the pass again.''

Lindsey watched the snow continue to fall, the cars and pedestrians slipping, the snowplows fighting a losing battle. ''Doesn't look like it's gonna be anytime soon.''

Rangers' winter cabin
Day 7, afternoon

THE LUNCH HOUR CAME and went, yet Naomi hadn't bothered eating. Keith's fever had increased as the infection to his shoulder grew worse. He slept fitfully. The antibiotics weren't helping, and with no long-distance antenna for the radio, she couldn't consult with a doctor. She suspected the bullet track's healing had caused a pus-filled cyst somewhere, and would need drainage and new antibiotics. Drainage usually meant tubes and surgery. If worst came to worst, she could always run a probe through his shoulder in hopes of puncturing the cyst and clearing a path for drainage, but that could involve the risk of heavy bleeding.

No radio, no doctor, no brother, no Lindsey, no clear weather, and to add to her worries, Ginger wasn't eating. Naomi had never felt so alone. In truth, she'd never *been* so alone. She'd always had the comfort of her twin and her parents, then her husband as well. Even after her husband had died, she'd still had Eric. Only now there was no one except a very sick man whose love for her might cost him his life. The fear she felt almost matched her shame.

Eric never falls apart without me. Even when he and Lindsey split up, he carried on. He stood on his own two feet... So did Lindsey.

Naomi seriously wondered if she could do the same. She suddenly realized just how different she and her twin were, and how alike Eric and Lindsey were. They were independent people who made their own decisions, lived by the consequences of those decisions, and didn't need each other as a security blanket, but as a true helpmate. Despite their age being the same, Eric had always been the dominant twin—but only because Naomi had preferred it that way. She had wanted him to make the tough decisions, so much so that she'd even followed him into the ranger service after her husband died instead of remaining at the urban hospital that had employed her.

No wonder Lindsey didn't want to marry Eric. Who'd want me along as baggage?

And with the innate honesty that marked her whole family, she realized something else. *I had problems in my marriage because too many times I turned to Eric instead of Bruce. If he hadn't died, we might have ended up in divorce court. It would've been my fault. Except for Eric, I've never really trusted anyone—not even myself. God, I'm such an idiot.*

And now a man might die if she didn't make the right decisions. A dog, too...

She might die, as well, if she didn't get hold of herself. She started to cry, her face in her hands, then she yanked her hands away and jerked her chin up. This was no time for tears. First, she'd check on Keith again. Second, go outside to get more wood and check on the mobile radio antenna. Third, cook up some lunch and insist that she, Keith and Ginger eat, even if she had to force-feed the dog. The dog was a ranger, and Naomi had sworn to guard the health of them all.

Then she'd get out her medical books and read up on anatomy and the surgical procedure for lancing a deep wound. She couldn't count on anyone right now except herself.

Naomi refused to wipe at the tears on her cheeks, refused to acknowledge that they were even there. She checked on Keith, pulled on her outdoor gear, grabbed the wood basket sling and headed outside into the falling snow.

KEITH OPENED HIS EYES at the sound of the front cabin door closing. He immediately noticed that Naomi's boots and gear were gone. Despite his fever-induced vertigo, he rose, retrieved the rifle and staggered to the window to make sure he could see her and anyone else who might venture into the area. With Ginger not eating again, he didn't trust the dog to alert them to intruders. He saw Naomi stumble through a particularly deep drift of snow. Her slight bulk was obviously no match for the elements, and since the others' departure, shoveling detail had been abandoned, other than keeping the doors clear.

He leaned against the window ledge, rifle at his side. She was a skilled medical caregiver. Keith knew that firsthand. But she was lousy at taking care of herself, which made her a lousy ranger. Unlike Lindsey or Eric or Keith himself, Naomi refused to acknowledge her limitations, or worse, deluded herself about her abilities. That made her a disaster waiting to happen, just like Eva.

Why on earth did she ever became a ranger? Then he swore, since of course he knew the answer to that question. She couldn't bear to be separated from Eric. Only in this case, the family business hadn't been as kind to Naomi as to her twin. Keith knew her parents were professional adventurers. They traveled all over the world, climbed mountains, navigated jungles, rafted down uncharted, rapid-filled waters. Eric must have inherited some of their stamina; he had no problems with physical or mental challenges. He wouldn't have been appointed head ranger if he had.

So what did Naomi do? Lean on her brother whenever possible—only now her brother was missing. Keith didn't bother pretending confidence when Naomi wasn't around. Eric and Lindsey were either safely away with Pam, or dead. In a Yosemite winter, there was very little middle ground. Keith would've given anything to help Naomi more—but he could hardly stand, let alone do his share of strenuous work. He felt the same helplessness he'd felt when Eva had disappeared.

Some places aren't for any man or woman to try and tame. Yosemite's one of them.

He closed his eyes, but only for a few seconds. He continued to watch Naomi until she came back with the load of wood, waiting to open the porch doors for her.

"Thanks," Naomi gasped, barely able to get in the door with her load.

"Here, let me help."

"No, I can manage. Lock the doors if you're up to it and get back into bed."

Keith heard the firmness in her voice, saw the huge load she'd slung over her shoulder, felt his own unsteadiness, and for once didn't argue. *She might be a bit lacking in the common sense department, but at least she's got nerve.* Not that nerve was much of a defense against a high-powered rifle. Nor would it console Naomi if her brother, along with Lindsey and Pam, were dead.

I wish I knew how they're doing. Still, Ric and Lindsey were tough enough to protect Pam and to survive. He only prayed the same could be said of himself...and Naomi.

Motel
Day 7, 9:00 p.m.

LINDSEY'S LONG NAP HAD not materialized. The issuing of new gear had taken longer than anticipated; so had replenishing their trail mix and other dried foods. Coupled with the drive up and back in the snow, it'd had been dark before they'd arrived back at the motel with a hastily purchased take-out order of pasta, salad and garlic bread. Both passed on going to a restaurant for a nicer dinner with wine. The weather forecast predicted heavy snow until midnight. Neither wanted to be on the slippery roads with backed-up traffic, not to mention the slow-moving snowplows, in the dark. By the time they'd made it back to the motel with the food, it was far too late for a nap. So they planned to eat dinner and go immediately to bed.

Eric grimaced. "This sauce is terrible."

Lindsey sat cross-legged on the bed, where she'd joined him, and was still eating her salad. Eric rarely complained about food. "Maybe we should've ordered the pizza, instead."

"Not if they use the same sauce. Here." He held out his fork with a fresh twist of pasta.

Lindsey leaned over and opened her mouth for the bite and quickly confirmed Eric's suspicions. "It tastes like ketchup over noodles."

Eric slid aside his plastic bin of spaghetti. "At least the garlic bread's good."

"We have some leftovers from yesterday in the mini-fridge," Lindsey reminded him. "Plus trail mix. Want me to get you some?"

"No, thanks. I'll fill up on bread and salad. If nothing

else, the portions are generous.'' He sighed. ''I'm getting too old for this.''

Lindsey's heart went out to him. She reached for his hand across the jumble of plastic tins, forks, napkins, bread. ''What do you want, Eric?''

He raised his head. ''For starters, some decent food.''

''I mean, what do you *really* want?'' she asked.

He paused, then answered. ''A home. Family. You. Mostly you.''

''Oh, Eric…after everything that's happened between us—thank you for that,'' Lindsey said in a shaky voice.

''What do *you* want?''

Lindsey hadn't expected his answer, or his question. ''I don't know,'' she said honestly. ''I thought I did…but I'm not sure anymore. It seems I'm always on the fence, damned if I do and damned if I don't. When I worked with canines, you weren't happy. When I worked without them, I wasn't happy. If I stay here, I miss my family. If I go home, I miss you. After four years, I still miss you…especially our friendship.'' She stopped before breaking down into tears. The time for that was long past.

''Thank you for that,'' Eric said, quietly echoing her earlier statement, their hands clasped.

Lindsey smiled. ''You're so lucky, Ric. You know what you want out of life, personally and professionally. I'm still trying to balance the two without driving myself crazy. But every time I think I've got the right combination—chaos.'' Her smile faded, and she lifted her face, her expression serious. ''I don't know if I'll ever get it right, but I keep trying.''

''Do you think maybe…we could give it another try?''

''Oh, Ric, I don't know. It's tempting, but I just don't know.''

Behind them, the TV Eric had earlier turned on continued with the news. When the anchorman announced the weather would be next, "after these commercial breaks," they looked at each other, then at the TV, and their fingers awkwardly slipped apart. Lindsey ate some more of her salad and the now-cold garlic bread as Eric turned up the volume using the remote.

Ten minutes later he turned it off, and kept the conversation on business. "The snow should stop sometime tonight, and the next three days are clear. If we leave day after tomorrow, that gives us an extra day's rest."

"But if we leave tomorrow, that gets us back to Keith and Naomi one day earlier."

"I'll admit I've considered it. But are you up to it?" Eric asked. "And be honest, Lindsey. There's a lot riding on this."

"I'm ready to go. We've got all our gear and supplies. I'm mobile, unlike Keith. As a result of his injury, Naomi can't leave, either. That worries me where Wilson's concerned."

Eric repeated Mrs. Wilson's words. "He's even more dangerous around strangers, Joyce said. That's why I want you to be sure about coming back with me."

"Trust me, Eric, I'm up to the task. I'll have plenty of time to rest when I know everyone's safe."

"Good. Frankly, I'm worried Wilson will make an attack on the cabin once the weather's cleared."

Lindsey's eyes opened wide. "But he doesn't know we're not there! It's four adults against one. Three, if he realized Keith was hurt."

"He can't have food and fuel stockpiled like we do. He'll need those soon, and he'll want his daughter. If he still thinks we're all in the same place, sooner or later he's going to be forced to move. I want to be there. Keith and Naomi aren't capable of dealing with him."

"They should both be in the hospital," Lindsey agreed. "Ginger belongs with me, and Wilson belongs in jail."

Eric nodded. "We'll get a good night's sleep, and if weather permits, leave at first light for the base of the pass. I'll give the main office a call and make arrangements for them to pick up the vehicle there."

By the time they were ready for bed, all the plans had been worked out to their satisfaction...except that this time, Eric didn't offer to hold Lindsey throughout the night, nor did she ask. She slept in her bed alone, the distance between her and Eric seeming as great as the distance between the motel and the rangers' cabin in Yosemite.

Or greater...

CHAPTER SEVENTEEN

Tioga Pass, entrance to Yosemite
Day 8, noon

"WE'VE MADE GOOD TIME," Eric said as he and Lindsey rested at the top of the pass.

Lindsey nodded. "And it's downhill all the way from here. Goodbye, climbing boots and snowshoes. Hello, skis."

"And rifle. And extra caution," Eric added.

"Of course," Lindsey said lightly. So far, they'd had no complaints. The earlier avalanche had made their ascent of the pass less dangerous at least, as far as snow slides went. While the temperature was below freezing, there was no wind or any subsequent chill factor. The sun shone brightly in the winter-blue sky, and the snow reflected back some heat. The physical activity had helped to work out most of the soreness in her muscles, and what remained would certainly be eased on the downhill part of the journey.

Eric bent toward the sled to start exchanging one set of footgear for another, and to retrieve and load the rifle. Lindsey followed his example with the footgear, then poured their cups full of hot cocoa while he used the binoculars to study their descent, mentally working out the safest trail. She'd insisted on having their predawn breakfast at the truck stop with the fantastic coffee, and wished they could've filled both their large thermoses

with more of it to take with them. Unfortunately, coffee
and its diuretic properties could cause dehydration. Hot
chocolate or sports drinks were the norm for longer treks.
Both preferred warm drinks to cold. When Eric finished
with the binoculars, she passed him his cup of cocoa. He
took a sip and frowned.

"It can't be cold, yet," she protested.

"No…" He continued to sip, his expression thoughtful.

"Then what?"

"I'm going to cache the sled and snowshoes," he said,
using the Old West term for safely placing or burying
gear that mule-drawn wagons could no longer afford to
carry, but was too valuable to dump. "Whatever we need
can go in our packs. I want to travel light and fast."

Her pulse sped. "Did you see something? Wilson?"

"No, but that doesn't mean we won't. The skiing conditions are too good for him not to be out and about. I
know I would. We've got more sleds and snowshoes at
the cabin. I want to reach it as soon as possible. You up
to it?" he asked.

"As long as the sun holds out…" She lifted her cup
and grinned. "I could even climb Mount Lyell," she
said, naming Yosemite's highest peak.

"Let's settle for the main cabin first," he said, grin-
ning back at her. He drained his cup, replaced it and the
thermos in his pack, then adjusted the rifle's carrying
strap and gathered his ski poles. "Ready?"

"Whenever you are."

"Let's go."

Rangers' winter cabin
Midafternoon

"I WISH YOU'D GO BACK TO BED," Naomi said, fretting.
"This can't be good for you. We have Ginger to keep
watch."

"Ginger's not eating—she's getting weak. I don't trust her." Wrapped in a blanket, Keith had moved a chair next to the window, his rifle resting in his lap. "If I'm gonna die, I'm taking Wilson with me. Sooner or later he'll come here. He's got nowhere else to go."

"You're not going to die. You'll be fine before you know it," Naomi said firmly, although Keith's fever-flushed cheeks, shaking hands and hunched figure said otherwise.

"Don't treat me like an idiot. I'm not."

"I am," she replied quietly. "I'm sorry you're stuck with me as your only backup. I don't belong out here, Keith. I never did. I've just been trailing after my twin."

Keith didn't argue, a fact that hurt, but not nearly as much as avoiding the truth. She continued while she still had the courage.

"Except for my medical skills, I don't expect any vote of confidence. But I want you to know I'll do my best for you—for us both."

"Well. At least some good's come out of this mess."

Naomi straightened and lifted her chin. "If that's what you want to call it. I'd like you to do something for me."

"What?"

"Teach me how to use that rifle."

Museum cabin

WILSON TOOK STOCK OF HIS meager supplies. The food and fuel would only last another two days, and Yosemite didn't provide much of either in the winter. Fortunately, the snow had stopped, and he suspected tomorrow's weather would be clear as well. Once the sun began to set and visibility became limited, he intended to make an assault on the cabin. They wouldn't expect him that soon, and he might as well shoot it out now, instead of starving or freezing to death later. He'd also find out if Pam had really gone with the other two. If not, he'd retrieve her, then somehow he'd get her across the border to Canada. Maybe he should consider Mexico. He hadn't decided, yet.

He checked his watch, then studied the sun's position in the sky. He'd leave in half an hour, before the sun started to set. That would give him enough twilight for his raid on the cabin, and he'd be ready for a good dinner afterward.

Courtesy of the rangers' pantry.

"I WISH THESE RADIOS WORKED." Their radios hadn't connected with the cabin, yet. "How much longer until we reach the cabin?" Lindsey asked. "Another half hour?"

"If that," Eric replied. They'd stopped for another break—which Lindsey hoped would be their last before making the cabin.

"We should get there about sunset if we keep up our pace," he said. "I don't want to be out here after dark if at all possible. Not with the way the temperature's dropping."

"Let's go, then."

Twenty minutes later the cabin's general area with its copse of trees was in sight.

"My God, Ric, look! The whole antenna tower's missing!"

Eric, who'd been concentrating on carefully picking

out their trail in the failing light, turned his head at her exclamation. His sharp eyes caught the movement that Lindsey had missed. In seconds he'd tilted sideways in a fall that brought down both of them. Before Lindsey could question his behavior, he had his rifle out and fired off two shots. Those shots were echoed by two more coming from the cabin's direction—at least that was Lindsey's impression. Her eyes were full of snow from Eric's tackle. One remaining shot echoed in the High Sierra, then all was quiet. They remained silent and low to the ground, the coldness of the snow seeping through clothes and bodies, the cabin so close, yet so far.

Minutes ticked by, and more, then the last of the winter's short twilight blended into full darkness.

"Kick off your skis and poles," Eric ordered. "We'll hike in and keep low the rest of the way."

"Try to reach the cabin again by radio," Lindsey said urgently. "Or else we may have Keith shooting at us as well."

For the first time since they'd left, they connected with Naomi. Eric's conversation with her was brief and terse.

A tense, but thankfully short trek later, they reached the cabin door. Naomi greeted them with tears of relief, rifle in hand. "Thank God! Are you two all right?"

"We saw Wilson," Eric said grimly, guiding Lindsey into the secure porch area before him.

"I did, too. She may be off her feed again, but Ginger alerted us. Who shot first?" Naomi asked.

"I did," Eric said. Naomi ushered both of them into the inner cabin as Eric continued. "I know I didn't hit him—but I figured I might scare him away."

"When I heard the shots, I thought he was after us— I didn't know you two were out there until you radioed.

The big antenna's down. Thank God you're back.'' Naomi gave Eric, and then Lindsey, a big hug.

"How's Keith?'' Eric asked.

"Not good. We've got to get him to a hospital...*now*.''

FURIOUS, WILSON RETREATED only as far as he decided was necessary for safety. The rifle fire aimed his way proved that the two rangers had returned, which meant they'd definitely evacuated Pam earlier and their numbers were now back up to three healthy adults, two of whom could shoot. He guessed they'd trek out again with the wounded ranger. Time for him to change his plans. He'd let the rangers leave the cabin with their patient. If he was lucky, they'd take him straight to the same area they took his daughter—Lee Vining. There was no other town in the vicinity. Pam had to be there, whether the police had her or her mother did. With this weather, she couldn't have left the area, and if she did, she couldn't have gotten far.

Either way, the nearest group of buildings that passed for civilization was where the rangers would go, and where he needed to be. He'd find his daughter from there. And if he couldn't, then he'd head for the hospital in Lee Vining and finish the job with the ranger he'd wounded.

Day 8, 10:15 p.m.

LINDSEY AND ERIC SAT AT THE table with cups of hot tea. Ginger lay awake under the table on top of Lindsey's feet, in constant physical contact. Keith and Naomi both slept on the beds in the common room.

"I never thought I'd see your sister sleeping with a rifle.'' Lindsey reached down to stroke Ginger's upright head.

"I never thought she'd have the need."

They both stared at Keith, whose overall color and demeanor had rapidly deteriorated in their two-day absence.

"It'll be a rough trip out of here for him," Lindsey worried.

"It'll be rough on everyone—one of us will have to carry the rifle, and the others will have to haul two sleds uphill to the pass."

Lindsey's gaze turned toward the sleds they'd already packed and loaded for the morning's journey to town. One sled would carry Keith, but another would be needed for medical supplies, skis, packs, food and dog-transport in the very deep snow. There was no way Ginger could travel off trail, and with the recent snow and the immobility of Keith and Naomi, there were no old trails left or new ones broken.

"If you can handle the dog and the rifle, I'll take Keith," Eric suggested. "Naomi can haul the supply sled and spell us. She doesn't have the rifle skills we do."

"She's done okay so far even if she hasn't got off a shot," Lindsey said. "I do wish we had a working antenna. I swear I could yell farther than that old portable can transmit."

"It wouldn't make a difference." Eric took another gulp of his tea. "We could call for help all we want. No one would be able to get out here."

"I suppose…"

"You should get some sleep. You look exhausted."

"In a bit." Lindsey added more milk to cool her tea and stirred. "Are you coming back here? To finish out the winter?"

"If I have to. I'm not happy about it."

"What about your sister? She'll need a biopsy—maybe surgery."

"I know. But Lindsey, it was hard enough getting you to replace Eva. *Someone* has to stay on duty. Find Wilson. Protect others who may get stuck out here in the park. There aren't that many rangers qualified to do what we do."

"But Naomi needs you!" Lindsey protested. "And what about Keith? He doesn't have any family around here."

"The main office has already notified Keith's next of kin. I called my parents when we were at the motel. They should be back in the country in a week or so."

"A week? I think Keith and Naomi could use a little moral support before then." Lindsey stared at him in frank amazement.

"You'll be at the hospital with them."

"Me? I thought I'd be coming back with you."

Eric shook his head. "No. As far as I'm concerned, once Keith and Naomi are in the hospital and Ginger's safely out, your job is over. Sled or not, I can't possibly get Ginger up the outer side of Tioga Pass. Once she's in town, she'll have to stay with you."

Lindsey took in a deep breath. "Not if I stay here at the cabin with Ginger until you get back."

"No. I need you for the trip out, and I don't want to leave anyone here with Wilson still loose." He reached for her wrist and touched it lightly. "But thanks for offering. You're a ranger and a half, Lindsey."

Lindsey didn't reply at first. The thought of Eric back here alone shook her up far too much.

"I can't let you come back by yourself, Eric. If anything happened to you, no one would know, not with the main antenna down. Ginger can stay with Naomi for a while.''

The shock on his face surprised her. "You'd actually choose me over that dog?"

"For heaven's sake, this is not a popularity contest! It's a question of need. If you say the park needs a ranger on duty, then I'll be that ranger."

"So I'm just—what...a professional obligation?"

"Stop twisting my words!"

"It's hard to twist what I don't understand," he countered. "I never know what you'll say or do next."

"Would you *listen* to me for a change instead of trying to second-guess me? I'm not your twin—nor do I want to be!"

Keith moved restlessly in his sleeping bag, and both of them were cautiously silent for a moment. When Lindsey spoke again, she kept her voice low, yet emotion caused a hoarseness that had nothing to do with whispering.

"Four years ago, you blamed me for choosing my partner over you. You broke off our engagement because I asked for a few extra days to get over Missy's death. Yet you plan to put yourself in deliberate danger when others need you! After everything you've been through this past week, plus Eva's death, no one would expect you to trek right back out here, if at all! And you have the nerve to say *my* priorities are screwed up."

"Lindsey..." Eric began in a quieter voice, but Lindsey stood and left the table for the couch and her sleeping bag, Ginger at her heels.

"You say you can't understand me—well, I can't understand you. You have one set of priorities for yourself and another for the rest of the world. Where's this secret rule book you carry around? Because I'd sure as hell like to read it."

"I don't have to explain my actions when it comes to my job."

"As if you ever have! But let me warn you—you walk away from Naomi and Keith to play hero, you're running the risk of losing them, especially Naomi. Just like you lost me."

Eric's face blanched, but Lindsey went on.

"Doesn't Keith's opinion of you count? You think he's strong enough to get through this alone? Tracking after a madman instead of being with those who love and need you is wrong. You're not a cop…it isn't even your job! You might think it is, but it's not. What kind of ranger—what kind of *person* are you?"

"According to you, a coward," he said slowly.

Lindsey's chest tightened at his words. "I never said you were a coward, Eric."

His heavy silence accused her more than words ever could.

"Believe what you want," she said wearily. "I'm going to bed. Wake me when it's my watch."

Silence. The silence continued that long night, and during the next morning's trek out.

Day 9

THE NEXT DAY'S TRIP UP, through and down the windy Tioga Pass was bone-tiring for all four rangers and the dog. If it hadn't been for the continued clear, sunny weather and the absence of Wilson and his rifle, Lindsey wondered if she would've had the strength to make it. A depression had settled over her. She ached from head to toe, and suspected Eric did, as well. Naomi had silently

towed the handsled with supplies, but her own demeanor
had been far from cheery as she kept watch on Keith. He
hadn't been able to hide his pain, which had worsened
during the long trek up and through the pass.

Eric and Lindsey maintained an uneasy truce, Eric
never speaking to her except in her capacity as ranger.
Between her aching heart, her fears about the journey,
her exhaustion, and the desolate, harsh landscape, she
could find no beauty inside or out. She'd once thought
the day Eric had left her the most miserable day of her
life—until now. If one more thing went wrong, she was
afraid she might fall apart.

Her emotional resolve wasn't tested, fortunately. At
the bottom of the pass, the helicopter was waiting to take
them on, then set them down in the hospital parking lot.
That left Lindsey with Ginger and the gear at the ranger
vehicle, while Eric went in to get Keith admitted and to
assist Naomi in making an appointment to see a doctor.

Hospital parking lot
Day 9, late evening

LINDSEY TRANSFERRED THE GEAR from the two sleds into
the same vehicle that had been waiting for them when
they'd brought Pam in, and sighed with fatigue as she
loaded the empty sleds. She opened the door and let Ginger inside to lie down on the middle seat on one of the
sleeping bags she'd unpacked especially for the dog.
She'd watered and fed her after dragging the sleds from
the heliport to the parking area. The keypad code for the
ranger vehicle door was the same as earlier, and the ignition key was inside the glove box.

"Sorry it's not warmer, girl," she said, her eyes gritty
from fatigue. "But you'll be okay for now." Lindsey

stroked the soft head, then pulled her glove back on and headed for the Admissions and Information area to find Eric and Naomi. Since she'd been officially "discharged" as replacement, she forced herself to shove aside her devastation.

She found Eric in the main lobby. He immediately rose to his feet at her appearance.

"I was just about ready to come looking for you. Everything okay?"

"You tell me." She unzipped her jacket and sat down on the lobby couch, where he joined her. "How's Keith?"

"They just took him up to surgery. I saw him before he left."

"How's he doing?"

"He seems more worried about Naomi than himself. I've got the main office contacting his next of kin."

"Where's Naomi now?"

"Upstairs having a mammogram done. They're going to fit her in with an oncologist later this afternoon."

Lindsey nodded. "What's next?" she asked. "You want to drop me and Ginger off at the motel so you can come back for Naomi?"

"I'd already planned on it," Eric said. "Jack Hunter's booked us two rooms, one for you and Naomi, and one for me. He also asked if you want to fly Ginger back with you to San Diego, or if you'd rather the park system arranged for a rental car."

She couldn't believe the calmness in his voice, or how he couldn't seem to wait to get her out of his life. "There's no way I'd fly Ginger on a commercial airline. She's stressed enough already. Have Jack authorize a car. I'll camp out at the motel for a few days to rest up and make sure everyone's okay before leaving."

Most of the drive south would be relatively snow-free
once she cleared the mountainous areas and cut across to
the Sunbelt's coastal route. Plus, if she felt like shedding
some tears on the way home, she'd have privacy in a car
that she wouldn't have in a plane full of passengers. The
drive down the coast would be more than soothing; it
would give her time to decide what to do with her future.
One thing she already knew: she'd be without Eric in her
life...once again.

"Is Pam still here?" Lindsey asked. "I wanted to see
her before I left."

"If she is, it won't be for much longer. I saw her
mother earlier, and she told me Pam's going to be discharged today and moved to Children's Hospital in San
Francisco via the Life-Flight chopper. Seems she might
lose more toes, after all."

"Oh, no! That poor kid.... What time were they leaving?"

Eric checked his wristwatch. "In a few minutes, as a
matter of fact."

"Damn! Maybe I can catch them at the helipad. Which
way?" Lindsey asked.

Eric reached for her arm. "Come on, I'll show you."

They hurried through the halls, Eric in the lead, and
almost ran into Mrs. Wilson right inside the helipad
lobby.

"I left Pam's insurance card at the finance office,"
Mrs. Wilson explained breathlessly. "Only I'm not exactly sure how to get back there."

"I'll take you, and Lindsey can say goodbye to Pam,
if that's okay," Eric suggested.

"That would be a big help," Mrs. Wilson said. "She's
already in the helicopter."

Lindsey nodded. After getting permission from the

flight ops controller, she hurried onto the helipad. Inside, the flight nurse opened the hatch and kicked out the folding steps so Lindsey could get inside. But before she'd even reached the first rung, she felt a sudden tug on the neck of her unzipped jacket. Off balance, she turned and found herself staring into the muzzle of a gun.

"Where's my bitch of a wife?" Wilson asked. "You're not her!"

"I—I just came to say goodbye to Pam," Lindsey stammered.

"Who the hell are—wait a minute. I know you!" Wilson's eyes narrowed in fury. "You're the ranger with the dog who kidnapped my kid." Wilson shoved her toward the steps again. "Get in," he ordered. "You—" He gestured toward the trauma nurse. "Get out. Tell the police I'm taking my daughter and leaving. Anyone tries to stop me or follow me, I shoot the ranger. And that goes for the pilot after I land."

The pilot's eyes widened. The trauma nurse, a thin male with pale-gray eyes, stare at the gun.

"I said go! And latch the door after you." The nurse wisely didn't argue. He left the chopper and stepped aside as Wilson climbed into the front seat next to the pilot. "We're going for a little ride, Pam," he said, the gun now pointing at the pilot. "The ranger will keep an eye on you, okay?"

Pam's eyes filled with tears, but she was too afraid to make a sound.

So was Lindsey, for that matter. She took the nurse's vacant seat, fastened her harness, and took Pam's hand in hers. As the pilot increased the speed of the rotors and began to lift from the ground, Lindsey looked out her window, watching through the glass as the trauma nurse gesticulated wildly to the head of medi-flight operations.

As the chopper lifted even higher, she saw Mrs. Wilson and Eric through the glass doors. Mrs. Wilson screamed and tried to run outside. Eric stopped her, his arms around her waist as both adults tipped their heads upward toward the escaping craft.

The last thing Lindsey saw before they gained enough altitude to clear the hospital was the look of horror on Eric's face.

Lindsey knew it matched her own.

CHAPTER EIGHTEEN

Hospital administration conference room
Day 9, late evening

"HOW COULD THIS HAVE happened? Where's the police officer who was assigned to guard the room?" Eric demanded. "And how did Wilson manage to make it all the way from Yosemite to Lee Vining without being spotted? I thought there was a police dragnet on, for God's sake."

Eric, Naomi, the local chief of police, the head of hospital security and the hospital CEO, along with the hospital lawyer, had all gathered inside the conference room around a large rectangular table. Mrs. Wilson was hunched over in a plastic chair, firmly believing she'd never see her daughter again. Eric didn't hold with that belief, but he couldn't have relaxed enough to sit, even if the chairs had been the most comfortable in the world.

"It's the dead of winter, and our police force has less than ten members. We're a very small town, Eric," Chief of Police McClanahan explained.

"Maybe your officers weren't where they should have been," Pam's mother said. "How could he make it all the way in here without someone seeing him?"

"Mrs. Wilson, I know you're upset. My officer and a member of hospital security escorted Miss Wilson's stretcher all the way to the helicopter. Others are manning the roadblocks out. You told us yourself your husband's originally from this area. Obviously he found someone to help him—maybe warn him about the roadblocks so he could get past them. Or maybe he just caught a ride and pretended to be an innocent hitchhiker. We're not sure.''

"I hope you've checked out any old friends," Eric said, frustrated at the turn of events.

The chief nodded. "We're on it now, thanks to Mrs. Wilson's help. We searched the surrounding area and the helicopter before anyone boarded, and rechecked it when your child boarded, as well."

"You didn't do a very good job," Mrs. Wilson said, her voice cracking with emotion, tears running down her cheeks. "I told you my husband was dangerous! You turn your back for ten seconds and he shows up and kidnaps my daughter! *Again!* I just got her back!"

She broke down even more. Eric could tell the woman's stamina had run out. Naomi hurried to her side, handing her a tissue from the box sitting on the single large table.

The hospital CEO, obviously fearful of legal repercussions, immediately became defensive. "Security cleared takeoff with my flight chief, Mrs. Wilson. All would've been well if you hadn't jumped off the helicopter at the last minute to run back for…what was it?"

He turned toward the hospital's lawyer who filled in the blank. "Her daughter's insurance card."

"Pam's insurance card."

"The clerk forgot to give it back to me!"

"This hospital will *not* accept any blame in this matter."

Eric interrupted. "Is that all you're worried about—

lawsuits? My ranger's been kidnapped, along with this woman's child and the pilot. The kidnapper's already shot one ranger. *What are we doing to get our people back?*"

Chief McClanahan, definitely calmer than the hospital staff, spoke up. "I'll tell you, but first, please sit down. All of you."

One by one, they did.

"I've notified the nearby military bases to keep an eye out for them on radar," McClanahan said. "But so far, tracking's been impossible. The chopper's obviously flying low enough to stay below the radar. The mountains aren't helping matters. It'll be dark soon, so we won't be able to do much of a ground or air-based search. And—" he directed an apologetic glance toward Mrs. Wilson "—there's another storm front heading in tonight. Any rescue attempt will have to wait for morning."

The CEO swore. The lawyer took notes. Mrs. Wilson cried harder, close to true hysterics. Naomi tried to calm her. Eric felt his stomach knot even tighter.

"Has anyone called the pilot's family?" Eric asked.

McClanahan nodded. "Did you call the female ranger's?"

With a shock, Eric shook his head, realizing he hadn't even called the main office. Twenty minutes ago, Jack Hunter was arranging for a motel and transportation for Lindsey, Naomi and him. Twenty minutes—a lifetime ago. "Not yet."

"I'll take care of that," Naomi quickly volunteered. "Mrs. Wilson, why don't you and I go get some coffee? Then I'll need to check on our dog. I'm sure by the time we get back, the police will have some news for us."

Eric threw his sister a grateful glance as he pulled himself together and forced his mind off Lindsey—how he'd lost her to his foolish pride four years ago, and how he'd just lost her again. He'd actually, stupidly been prepared to say goodbye…to let her go home to San Diego. What kind of fool was he? A big one, obviously. But he was still head ranger—and if he had to track after that chopper himself and on foot, he'd do so. He concentrated on the business at hand.

"Why don't we regroup outside Keith's room in say, a half hour?" he suggested. Naomi agreed.

"Is your pilot a levelheaded man?" McClanahan asked after the women had left.

"Under ordinary circumstances, I'd guess he is," the CEO replied.

"You guess?" Eric echoed. "Don't you know? This is a small hospital."

The CEO flushed, and glanced nervously at the lawyer. "Not *that* small. Besides, I don't do the hiring. I can't know everything."

"Then you should check with Personnel and find out," Eric said tersely. "Give them a call and get back to us."

McClanahan nodded his agreement, and after a moment, the CEO and his lawyer disappeared.

"Not much help, are they?" the chief muttered. Then, without waiting for an answer, he said, "I don't think anyone, even the military, will be able to do much until morning. But we do have one thing in our favor. I talked with the helicopter mechanic. The fuel hadn't been replenished, yet…."

"That's because the chopper had just dropped off the injured ranger—the man Wilson shot."

"The bastard won't get far on that much fuel."

"There aren't many places around here that sell chopper fuel, even in the summer," Eric said. "It'll be easy to have those places watched."

"I'm already on it. And my staff's contacting the media. They're helping us put out an Amber Alert," he said, referring to the California law that waived a twenty-four-hour waiting period for a missing person if the person was a child, and enlisted media help. There had been no such law to help the real Amber when she'd been kidnapped and killed, but other children had been saved because of her plight. "You can't hide a helicopter for long. If anyone sees it, they'll report it. I'm hoping to hear something come first light."

Eric nodded. "Let your people know that Pam can't walk. Once they're out of fuel, I wouldn't put it past this guy to carjack someone."

"Yeah, I'm worried about that myself. The last thing we want is more hostages. The pilot's safe as long as the fuel holds out. And the felon will need a woman's help with the child while they're the air, I'm guessing."

"In the air, yes, but once the chopper's out of fuel—" Eric couldn't finish the thought, but the police chief did.

"One, maybe both, are expendable. Still, I've read this guy's profile. He won't give up any advantages, and that includes hostages."

Eric swallowed hard. Lindsey, a hostage—because of him. Because he'd asked for her as the replacement.

"Tell me about Lindsey Nelson," McClanahan said. "She have a good head on her shoulders?"

"The best," Eric replied fervently. "She's the calmest woman in a crisis I've ever known. And she has more than her share of luck."

The other man exhaled slowly. "Let's pray it stays that way. We could use some luck right now."

A pause, then Eric asked, "Anything else you need from me?"

"I've got your motel and contact number." Mc-

Clanahan reached inside his wallet. "Here's my card. Unless I hear anything sooner, I'll be in touch tomorrow morning."

The men rose, faces grim, and shook hands.

"Thanks," Eric said.

"Save it until the job's done. Let me know how your man's doing after surgery."

"Will do."

The police chief departed for his office, Eric for the elevator and the short ride up to Keith's room.

KEITH WAS STILL IN Recovery, according to the head nurse at the nurses' station, but was doing well; in about an hour, he'd be transferred to the private room the rangers' main office had authorized. In the meantime, Eric was welcome to wait in Keith's room, and was told his sister and Pam's mother were already there. Eric thanked the nurse, got the room number and went to rejoin the women.

Naomi and Mrs. Wilson immediately sprang to their feet, their "Any news?" and "Anything on Pam?" coming at the same time. As he shook his head, both women drooped, Naomi as much as Joyce.

"Keith won't be out of recovery for another hour, the nurse said. Let's go to the motel," Eric said. "There's a room booked for you and Lind—Mrs. Wilson to share," he said to Naomi. "The police will contact us there."

Naomi protested, but Eric insisted. He took her aside. "We need to get Ginger and Joyce inside and settled down. The dog needs to eat, and so do we. After that, they can stay at the motel and we'll come back. We're only a few minutes away."

Naomi allowed herself to be partially convinced. She went along with Eric's plan, but while Joyce ate in her motel room and Ginger did the same in Eric's, Naomi skipped the food and insisted on going back to the hospital. Eric didn't feel like eating, either, and soon the two were alone in the car for the drive back.

"How'd the needle biopsy go?" Eric asked at the first red light.

"I'm sore, but I'll live. I'm luckier than Lindsey. I wasn't jabbed with a gun. Eric, how could all this have happened?"

"God knows." The traffic light changed to green, and he cautiously pulled through the dark, slippery intersection. "What did your doctor say?" he asked, returning to the subject of his sister's heath.

"The usual mumbo jumbo. Mammogram not conclusive, biopsy won't be back for a couple days, we shouldn't make any uneducated guesses—blah, blah, blah. But from the way he acted..." Naomi frowned. "I'm not stupid. I suspect I'll be having surgery soon."

"Here?"

Naomi shook her head. "No. I intend to get a second opinion, and I'll go to San Francisco for that. I'll notify headquarters when the results are in. I'm holding off until then. Besides, I'm not doing a thing until Keith's back on his feet. I can't help him if I'm in a hospital bed myself."

"I'm sure he'll return the favor when it's your turn—if you let him." Eric took his gaze off the road for just a second to face his twin. "Will you?"

"I don't know. I expect to lose a breast, Eric. Why would Keith want to go through all that? And don't say because of love, either," she said, answering her own question. "I know breast cancer patients are strongly advised against pregnancy. I'd never be able to have children. That's if they get it all the first time. I could spend the rest of my life—however long that is—in and out of hospitals for chemo and radiation. Bad enough for me. Why should I let him suffer through it?"

"Because, believe it or not, he'll suffer more if you don't. Let him into your life, Naomi. He needs to be there."

A pause. "Like you and Lindsey?" Naomi asked quietly.

"As bad as things get—and God knows they're pretty bad right now—they always seem worse when we're apart...at least for me."

"And Lindsey, too, I suspect." Naomi swiveled to face Eric as far as her seat belt would allow. "It's time you and I let go of each other, Eric. I don't know whether or not things will work out for me with Keith and for you with Lindsey, but either way, it's time."

Eric couldn't believe what his sister had just said. "That's a hell of a thing to ask of me, and with you so sick! Who else will know what you want, what you need, except me?"

"No one if you don't step aside," Naomi said emphatically. "We can't be each other's better half anymore. I know it happens all the time with twins, but it's not—and it's playing havoc with our personal lives. It did with my marriage."

"You never told me that." Naomi hadn't come to Yosemite until after her husband's death, and she hadn't revealed the problems in her marriage—not in any detail. He'd assumed that her reticence about Bruce was due to her grief. "I didn't realize..."

"No, but it only happened because I let it," Naomi explained. "I may...just may...have another chance at a relationship. I'd be an idiot to pass it up. I want you to have that same chance with Lindsey."

"Did she say something to you?" he asked sharply, already hurting at his sister's words, but recognizing their truth. "Suggest this?"

"Oh, Eric, she'd never even think it, let alone say it. She's far too generous. We aren't—except with each other. Maybe other twins can keep their twin first and put their lovers second and make a go of it. We can't. Not anymore."

The hum of the car heater continued as the snow started to fall, wet, icy flakes that splattered on the windshield. Eric turned on the wipers and slowed his speed.

Naomi didn't speak again for a full three blocks. "You're upset with me, aren't you?" Naomi started to cry, and Eric realized his sister had been holding back tears since leaving the motel.

"Don't cry, sweetie. You were being honest, and there's a lot of truth in what you say."

"I'm not crying for myself." Naomi sniffed again. "I'm just so worried. Do you think Lindsey and Pam and the pilot are still...?" She couldn't finish the sentence.

Alive.

"I'll find them if it takes me the rest of my life," Eric swore. "If Wilson hurts any of them—he's going down."

Naomi shivered. Eric couldn't tell if it was from the cold or the icy coldness of his voice. Either way, it didn't matter. If Lindsey and the others didn't survive this, then Wilson wouldn't, either. It was as simple as that.

Medi-chopper
Night

THE WIND HOWLED AND MOVED the rotors of the chopper as another storm front blew in. The passengers were rocked inside as the wind rocked the main cabin. The pilot and Wilson remained in their seats; Lindsey still sat next to Pam. When the pilot had been forced to land due to the weather conditions, Wilson had ordered him to shut down the chopper to conserve what little fuel was left, even though the pilot warned him that without an engine heating block, the chopper might not start up again. At present, there was no heat in the cabin, and it grew colder by the minute.

Earlier Lindsey had dressed Pam in extra clothes from the bag Joyce had brought, then placed her back under the blankets on her stretcher. The child had actually managed to fall asleep, a good thing for her, but not for Lindsey. When Pam was awake, she'd concentrated on keeping her calm and comfortable. Now Lindsey had nothing but her tortured thoughts—and guilty conscience—to keep her company.

I yelled at Eric for wanting to stay behind and catch Wilson. Told him he had his priorities wrong. Guess I'll be eating crow when I see him again. If I see him again...

"I need some shut-eye," Wilson said suddenly. He waved the gun at the pilot, gesturing him to the back area of the cabin. "Go sit with the ranger. I should warn you I'm a light sleeper. Anyone tries anything and I start shooting."

The pilot, Jim, moved to the back of the cabin and perched next to Lindsey on Pam's stretcher. Wilson turned both front seats to face each other for a makeshift bed. Then he lifted his feet, tucked the gun within his crossed arms and closed his eyes. In minutes the sound of soft snoring told them their captor slept.

"Shall I rush him?" Jim asked in a softer voice. A young man, younger than Lindsey, he seemed ready to tackle the world—and probably get himself killed, Lindsey thought.

"God, no. This guy shot one of my co-workers, remember? He certainly won't miss hitting us in here." Lindsey looked to make certain Wilson still slept, then patted her ranger jacket. "I've got a better idea."

A few minutes later, Jim rose and crept toward the chopper door. Wilson was immediately alert, pointing the gun. "Where do you think you're going?"

"I need to go," Jim said bluntly.

"Unzip in here and use a medical container," Wilson ordered.

"I need to drop my pants."

"Too bad. Hold it."

"Can't. I've got a nervous stomach as it is, and being hijacked has made it worse. You'd better let me outside or this whole cabin is gonna reek from soiled underwear in about two seconds." Jim grabbed at his gut for emphasis.

Lindsey deliberately wrinkled her nose. "Please let him out, Mr. Wilson. Where could he go in this storm? And in the dark, no less?" She opened the supply locker and tossed Jim a packet of sterile towels. He caught it easily.

Wilson scowled, cranky at being awakened, and definitely annoyed. "Make it quick," he ordered.

Jim nodded, opened the door and stepped outside, then quickly latched it as Wilson complained to Lindsey, "Next you'll be wanting to go. Then the brat."

"I'm fine, and Pam's asleep." Lindsey deliberately yawned. "Don't worry about us." She stretched out next to Pam and covered herself with part of the child's blanket.

Wilson returned to his earlier position in the two

chairs, relaxed yet still alert. Lindsey closed her eyes. Right now Jim had the avalanche transponder from her jacket, the one she was required to wear in the field. She didn't want Wilson to find it, so she'd asked Jim to fasten it on the outside of the chopper with the tape that came in the packet of sterile towels. Wilson wouldn't find it there. Nor would he find the pilot, if Lindsey had her way.

"I want you to run as fast and as far as you can. You said you're local…know your way around. When the fuel runs out, he'll kill you," Lindsey had said with all certainty. "You're expendable to him."

"So are you," he'd countered.

"Wilson needs at least one hostage, and I won't leave without Pam. She's my responsibility."

"She's my passenger. You go." Jim had tried to convince her to change her mind, but the whispered argument hadn't lasted long when Lindsey told Jim how she'd spent her past week.

"I'm physically exhausted. I don't stand a chance out there," she said. "Besides, I may know the park, but you know the area outside it much better."

"All right," he finally agreed. "I do know of a hunter's cabin about half a mile from here. My dad and I used it last fall. All the locals know about it. I could hole up until the storm passes and it's light." Lindsey passed him some survival items, including her compass, some trail mix and the cigarette lighter she still had in her pocket. Jim had his own flashlight and batteries. After softly instructing Lindsey on how to use the chopper radio and turn on the cabin heat, plus telling her their present coordinates in case she had a chance to relay them, they put their plan into action.

"Just push this button when you get outside," Lindsey

whispered. "When the green switch lights up, it's active and transmitting."

Jim had carefully stashed the transponder and his supplies inside his inner clothing. Now he was out there, taking his chances with the terrain and the weather.

And Lindsey waited, counting the seconds with eyes closed, pretending to sleep. She prayed she and Jim and Pam would make it to safety. She also wished with every ounce of strength that she'd get to see Eric again.

I can't believe I was going to leave him. All this time I thought he didn't know what was important in life—when it was the other way around. I always want to do things my way. I should've married him and gone on the honeymoon. Everything was ready. Yes, Missy died, but I should've shared that with him, not shut myself away...shut him out. He and my whole family were there to support me. I didn't take advantage of it. And I was going home to San Diego without even a kiss goodbye. Now I'm stuck with an armed kidnapper in the middle of nowhere, and I might just have sent a young man to his death. I might never see Eric again.

She listened to the howling wind outside, resisting the urge to throw a pillow over her ears, and prayed she'd see morning in one piece.

Keith's hospital room

KEITH RESTED IN A DRUGGED grogginess that was closer to sleep than waking when Eric and Naomi entered the room.

"He's doing fine, so let's keep it that way," the doctor ordered. "A short visit, and no bad news. Security said one of you can stay the night if you want."

"That would be me," Naomi said.

"Remember what I told you—no sudden shocks. He's had a rough time of it."

You're telling me, Eric thought silently. He remained silent as Keith opened his eyes and focused his gaze on Naomi. The unguarded look of joy and love on Keith's face confirmed for Eric everything that Lindsey had told him. For the first time in his life, Eric felt out of place in the company of his twin. After a few reassuring words to Keith, he said his goodbyes and quietly slipped from the room to return to the motel, where Ginger and Mrs. Wilson were waiting.

He had to pass the heliport on the way to the parking lot. Its stark, empty landing pad in the cold darkness seemed to reprove him. With an icy grip around his heart, he forced himself to stop.

Where are you, Lindsey? How will I ever find…?

He stopped, the icy grip on his heart lessening. *She still has her winter survival gear on…just like me. I didn't change at the motel, and Lindsey never even made it there. That means…*

His right hand immediately traveled to the avalanche locator beacon that remained attached to his parka.

I know Lindsey! She would've turned it on the first chance she had!

Despite the ice and falling snow, he ran back to the hospital's phones. He had to get hold of Jack Hunter and the chief of police. And then he had to search his gear in the back of the car for the more powerful locator device.

LINDSEY CONTINUED TO FEIGN sleep, not hard to do. Her exhausted body had relaxed under the warmth generated by the sleeping Pam. She tried to guess how long it had been, wished she dared look at her wristwatch, and wondered how soon before Wilson went after Jim. She didn't have to wait more than a minute or two.

"That son of a— I told him not to take long!" Wilson peered out the front bubble window of the chopper, trying to catch some glimpse of the pilot. "Where the hell is he?"

Lindsey sat up and rubbed her eyes. "Huh?" she said, wishing she was a better actress.

"You stay put," he ordered with another wave of his gun for emphasis. He hurried to the door latch and lifted it with one hand. Nothing happened. He lifted the latch again. Still nothing. Wilson swore a vicious expletive, pocketed his gun and used both hands. The door remained jammed shut, secured from the outside. Wilson swore again and reached for a large flashlight.

Hot damn, Jim, you bought yourself some time! Lindsey thought as Wilson continued to work at the door, pushing his shoulder against it. Finally the latch popped open at Wilson's weight, and he fell out, head first, into the snow. *No wonder you wanted me to know our present coordinates! You planned on jamming the door all along!*

Immediately Lindsey was on her feet, grabbing at the door and locking it securely. She dashed to the front of the helicopter, turned on the battery-operated control lights the way Jim had explained, and reached for the radio. She keyed the mike and spoke into it, using the chopper's call sign, begging the hospital control desk to answer her with a frantic "Over?"

"Lee Vining Hospital here, Life-flight One. Over?"

"This is Ranger Lindsey Nelson. Your pilot's escaped and is headed for a nearby hunting cabin. Said you'd know where. I turned on my—" She started to tell them about the transponder and give their coordinates, but the noise of a bullet passing through the Plexiglas of the cockpit—followed by Pam's scream—cut her off. Startled, she accidentally dropped the radio mike, then froze as she looked straight ahead. Wilson held the flashlight toward himself, and the light showed him pointing his gun straight at her.

Lindsey made no move to retrieve the radio mike. Instead, her hands in the air, she slowly backed toward the helicopter door, unlocked it and let her captor back in as a terrified Pam sobbed on her stretcher.

Hospital flight dispatch room

ERIC LISTENED TO THE dispatcher relate the circumstances of Lindsey's short radio contact to McClanahan. He'd planned to contact Jack Hunter via radio from the dispatch center, and happened to be there during her frantic call. The sound of gunfire had made him break out in a cold sweat. When the broadcast went dead, he'd instructed the dispatcher to radio the chief, who'd arrived soon after.

"So the pilot's escaped, and we don't know the status on the other two hostages?" McClanahan asked the dispatcher.

"Not that I could tell. The transmission was so short—"

"I know what she didn't get time to say," Eric said. "She's wearing a homing beacon. You get me to that hunting cabin, and I can find her from there."

"You got access to a locator unit?" McClanahan asked.

Eric showed him the personal transponder he had in his jacket. "They're two-way. Any of us can switch them from transmit to receive. But I've got a stronger unit in the back of my truck. Let's go."

LINDSEY WIPED AT THE TEARS on one of her cheeks. Wilson had punched her hard in the face when he finally returned without Jim. Already her eye was swelling shut, tearing from pain. Pam continued to wail until Wilson threatened her as well, then she buried her small face in a pillow to muffle her crying. Wilson ranted and screamed, finally ripping the radio mike from the console. Bare wires trailed from the unit as he threw it at her. Lindsey ducked, and it bounced off the locker behind them.

"I hope your pilot freezes his ass off. So, who planned the escape?" Wilson asked, his posture threatening as he hovered over her. "Whose idea was it?"

Lindsey shook her head, unwilling to be honest yet knowing she didn't lie well. "I didn't know he was going to latch the door from the outside!" she said honestly. "I swear he didn't tell me!"

"Lying bitch." Wilson raised his hand as if to strike her again. Lindsey ducked, covering her head. The blow she waited for didn't fall. Instead, she heard Wilson click off the safety on his handgun.

"Give me one good reason I shouldn't kill you like I killed that last ranger."

Lindsey cautiously dropped her arms and raised her head, one hand reaching for Pam's shaking body, the other pressed against her swollen eye.

"But...Keith's not dead," Lindsey said, confused. "He's recovering at the hospital."

"Not the male ranger," Wilson said contemptuously. "The female one—the one I buried in the snow."

"What?"

Wilson smiled with evil satisfaction. "She came across me and Pam earlier, only she was downwind and downhill. Didn't take much to start that snowslide. Saved me from wasting ammo and the other rangers from learning my location. Until you showed up to replace her.''

This time tears spilled from Lindsey's eyes. ''You killed Eva?'' she whispered in horror.

His smile chilled her. ''Nope, the snow did that. I just helped it along.''

Lindsey began to shake with fear, willing herself not to give into panic and hysteria as Wilson continued.

''Come daybreak, the three of us are going on a little hike. As long as you carry my daughter, you stay alive. When you can't...I leave you for the elements. They won't be able to prove murder, even if they do find you.''

Lindsey thought of the sorrow Eric, Naomi and Keith felt over Eva's death. *Will I ever get a chance to tell them about her? Will I ever see any of them alive again?*

Sheriff's truck

''HOW LONG WILL THE BATTERIES in her transponder work?'' the chief asked.

''A good twenty-four hours.''

''I hope that's enough time for us to find her.'' McClanahan nodded, driving the four-wheel-drive truck with the snowmobiles in the covered cab. Another police truck followed, with two more officers. ''If we get any more snow, we won't be able to use the snowmobiles. We'll have to hike—and leave the dog in the truck.'' McClanahan glanced quickly at Ginger between Eric's knees. He'd insisted on bringing her.

''How much has fallen?'' Eric asked, peering through the windshield. Even on high, the wipers were barely able to keep pace with the precipitation.

McClanahan shrugged. ''Easily close to five,'' he said.

"We'll get more if this storm doesn't blow itself out soon."

"We've got to get to that hunter's cabin quickly," Eric told him. "We usually start setting charges and firing the avalanche cannon for every six inches of snow we get."

"Whaddaya use?" McClanahan asked with curiosity.

"Two-pound charges—anywhere from three hundred to three hundred and fifty of them."

The chief whistled. "Wouldn't catch me messing around with that stuff."

"Keith's our explosives expert. He's as good as they come."

"The parks should close down in the winter, especially to cross-country skiers or snowmobilers stupid enough to risk killing themselves."

"Can't. The parks are—"

"Public land," McClanahan finished for him. "I know. It stinks."

"We tell visitors about the dangers, do our best to keep the slide risks down, but we're powerless to prohibit entry."

"They should change that law," McClanahan said. "Friend of a friend of mine got killed when a slide caught him on public land. It only moved fifty yards down the slope, but it compacted itself as dense as ice. Guy never had a chance." He took his eyes off the road for just a second to meet Eric's. "I won't order my men into danger. I've seen how snow kills."

Eric thought of Eva. *So have I.*

"If you're worried about your men or yourself," he muttered, "save it. Suicide missions aren't my style."

"Then we understand each other," the cop said. "Frankly, if it were only Wilson trapped out there, I'd leave him to the weather and sleep with a clear conscience.''

"But it isn't only him. Is it.''

The cop had nothing to say to that, and the two trucks continued on their way in the whirling flakes toward the old hunting cabin.

CHAPTER NINETEEN

Medi-chopper
Day 10, dawn

LINDSEY AWOKE SHIVERING from what was already a fitful sleep. The temperature inside the cabin had dropped dramatically. Even with her winter gear on, she was cold. She quietly placed her half of the covers more firmly around Pam, who still slept, and checked her skin. The child's face felt cold, as did the little wrists above her mittens. Lord only knows what further damage was being done to the girl's feet, Lindsey thought.

Worse yet, despite the morning hour, it was still dark inside the chopper cabin. She confirmed the morning with a glance at her lighted watch face. A heavy layer of snow, so heavy that it blocked most of the light, must have covered the cabin's Plexiglas. She couldn't hear anything clearly. Lindsey almost pounded on the nearest glass to try to dislodge the snow, then stopped.

In the background she could hear Wilson's soft snoring. He was still in the front of the cabin, while she and Pam remained closest to the chopper hatch. Lindsey stared at the sleeping girl, her throat tight.

This idiot's never going to let his daughter go. He'd kill us first. I've got to try one last time to get out of here. If I can get free, I know Eric will find us.

Lindsey had no elaborate plans. The most she hoped was that she and Pam could get out the door before they were shot. If Wilson woke up, she'd say they needed to relieve themselves after the long night. If they did make it outside, Lindsey planned to wait under the chopper, then tackle him as he came out.

Maybe I'll get his gun. Maybe he'll fall and hurt himself. And maybe I'll win the lottery today and fly off to Hawaii for a suntan.

She knew her plan was risky and would probably get her another black eye or a bullet in the back. But all her instincts—instincts she'd always trusted to keep her alive as a ranger—told her it was now or never.

Lindsey said a quick, desperate prayer, then placed her palm over Pam's mouth to wake her. The child's eyes flew open as Lindsey bent and whispered in her ear, "Shh. We're going outside."

She gave no other explanation, nor did Pam ask for one. Lindsey helped the girl sit up and wished she had boots or shoes for her heavily bandaged feet. After allowing herself a final thought of Eric, she grabbed the child's waist with one arm, reached for the door handle, pushed down on it...

And threw herself and the child headfirst out the open door.

Wilson's roar of anger filled her ears even before she and Pam hit the deep, soft snow. Out of the corner of her good eye, she saw him come after her, gun pointed. His heavy frame hit the side of the hatch, shaking the helicopter. All of the night's accumulated snow, which had covered the chopper, fell on top of him and knocked the gun out of his hand.

Lindsey did the first thing that came into her head at the sight of this miracle. She bounded as fast as she could through the snow, Pam in her arms. She kept going, expecting to feel a bullet slam into her back at any second. Behind her, she heard Wilson cursing as he searched for the gun, but it was just dawn, the light was faint, the snow deep, and Wilson hadn't been awake long enough to be fully alert. By the time he found his gun, Lindsey had made the cover of a small copse of trees.

The first bullet Wilson fired at her missed.

Lindsey dropped to the ground, the tree trunks between her and Wilson providing shelter. She prayed Eric and the authorities were close enough to hear the noise, then she heard an ear-splitting crack—not the sound of a bullet, but the ominous sound of snow shifting and groaning, layers of ice and snow splitting.

Oh, God, not again! She hunkered even lower with Pam on the downside section of the copse of trees. Then the heavy blast of the displaced mass of air tore at her body, followed by the stinging needle-sharp fierceness of moving snow and ice.

ERIC, MCCLANAHAN AND ONE of the cops made their way through the hilly expanse of snow, which continued to fall in what looked more like chunks than flakes. Earlier they'd discovered the pilot in the hunting cabin. He'd brought them up to speed regarding the hostages and their situation.

"You're not that far from the chopper. Shouldn't be hard to spot it when the sun comes up, especially with that big red cross on the side," Jim had said, then wished them luck. Accompanied by one of the officers in the second truck, he'd retreated to the warmth of the vehicle while the other three had gone on.

The new snow was deep, but the snow beneath it had frozen to a hard crust that supported the three men and

Ginger. Eric towed the ranger sled with medical supplies and snowshoes, in case the crust grew unstable in the warmth of the day. For now, he preferred the hard footing for speed. Lindsey's transponder was still beeping strongly, and the local authorities knew their way around this popular hunting area even in the faint light.

"How much farther?" Eric asked McClanahan, when they'd stopped for a breather. While the chief checked his navigation, Eric searched the area ahead with his binoculars.

"I figure another fifteen minutes or so. We should make good time with the sun fully up. With the ground cover and all, maybe we can take—" McClanahan never finished his sentence.

The sound of a discharged firearm filled the air, followed by a second cracking that grew into the earsplitting roar of an avalanche.

None of the three men moved. They were off to the side of the moving snow. Eric thought he heard McClanahan yell, "We're safe," but the thundering roar made speech impossible.

"Lindsey..." His lips formed the words in horror as he watched the night's accumulation of snow on the nearby slope—and the layers below, made slippery by lubricating meltwater—cover the wooded area where the chopper was hidden.

Before the snow had even stopped moving, Eric reached for his watch and set the chronometer to tick down from fifteen, the average number of minutes an avalanche victim had before suffocation set in. He hoped it might be more, since the three were inside an enclosed aircraft. *Please, God, let the chopper stay upright and intact. The slide wasn't that big.... It didn't travel that far....*

He heard McClanahan say to the officer, "No sense taking the covered route to the hostages now. Let's head straight on in."

But Eric was already leading the way, his receiver picking up stronger and stronger signals as the party moved across the crust of undisturbed snow to arrive at the slide area. Quickly they changed to snowshoes, the receiver still beeping.

They advanced to the edge of the slide, then cautiously climbed upward to continue their trek. The pinging noises weren't coming close enough together for them to dig, yet, but Ginger suddenly stopped, her whole body quivering.

"Come," Eric commanded, but the dog stayed where she was, nostrils flaring.

"What's going on?" McClanahan asked. "Do we dig here?"

"I don't know...." Eric said uncertainly. "The slide couldn't have moved the chopper this far, could it? It wasn't that big."

"What, the helicopter or the slide?"

"The slide—the slide wasn't that big." He checked his receiver. The pings still weren't signaling their usual X marks the spot."

"Maybe the dog smells some rabbits," McClanahan suggested.

"Come on, Ginger," Eric urged again. Ginger paused, then ran toward the area at the bottom of the slide, where just the tops of the trees showed. Eric yelled the dog's name, and she froze, unwilling to return, but uncertain about continuing.

"That chopper couldn't have been dragged into the trees—not with the pines standing straight up like that," McClanahan said.

"Or could it?" the other officer asked.

Both policemen swiveled toward Eric, who held the receiver in his hands. "Which way?" they asked. "Where do you want us to dig?"

Eric took in the snow before him, the waiting dog, the shovels strapped onto the sled. He heard the beeping of the receiver. Then he looked at his watch, and saw that five of his fifteen minutes had already gone by.

"What's the word, Ranger?" McClanahan repeated. Eric was the avalanche expert. They looked to him for orders.

For the life of him, Eric didn't know what to say…what to do…as the minutes ticked on.

LINDSEY FELT WARM BLOOD from her nose seep onto her face as she started to dig a breathing space in the dark silence that had descended on her. That movement sent shooting pains through one arm—pains that meant the serious injury of broken bones. With her one good hand, she frantically felt for Pam's face and managed to clear the girl's nose and mouth.

"You okay?" Lindsey whispered. She tried to move her legs, an unsuccessful attempt. She tried to shift her back, as well. No pain, but no movement, either.

Pam tried to nod, could barely move her head, and whimpered, "It's dark." She sneezed snow out of her nose, then whimpered again.

"Don't be scared," Lindsey said. "Just breathe slow and easy. I'll take care of you." She didn't say anything more, trying to prevent her own panic and overuse of precious oxygen. Instead, she moved her good arm and hand—both gloves had stayed on this time—and slowly, agonizingly, began to dig straight up, hoping she could

break the surface, hoping it was within reach of one piti-
fully short arm that suddenly seemed to weigh a thousand
pounds.

ERIC'S CHEST HURT SO MUCH, he thought for a moment
that his heart had actually stopped beating. The dog
wanted to go one way, the beeper on his receiver said to
go another. Lindsey had to be inside the helicopter, didn't
she? So he should go with his instincts and ignore the
dog. Only his instincts were telling him that perhaps the
dog made fewer mistakes than the technology—unless
the chopper *had* been blown apart against the trees, and
the three occupants were scattered throughout the snow.

Dear God, what should he do? Trust Lindsey's life to
a dog—a dog who didn't even obey his commands? But
that dog could smell differences on a cellular level. Naomi was proof of that, wasn't she? And he wasn't really
trusting a dog as much as he was trusting Lindsey and
her judgment.

"We'll split up," he said, sounding more confident
than he felt. "You two take my backup receiver and the
sled. I'll take a shovel and follow the dog."

INSIDE THE DARKNESS, Wilson swore. *Damn this snow,
damn that bitch of a ranger, and damn the daughter of
my bitch wife!* With muscled strength fueled by anger and
adrenaline, he pushed snow away from his face and
moved both his arms slowly upward. He knew the trees
and the chopper had to have taken the brunt of the slide.
He also knew the snow above him wasn't that deep, since
the chopper had remained upright amid the trees he had
forced the pilot to land in. And judging by the way he
was able to move, it wasn't that packed around him, either.

He hoped the pilot was crushed to death, along with

the ranger. As for his daughter, if she was dead, it wasn't his fault. They should arrest the ranger for kidnapping, not him. Maybe he'd sue the ranger service—from out of the country, of course. Nothing, no one, should stand between a man and his family.

Wilson managed to displace enough loose snow so that he could stand upright, which made digging even easier. Why, he could even hang on to parts of the helicopter and pull himself to the surface. His gun might be lost, but if that ranger still breathed, he could still kill her, even if he had to choke the life out of her with his bare hands.

First…he needed to get free.

PAM NESTLED EVEN CLOSER against Lindsey's broken arm, causing Lindsey to gasp. She suddenly remembered how a woman and child in a similar position had been immortalized forever, covered by the ashes of Mount Vesuvius in ancient Pompeii. Lindsey had one arm straight up as far as she could move it and hadn't broken the surface. Nor could she use her other arm, the one painfully anchored around Pam's waist. Broken bones, Pam's position in her lap, plus the heaviness of the snow on them both proved impossible to conquer.

I hope my beeper's still working. Are you out there, Eric? I'm so cold, and Pam's not answering me anymore, even when I call her name. The air is so heavy. We're running out of time!

ERIC FOLLOWED GINGER, who seemed to have no difficulty traversing the new packed surface of slide material. "Seek, girl," Eric encouraged, while watching his own footing. The dog trotted steadily on, then stopped above the snow and began to dig, front paws and nose tunneling through the snowpack. Eric quickly joined her, using his folding shovel and throwing the snow to one side.

From his location, Eric could see the two policemen heading downhill and farther away from him, but he didn't stop his efforts, nor did the dog. Down they tunneled, a foot, two feet, a yard, then Eric was waist-deep in the hole he'd dug, and still no sign of a human. By now Ginger waited outside the hole. Not even an article of clothing appeared as the minutes ticked by. If it wasn't for Ginger's frantic whining, he would've joined the other men, but the dog grew more and more excited. Suddenly, Ginger launched herself into the hole, tipping Eric sideways and knocking the shovel out of his hands. Unable to dig with the dog inside the hole, Eric tossed aside the shovel and moved out of the dog's way as she worried and clawed at the snow…and exposed the tip of Lindsey's glove.

WILSON STRUGGLED HARD, grabbing onto the helicopter's frame and using every ounce of strength he had to pull himself higher through the snow and toward the surface. The helicopter seemed to shift slightly as he hauled himself upward, inch by inch, through the snow.

The snow can't be packed down that hard if I can move the chopper frame, Wilson told himself. *I'll be out of here in a few more minutes.*

Using his hands and feet to feel in the dark, his eyes starting to make out the faintness of daylight through the snow above him, Wilson knew he didn't have far to go. He hooked his foot in what seemed to be a convenient hole. He couldn't see what it was, but it felt firm beneath his boot sole. He shoved his foot more firmly into the hole and strained upward. The jagged opening in the superchilled Plexiglas, already damaged by a projectile cavity and greatly enlarged by the slide, couldn't take the weight of the snow-covered man. Brittle from the cold, the cockpit glass shattered, taking Wilson and all the snow above him down farther. Still conscious, he fell backward, his weight pressing his leg against the edge of glass his own bullet had weakened. The glass sliced through muscle and vessels, stopping only at bone.

"SON OF A—the receiver's just gone dead!" McClanahan swore. "The pings were coming good and close, too."

"Maybe we should just start probing around here," his co-worker suggested.

"Maybe I just need to get a new battery from the ranger," McClanahan said. "Dammit, there's a lot of snow below us."

"I'll probe if you want to hike over and get the spare," the other man said.

"If that's even the problem. I don't wanna be the one to tell Joyce Wilson we lost her kid because—"

Eric's excited shout interrupted their conversation. "I've got a live one! Give me a hand!"

The two men, cheered by the news, hurried uphill to Eric's location and joined in the rescue attempt. They left behind Wilson and the helicopter—its top rotor mere inches from the surface. Wilson was still alive, his injured leg staining his prison of snow.

LINDSEY COULD BARELY BREATHE, nor could she tell if Pam was breathing. Lindsey's lungs hurt so much from lack of oxygen that at first her numbed fingers didn't even register the cold as Ginger's teeth yanked off her glove. But when warm human skin touched her fingertips, she instantly recognized Eric's touch. Tears ran down her face and into the small air pocket she'd dug around her face as she forced her oxygen-deprived and weakened muscles to respond. Her fingers curled slightly, and she felt his hand curl around hers. She heard his voice, muffled and faint. Although she couldn't understand the words, her joy was boundless.

"Help's here, Pam," she whispered as three pairs of hands and a set of paws dug at her, clearing away snow. Eric's hand grasped her good one as they lifted a limp Pam from her lap, shoving an oxygen mask onto the child's face.

"She breathing?" Lindsey asked, not aware that her voice was a faint whisper.

"She's breathing, sweetheart."

Lindsey closed her eyes in relief. She opened them again and cried out as Ginger jostled her. She yanked her good arm away from Eric to cradle her injured one.

"Where are you hurt?" Eric demanded. McClanahan dug a wider hole around her as Eric held back the dog, while the EMT police officer tended Pam.

"My arm. It's broken."

Eric deftly caught the splint the EMT tossed him, and released Ginger. "Did you hit your head? Can you see out of your right eye?"

"Wilson did that," Lindsey said. "He killed Eva, too. He told me." Then, to her horror, she began to cry. When a grim-faced Eric splinted her arm, a myriad of emotions shook her body. Grief, relief, joy, horror and pure shock—they couldn't be contained. She couldn't stop her sobs as Eric and McClanahan gently lifted her stiff, chilled body from the hole and out into the bright light of day. She continued to cry as Ginger licked her face, and cried as she was given her own oxygen mask. Only when Eric took her onto his lap and held her tight did she begin to settle down.

"Jim?" she asked, remembering the pilot.

"Safe and sound with us," Eric said, his arms tightening around her.

"Everyone's accounted for but Wilson," McClanahan said. "I heard the chopper's transponder right before we found you. We should…" He jerked his head toward the buried helicopter's location.

"Lindsey, love, I have to go, but I'll be right back," Eric said, gently transferring her from his lap to the silver solar blanket waiting for her on the snow. He then carefully covered her with another, and adjusted her oxygen mask. "Okay?"

Lindsey nodded and closed her eyes. She heard Eric's "Keep a close eye on them both" to the remaining officer before he called Ginger and set off with McClanahan, shovels in hand.

DESPITE HIS GLOVES, Eric's grip on the shovel was so fierce that it hurt his fingers. Lindsey's words echoed in his head. Wilson had hurt her—and had killed Eva. And now he had to leave the woman he loved to rescue an enemy. He barely noticed the beep of the transponder, as he concentrated on using his probe, and on Ginger's frantic searching. Fury over Eva's death waged with joy at Lindsey and Pam's rescue.

"Think I've got something!" McClanahan sang out. He and Eric efficiently started digging, and just a few feet down uncovered one of the helicopter blades. "The transmitter was with the chopper all along, yet your ranger and the child weren't here. I don't think they were thrown—they must've gotten out before the slide."

Eric couldn't respond. For a moment, his shovel remained motionless in his hand. *If I hadn't trusted Lindsey's expertise and Ginger's instincts, Lindsey and Pam would be dead right now.* Suddenly he understood the bond between canine and human, the great respect Lindsey had for the dogs she worked with.

He changed his position to dig closer to Ginger's location. He didn't respect Wilson, but he did respect life. He always had. Eric put his back into his work and shoveled harder.

WILSON HEARD THE MUFFLED sounds of digging above him. *About damn time,* he thought, his brain muddled with loss of blood. *If it's the police, they'll be in for a surprise.* One good thing about his fall, it had reunited him with his gun. He'd shoot them all and get the hell out of here. He'd come back for Pam later, maybe in a few months, when the police heat had died down and his cut leg healed.

Wilson shifted beneath the snow so as to bring his gun more to the ready. Such was his confusion, his mortally weakened condition, that Wilson didn't even realize he'd dropped the gun.

ERIC CONTINUED TO DIG. Suddenly, Ginger backed away from their location. Her ears flattened, pinned against the side of her head, as her lips pulled back in a grimace.

"Hey, what's wrong with the dog?" McClanahan asked.

Eric knew. He watched Ginger sit on her haunches, saw her nose wrinkle at the new smell—then saw her nose point to the heavens as she keened her death howl.

"Hell," the chief spat out. "That can't be good."

"I'm done here." Eric folded his shovel and fastened it back onto the sled. Ginger at his side, he turned away from death and back to life.

Back to Lindsey.

CHAPTER TWENTY

Hospital
Day 10, noon

LINDSEY MOVED RESTLESSLY on her hospital bed. Her broken arm, now in a lightweight fiberglass cast, throbbed miserably, as did a cracked rib. She tried to find a comfortable position, alerting Naomi, who was sitting in the room. Pam was down the hall, reunited with her mother.

"I thought you were asleep," Naomi said. "Should I call the nurse? Do you need more pain meds?"

Lindsey shook her head. "I just need Eric back. I won't be able to rest until I know he's safe and sound."

"He's safe, Lindsey. He's at the main ranger office right now."

"Are you sure Wilson's dead?"

"We are. The man can't hurt anyone now, I don't know if you remember, but Eric was working Ginger. That's how he found you and Pam in time. He trusted the dog—not the transponder."

"I remember...." Despite her panic at the time—due to oxygen deprivation—she remembered Eric and Ginger rescuing her as a team. "Hard to believe."

"Not really. He loves you, Lindsey. He's never stopped. You know that, don't you?"

Lindsey nodded and adjusted the pillow under her injured arm, careful not to jar her side. "How's Pam?" she asked.

"With her mother. San Francisco Children's Hospital was going to send a helicopter for her, since this hospital's is out of commission, but Pam doesn't want to get on another chopper. She went ballistic just hearing about it."

"I can't blame her."

"They suggested sedation, but her mother refused. Said she isn't going to force her. Instead, they've flown a doctor here to treat her frostbite. From what I heard, she'll need some more debridement surgery, but it looks like she won't lose any more toes."

"Thank God. Does she know her father's dead?"

"Her mother told her, but no details."

"What details?" Lindsey asked.

Naomi hesitated. "Eric said I shouldn't upset you."

"I want to hear, Naomi. I *need* to hear."

The other woman slowly exhaled. "Eric and the police went back out after they brought you and Pam here. The pilot wasn't hurt, so he went back, too. He wanted to check out his craft. Dispatch said the rescue team recovered the body a little while ago. Eric told me about it later, while you were still with the doctors." Naomi paused.

"And?" Lindsey urged.

"Seems there was a pocket beneath the helicopter where the snow didn't pack tightly. That's where Wilson was. He managed to get himself upright and was climbing his way out of the snow using the helicopter frame to assist him. Somehow, he managed to slip and get entangled in the wreckage. He injured himself and died from his injuries."

"Just from a slip?"

"Wilson cut a major artery, Eric said. No one could have saved him."

Lindsey suspected Naomi wasn't telling her the whole story, but she didn't press for details. For now it was enough that the man could never hurt anyone again.

"I feel sorry for him," Lindsey said quietly. "Being trapped in the snow, dying like that."

"That's how he killed Eva. I say he got what was coming to him," Naomi said fiercely, tears in her eyes. "And thanks to him, we blamed Eva all this time, too!"

Eric must have told Naomi that Wilson had confessed to Eva's murder. "Still, it's a horrible feeling, being buried alive. I wouldn't wish it on anyone." She shivered at the memory of her own close call. Naomi approached, smoothed Lindsey's covers and, still standing, held her good hand and patted it, even though she was the tearful one, not Lindsey.

"Well, it's all over now," Naomi said briskly. "You just relax, and I'll stay here until Eric comes."

"You don't have to do that," Lindsey protested. "You should go back and stay with Keith. How's he doing?"

"Fine. He knows I'm here and sends you his best. I promised Eric I wouldn't leave until he returned," she explained, then quickly added, "And even if I hadn't, I still wouldn't go. You wouldn't leave any of us behind."

"Yeah, Super Ranger, that's me," Lindsey said with a wry twist of her lips, staring at her throbbing arm. "I think I need a vacation," she said, closing her eyes.

"Definitely some rest." Without releasing Lindsey's hand, Naomi pulled her chair close to the bed.

"I have a confession to make," she said suddenly.

Lindsey opened her eyes.

"I'm the one who asked for you as a replacement,"

she admitted. "I want to be your friend. And your sister-in-law. I needed the chance to set things right, so—"

"You?"

"Yes. I know it was wrong. I didn't even tell Eric. Can you ever forgive me?"

Lindsey smiled. "No problem," she said, closing her eyes again, feeling the warmth of Naomi's fingers around hers.

WHEN SHE OPENED HER EYES, almost two hours had passed. Keith, in hospital pj's and robe, with a portable IV, sat in a wheelchair near her bed.

"Hey, partner. Feeling better?" he asked.

"Keith! My God, you look great," Lindsey said, truly delighted.

"Better than the last time you saw me." Keith grinned. "And since the doctors said I could sit up, I got a nurse to wheel me here. I decided I'd check up on you. How ya doin'?"

"I'm warm and breathing, with no complaints. Except for my hair." Lindsey pushed away the straggling mess in her eyes, suddenly aware of Naomi's absence. "Where's Naomi?"

"On the phone at the front desk. Eric called her to get some last-minute details for the main office. He's requested sick leave for all three of us."

"When's he coming back?

"Soon, I expect." Keith paused. "Lindsey…"

"Hmm?"

"I owe you an apology."

"For what?"

"After Eva died— God, I still can't believe that bastard killed her…. The three of us were at our wit's end," he said frankly. "Naomi and Eric always talked about you. Even Eva used to complain, saying she was tired of living in your shadow. I figured you were the replacement we needed. Only I never figured on you getting hurt.''

Lindsey shook her head in confusion. ''I don't understand. I thought—''

''*I'm* the one who asked Hunter to send you here. Lindsey, I'm sorry. It wasn't my place to make that decision,'' Keith said. ''I should've gone through proper channels, gone through Eric. I nearly got you killed—and...and I felt you ought to know.''

Lindsey almost explained that Naomi had had the same idea, but didn't have the energy. Nor did it make any difference now. ''Apology accepted,'' she said graciously.

Keith exhaled heavily with relief and returned her smile. ''Thanks, Lindsey. You're a class act. Friends?''

''Only if you never volunteer me again,'' she teased. ''There's such a thing as being too popular.''

''You're one lucky lady,'' Keith said fervently. ''We've all been lucky.''

Lindsey's smile faded. *If I was really lucky, Eric would be here. Where is he?*

ERIC RUBBED AT HIS RED EYES with a weary hand. He'd finally finished the last of the paperwork required by the hospital, the rangers' office, the police and the coroner, since he'd been the one to uncover Wilson's body.

Finding the man hadn't been a pleasant experience. One of the police rescuers, the EMT, had shaken his head at the gash that had killed Wilson, while Ginger had cringed and whimpered at the smell of death. Eric could only try to settle the dog and pity the waste of human life. He thought of Eva, of Keith's shoulder and Lindsey's injuries, Pam's missing toes, Joyce's anguish. The man's death couldn't undo that damage. But perhaps Pam and her mother could now live a normal life.

Like the one he wanted for Lindsey and himself. *If she'll still have me... If she isn't furious that I wanted her here—asked for her as the replacement.... Damn, I'll have to tell her. No more misunderstandings between us. I nearly lost her three times, and twice this week. Never again.*

He ached to be at her side instead of with officials and paperwork and computers and phone calls. But that was his job—and there was no one left on his team to help. Hell, he was lucky he even *had* a team, after everything that had happened. Lindsey's revelation that Wilson had deliberately started a slide to kill Eva and keep his location safe had shocked him. He'd insisted on calling Eva's family himself and telling them of the latest developments. They deserved to know about Eva's death, and they needed to know that Eva's killer was dead. No matter how late the explanation came, the truth needed to be told....

Or at least as much of it as would benefit the living. He'd told Pam's mother that Wilson had died quickly in the slide, sparing her the details, and had made certain that none of the police officials would share that information with the family, unless they insisted on a formal report. He had also requested that Naomi not share the news with Lindsey at present.

Lindsey's hysteria when he'd finally pulled her out of the snow had shaken him badly, for she was the strongest woman he knew. He couldn't imagine the fear she'd gone through, and knew for certain that she'd carry those memories the rest of her life. So would he. He figured she'd never return to Yosemite. Naomi or Keith, either. He'd have to go back alone, at least until the end of winter and the first spring thaw. Fortunately he'd leave Naomi and Keith in the competent hands of loving family.

And Lindsey... Would she ever forgive him for both past and present mistakes? Would she ever want to become his wife, considering the rocky history they shared?

Now that he'd finished this damned paperwork, he intended to find out.

Lindsey's hospital room
Late afternoon

LINDSEY FINISHED WATCHING the local news. Pam's rescue and her father's death had been reported. Her family had called from San Diego, and so did Wade. Lindsey didn't know who'd been more upset, her parents or her ex-fiancé. The phone rang most of the afternoon. Everyone, including her parents and sisters, wanted to come up to take care of her, but for now, Lindsey had asked that they wait.

"You'll need help getting the dog home. What aren't you telling us?" her sisters, and particularly her mother, demanded to know.

"Wait until I find out what's going on," she said when she had her oldest sister Kate on the phone. "I don't care what the reporters are saying, I'm not at death's door, and I don't want any visitors right now."

"I can convince Mom and Dad to hold off a bit, but I doubt I can convince Wade," Kate said slowly. "What do you want me to tell him?"

"He's already called. I told him myself."

Kate remained tactfully silent, but Lindsey continued. "It's over, Kate. I think he already knew that before we talked."

"How'd he take it?"

"He was a good sport. When I told him the hospital had to cut off his ring, he said he shouldn't have tried to give it to me in the first place. Said he pretty much figured it was over that day at the airport."

"Poor guy."

"Yeah. He was great on the phone. He even said it's probably for the best, and wished me well."

"Must've been hard on him. Did you give him a reason?"

"No. What could I say that wouldn't make him feel worse?"

"Ah. Eric?" her sister wisely guessed.

"I'm still waiting to see him, so stall everyone, would you? I've got a broken arm and a cracked rib—painful, but that's all. I wouldn't even have stayed the night if I had someplace other than a motel to go."

"All right, I'll do my best," Kate said. "But you call me back as soon as you know anything," she insisted.

"I will. Thanks, Kate. You're a lifesaver."

"No, you're the lifesaver. Take care of yourself. I love you."

"Love you, too. Bye."

Lindsey had just hung up the phone when a knock sounded on her door. "Come on in."

Eric entered. To her surprise, he had Ginger with him.

"Hi," she said. *I won't get anywhere with this man if that's all I can come up with.*

"Hi, yourself." Eric closed the door behind him and took the room's only chair—but not before kissing her on the forehead and inquiring about her arm. He quietly told Ginger, who needed no urging, to lie down.

"Been one hell of a day," he sighed. "I don't know where to start."

Lindsey waited patiently. Eric looked as tired as Ginger. She watched his hand drop down to the animal's head and lightly stroke the fur. "Where's your ring?" he asked.

"They had to saw it off in the E.R. My whole hand and arm swelled up, and it was cutting off my circulation."

"Sorry about the ring," Eric said.

Something in his expression gave her the courage to say, "I'm not. Wade put it on at the airport, and I couldn't get it off. I never wanted to wear it here in the first place, and I told him that."

Eric's head lifted. "Any particular reason?" he said, his voice strained.

"Yeah. You." Suddenly nervous, she couldn't go on.

"I still have your old ring." He reached for a chain on his neck and pulled it out. Along with the cross she'd given him to wear long ago was her original engagement ring. "I never wanted it back. Keep it, Lindsey. Do whatever you want with it. Sell it, toss it…wear it." He held it out to her, silently asking the question they both knew needed to be asked.

"I think I'll wear it." She opened her palm and he placed it there. The ring was warm from his body, and before she knew it, she'd slipped it on the ring finger of her uninjured hand. "It's a perfect fit," she said in awe.

"I know *we* aren't," Eric said slowly. "But we'll do it right this time." Before she had a chance to answer, he went on. "I never stopped loving you."

Lindsey felt her eyes fill with tears of joy as her breath caught in her throat.

"I've learned a lot of things these past ten days, Lindsey. I never understood how it was with you and dogs. I lived with Ginger here for four years and never understood. But when we were going to search at the location where your receiver transmitted, and Ginger wanted to search elsewhere—something happened."

"You understood her," Lindsey said softly.

"I did. And I had to make a terrible choice, Lindsey. Trust modern technology, or trust what you and your dogs tried to teach me. When I decided to listen to Ginger—to you—I put your life and our future in her hands. Pam's life, too. I've never felt that kind of trust before. Not even with you. But after I decided to trust Ginger's nose…"

He paused, looking for the words. "Not only did the dog and I bond, but I suddenly understood you, and your way of life, in a way I never had before. I owe you an apology, Lindsey, for the past. I *didn't* understand. I didn't trust myself with anyone except Naomi. That's not true anymore."

Lindsey adjusted the pillow under her casted arm. Hope began to beat strongly in her heart. "So then there's nothing to stand in the way of us getting married?" she asked.

"If we can stay together this time."

"I never really let you go, not in my heart," Lindsey said. "And God knows I should've tried to explain things better about Missy. I'm not your twin, and you can't read my mind. I had no right to expect you to. We all react to death in different ways." She reached for him, moving forward to loop her uninjured arm around his neck.

He held her as tightly as he dared, her bruised cheek beneath the black eye resting on his shoulder.

"We still have some things to work out," he said, stroking her hair, his blunt words at odds with the happiness on his face. "I have to go back to the cabin and finish out the winter alone. I hate to leave you there, and

I'll transfer out as soon as possible, but they can't find a replacement on such short notice. I'm all that's left.''

Lindsey raised her head from his shoulder so she could meet his gaze. "I know," she said, remembering how she'd felt pressured to return to Yosemite to help a child she'd never met. "There just aren't enough of us to go around."

"You okay with that?"

She wasn't, not really, but she knew about duty and obligation, and knew what he needed to hear. "I am."

"That's one problem down. Two to go."

Lindsey let him take her good hand in his and bring it to her lips. "What's next?"

"I want to keep Ginger. Learn to work with her. I've lived with her four years, Lindsey," he said quickly. "It's not as if I'm a stranger. And I think Eva would want me to have her."

"I'll have *you* around, so I'll see plenty of Ginger," Lindsey said graciously. "And since the two of you saved my life—and Pam's—I'd hate to break up a winning team."

"Thanks for understanding." He continued to hold her hand with his own.

"You said one more problem?" Lindsey prompted.

"Yeah. This is kind of off the subject, but..." He lifted his face, definitely embarrassed. "I'm the one who asked for you as a replacement. I hope you can forgive me, even though—"

Lindsey didn't hear the rest. She burst into laughter. Ginger rose from her spot on the floor to put two paws on the bed. Her joy and sheer relief at rediscovering the love she'd lost made it impossible to speak for a moment.

Naomi, Keith and Eric had all secretly asked for her as the replacement. Finally she was able wipe her eyes, take his hand again and murmur, "I'm glad you wanted me, Eric. I wouldn't have it any other way."

CHAPTER TWENTY-ONE

Yosemite Valley, Bridalveil Fall
Summer

THE WEDDING GUESTS ENJOYED the afternoon sun, the picnic and barbecue-style food, against the soothing background noise of Bridalveil Fall. The spring thaw and roar of millions of gallons flowing down the Sierra Nevada was over. Now the waterfall was a delightful, misty shadow of its earlier massive torrent; indeed it looked like a lacy bride's veil as the High Sierra breeze blew intricate patterns into the falling spray.

Friends and family gathered around the picnic tables, while dogs beneath the shady trees kept eyes, ears and noses on guard for bears, deer, rabbits or, better yet, people who accidentally or deliberately dropped hot dogs or hamburgers their way. The casual atmosphere and clothing didn't take away from the joy of ceremony soon to begin for the engaged couple.

Lindsey sat quietly in the small rangers' cabin as her mother and sisters fussed with last-minute details of her hair and veil. Her father was with Eric in the wooded alcove outside the cabin while Kate's husband had generously offered to keep an eye on the family dogs, which now included Ginger. Despite the crowd of women in the room, Lindsey's thoughts were elsewhere as she re-viewed the past few months.

JACK HUNTER HIMSELF had offered to replace Eric at the rangers' cabin in Tuolumne Meadows, leaving Eric free to stay with his whole team at the hospital. When every-one had recovered, he went back to Yosemite.

The past few months had been hectic, and full of changes and surprises. This time, those changes were welcome.

As Naomi had promised, she hadn't checked into a San Francisco hospital until Keith was out of the Lee Vining hospital, his shoulder in a sling. The doctors had assured him it was healing well, and except for the scars, there would be no lasting ill effects from Wilson's murderous attempt. Keith and Eric had then accompanied Naomi to the San Francisco hospital, where she underwent surgery. The tumor Ginger and Lindsey had discovered *was* ma-lignant, but according to the doctors, hadn't spread into the lymph system due to early detection. Naomi had opted for only partial removal of the affected breast quad-rant by the oncologist and then repair by a plastic surgeon during the same operation, a new innovation. She'd had survived chemo with spirits and—as is rarely the case—hair intact.

"I'm the luckiest woman in the world," she'd told everyone during her stay in the hospital. "I've got my health, a new husband, and I even got to keep all my hair for the wedding photos. I couldn't ask for anything more," she said, holding Keith's hand from her bed. "Except for Lindsey to be my sister. For heaven sake's, Eric, when are you two going to tie the knot?" she kept asking. Lindsey had flown home to San Diego to recover at her parents', leaving Ginger with Eric.

Naomi's admiration and respect for Keith had turned into something more. "It isn't the same kind of love I had for my first husband," Naomi confessed to Lindsey via phone one evening. "A part of me will always love Bruce. But being with Keith has made me happy again in a way I never expected. Somehow, when I'm with him, I don't miss Eric. I couldn't say that about my first marriage."

"Keith's a good man," Lindsey had said. "What are you two going to do?"

"Keith'll be going into antiterrorist work with the San Francisco bomb squad," Naomi said. "I can't say I'm thrilled, but it's what he wants."

"What about you?" Lindsey asked. "You can't go back to being a ranger."

"No, and even if I could pass the physical, I wouldn't. I think I'm going back to school," Naomi said. "Take some more medical classes. Ever since Keith's shooting, I've felt that I need to learn more, to be more than just a paramedic."

Lindsey smiled. "Are we talking Dr. Naomi?"

"I don't know, yet. It depends on my health—if the cancer comes back," she said bluntly. "I don't know if I've really beat this thing. It's too soon to tell. In any case, I want to make sure I have enough free time from my studies for the people I love. Like Keith, and Eric. And you."

Naomi had married Keith in a small ceremony at the hospital chapel the very day of her discharge, without pomp or circumstance. When Keith started his explosives training with the San Francisco Police Department, she returned to school again, part-time, taking premed courses. So far the couple had remained healthy as well as happy.

Another couple had been married soon after, too. Joyce Wilson had been forced to stay in town for an extended stay, thanks to her daughter's condition. She found herself receiving frequent visits from the chief of police at both the hospital and Joyce's motel. McClanahan, a middle-aged childless widower who'd taken a shine to Pam, had fallen hard for the mother. The ex-Mrs. Wilson, now Mrs. McClanahan, had called Lindsey herself.

"I know everyone says it's too soon, but I don't care. He loves us both, he'd never hurt us, and he's a police officer," she said wryly. "I have to admit that's very appealing. I'll be safe, and so will Pam. He'll be a good father and husband. That's enough for me."

Pam had recovered from her ordeal and was in therapy. Isolated as he was, Eric couldn't make it to the wedding, but Lindsey had attended. She saw plainly that the romance was somewhat one-sided, but Pam's mother had married for love the last time. Maybe Joyce felt that a sensible affectionate marriage would serve her better. In any case, the couple seemed more than compatible, and the police chief was definitely in love. So was Pam.

Lindsey had chatted with Pam during the wedding.

"My new daddy's getting me a puppy!" Pam had whispered, wriggling and rustling her frilly formal dress during a particularly lengthy and sadly dull wedding sermon. Joyce sat on one side of Pam, and she and McClanahan had insisted that Lindsey join them in the bride and groom's pew. "I want one just like Ginger!"

"I'll bet you're excited," Lindsey whispered back. She slipped her arm around the child, who, except for the gaily-beaded soft white moccasins she wore on still-sensitive feet, bore no outward traces of her terrible ordeal.

"Uh-huh. As soon as we get back from the honeymoon, I get my dog. I want a girl and I wanna name her Ginger. But Mom says…''

Joyce made a gentle shush. A happy Pam ignored her mother. Lindsey doubted she'd even heard her, Pam seemed so excited. "Mom says the puppy'll want her own name, but *I* think she's wrong. My new daddy—" Pam leaned forward to point at the man sitting next to her mother "—said I should ask you."

Another "shh!" hissed from behind, this one not so gentle. Lindsey picked up Pam and settled her on her lap, her mouth inches away from the child's ear.

"Ginger is a color," she whispered. "How about if we pick something that describes the puppy's fur? How about—oh, maybe Daisy? Or Sunny?"

Pam frowned, then brightened. "Could I name her Pumpkin? It's orange, and Ginger is orange-y."

"I think Pumpkin is a perfect name," Lindsey agreed.

"We're gonna have so much fun," Pam squealed loudly, forgetting to whisper.

A pause in the sermon and a disapproving stare from the presiding minister had Lindsey flushing with embarrassment. The "new daddy" beckoned Pam with a crooked finger and kind smile, and she happily left Lindsey's lap to sit between the bride and groom.

The last Lindsey heard, Pam did indeed have a new golden retriever puppy named Pumpkin. Lindsey held out hope for a stable future for them all.

Her own wedding hadn't come about as soon as she'd wished. Although Jack Hunter had replaced Eric at Yosemite while Naomi had her surgery, it was only temporary. Eric had spent the remainder of the winter back at Yosemite. Lindsey went home to recuperate at her parents' and missed him terribly. However, the one bright spot was knowing Eric wasn't alone. He and Ginger had remained together, and Eric had hand-towed the dog on the sled for the long trek back into the isolation of Yosemite. If Lindsey had once had doubts about Eric's love for her, those doubts were gone. He'd trusted her life and his future happiness to Ginger—because he had finally trusted Lindsey herself.

He finished out the rest of the winter doing avalanche control, working the dog and packing up Keith's and Naomi's things, as well as his own, in the cabin where he'd spent the past seven years.

"I can work anywhere you want," he'd said at their last meeting. "As long as we're together. Just let me know."

Lindsey had been afraid he'd change his mind, and expressed her concern over Eric's giving up his way of life for hers. "What if you come to resent it? And me?"

"I'd resent it if you kept me out of your life," he said quietly. "I've done my part here. It's time to move on."

Lindsey had felt uneasy about the whole situation. She'd discussed it during her counseling. Lindsey had developed a full-blown case of claustrophobia after twice being buried in the snow. She hadn't even been able to get in a car unless all the windows were down. Back in San Diego, she'd worked on behavior modification techniques in therapy while her bones knit and arm healed. After six weeks, the cast was removed, and she began to work with the new dog chosen for her out of the "in-training prospects" at her parents' kennel.

Rocky was a beautiful black-and-tan German shepherd who showed great promise in multiple search-and-rescue techniques, both in rural missing persons and urban collapsed-structure and earthquake rescue. Like most of his breed, he loved to work. He definitely loved having Lindsey as a full-time partner, and had a devilish sense of canine humor and independence, not always appreciated by more serious law-enforcement owners. He made Lindsey laugh the very first time she met him. Her wise mother immediately said, "Forget police work for Rocky. *This* is the rescue dog for you," and brought her the leash.

Rocky and her family had helped with her loneliness while Eric was gone, but she missed him constantly. She'd also missed her youngest sister. Lara had met the hospital's helicopter pilot, who'd kept in touch with Lindsey during her recuperation. Lara had suddenly transferred up to Lee Valley and joined the police force there to be closer to Jim. Much to her parents' shock, she'd already moved in with the bold man who had vowed to protect Lindsey and Pam with his own life.

"I'm not getting married until I'm good and ready," Lara explained to Lindsey in private. "And it's not as if I'm pregnant or moving into a brothel. Mom and Dad are *so* old-fashioned!"

"You'll understand when you have your own daughter," Lindsey said, seeing both sides.

"Well, I don't have any kids, and they aren't in my immediate future, either. Besides, it's a small town and there aren't any apartments for rent. The opening on the police force is now or never, so I'm taking it before someone else does. This is the guy for me. I don't need to wait four years to be sure."

Lindsey had winced inwardly at her younger sister's honesty, but only said, "Mom and Dad will miss you. So will I."

Lara grinned and kissed her cheek. "Only until you get Eric back in your arms. Then you won't miss me at all."

IT HAD BEEN A LONG WINTER and a very late spring before the snowpack melted and Eric could leave his duty station with a clear conscience. The Hetch Hetchy watershed filled reservoirs for the massive Central Valley population, and the park and roads were clear of snow and open to the public. Bears awoke, deer migrated back to the lush, grassy meadows, and Lindsey was able to see Eric again. Their separation had been rough, and their reunion was tinged with regret over all the time they'd spent apart. They finally reunited physically, and they planned their wedding—*today's* wedding. Their personal happiness wasn't in doubt, but their professional future still seemed uncertain.

"You're awfully quiet," her mother said, finishing with her hair. "Are you nervous?"

"I need to see Eric," Lindsey said suddenly.

"But it's bad luck!" her mother protested.

"You're not going to call this off again, are you?" her oldest sister asked warily.

Lindsey's mother turned as white as Lindsey's veil.

"No, I just want Ric." Lindsey stood, lifted the lacy folds of her long dress and hurried out of the cabin and over to the men. Her father and the others stared at her as she burst onto the patio area in the alcove.

"Ric?" she called out. "I need to talk to you."

"You're not getting cold feet, are you?" her father asked.

"I want to talk to Eric." She determinedly made her way through the men to the one she loved, handsome in his formal wedding attire.

"Can we go for a walk?" she asked.

"If you're leaving me at the altar again…" he said, his voice hoarse.

"Would everyone please stop saying that!" Lindsey

looked around at the men, and then the women who'd hurried after her and had joined them on the pavilion. "I'm not! I just wanted…"

Everyone stared at her, waiting breathlessly. "Maybe it's better that you all hear this," she decided. She faced Eric and took both his hands in hers.

"We've spent so much time apart. I thought that since everything's going so well with both our families, we should stay in Yosemite one more year."

"Through another winter?" Naomi gasped out loud.

"Yes." Lindsey continued to watch Eric. "Rocky hasn't been trained in snow rescue, yet. I can't do that in San Diego. And I thought…well…since they haven't found anyone to replace you or the team…maybe we should stick around until next summer. That way they'll have trained staff who really want to stay here. We'll feel better about leaving, and we can go from there."

Eric blinked in surprise. "But…I thought you hated it in Yosemite!"

"I hated being caught in the avalanche. I hated how people were killed, and hurt." Her voice dropped so only he could hear. "I especially hated how I hurt you."

"But…the counselor said…"

"She says I'm fine. *I* say I'm fine. I also say we have a lot of time to make up for, and people like Pam need good rangers in Yosemite. Why not a year-long honeymoon with just ourselves for company?"

Eric moved closer, his black pants brushing against the full skirt of her dress. "Lindsey, that's very generous, and I love you even more for it, but Jack said he'll personally take my place if he can't find anyone by the start of fall."

"He *found* someone, Eric! Me! I'm the perfect replacement, only I never realized it! I've missed being here with you. If we're together, a year here is nothing at all. Your training kept Pam and me and Keith alive! What kind of ranger—what kind of *person* would I be if I left the park and made *you* leave the park without a capable, willing rescue team to replace us?''

There was a pause as Eric squeezed her hands even tighter. ''Sounds like you know what you want.''

''I do. And if everyone would stop eavesdropping,'' she said, deliberately speaking louder, ''we could get this show on the road and I could say 'I do' again!''

Everyone broke out into cheers and applause. Ginger, unhappily away from all the excitement, ducked her head and slipped out of her collar, leaving a barking Rocky still tied. Ginger ran over the soil made damp from the waterfall's spray, threaded her way through the crowd on the pavilion and emerged in front of the couple. Barking happily, she jumped up, muddy front paws making contact with the side of the bride's dress.

The women moaned, and the men made unsuccessful grabs for the energetic dog, who led them all on a merry chase.

The bride and groom, their lips on each other's in a loving kiss, ignored the crowd.

''Let's get married,'' the bride murmured, her arms around the groom's neck.

''I love you,'' the groom said, the two of them contentedly remaining in each other's embrace.

JACK HUNTER, WEDDING GUEST, watched as Keith restrained Ginger until Naomi hurried over with the slipped collar and leash. The women assured Lindsey that the mud wasn't much, and it wouldn't show in the wedding pictures since it was on the side of the dress instead of the front, and they would sponge it out right now so it didn't stain.

Jack grinned. Lindsey Nelson hadn't heard a single word in the entire melee. Her face—what he could see of it—shone with happiness, and she hadn't bothered to glance at her dress to check the damage even once. Not once.

He'd made the right choice, no question. He silently congratulated the couple, then congratulated himself on another job well done. No one could have replaced the opening Lindsey Nelson left four years ago—except Lindsey Nelson herself.

In the welcoming warmth of a summer sun, in the celestial beauty surrounding the rainbow around Yosemite's Bridalveil Fall, *anyone* could see that.